I turned the car to the gravel shoulder and leaned back in my seat, closing my eyes. "I don't need this. I don't need any of this," I said thickly. I turned and looked at Sam, transparent as tissue paper, iridescent as mother-of-pearl. "Why are you doing this to me? My life was fine until you showed up. Since you've been—whatever—everything that could go wrong *has*. My editor's all over me. H.P.'s about to be all over me. And it's only going to get worse if you start nagging me to play Suzie Detective. I *need* this damn job, Sam. Everything you ever touched turned to trash. You were a royal screwup when you were alive, and you hurt me like nobody else has ever hurt me before or since. For all I could care, you can rot in hell—literally." And suddenly, cynical hard-boiled me, I burst into tears.

Well, it happens. I never said I was made of stone. . . .

SLOW DANCING WITH THE ANGEL OF DEATH

Helen Chappell

FAWCETT GOLD MEDAL • NEW YORK

A Fawcett Gold Medal Book
Published by Ballantine Books
Copyright © 1996 by Helen Chappell

http://www.randomhouse.com

Library of Congress Catalog Card Number: 95-96238

ISBN 0-449-14983-8

Manufactured in the United States of America

First Edition: May 1996

10 9 8 7 6 5 4 3 2 1

Acknowledgments

The persons, places, events, and specific geography of this book are entirely of my own creation. Any resemblance to any persons living, dead, or still trying to make up their minds is pure coincidence.

I am deeply indebted to fellow "recovering reporter" Arline Chase, the Hon. William S. Horne of the Circuit Court of Talbot County, Maryland, and environmental writer Tom Horton for their advice, input, and technical support. Any factual mistakes are entirely my own. I certainly had the best advice from some wonderful friends and mentors.

The world's wetlands are disappearing fast; we all have to do what we can to preserve them for our future as a viable planet.

There is no such bird as a red-headed hawk.

But there ought to be.

ONE

•

Just to Make Sure
He Was Dead

If you were Sam Wescott's ex-wife, you'd go to his funeral, too.

Just, you understand, to make sure that he was really dead.

Actually, I was part of the cluster of mourners because my editor told me that I had to be there. It seemed my former father-in-law had personally requested my presence. And what H. P. Wescott wants, H. P. Wescott gets.

At the *Watertown Gazette*, where the motto is DON'T OFFEND THE ADVERTISERS, Wescott Real Estate and Development Corporation is a major advertiser. In a small place like Santimoke County, H. P. Wescott is a nine-hundred-pound gorilla, as in "Where does a nine-hundred-pound gorilla sit?" Anywhere he wants to, if you know what I mean, and I think you do.

So, there I was, on the hottest day of the summer, standing beside Chesapeake Bay, dressed in basic black and dark sunglasses, doing my best to be invisible, lurking in the background beneath some scraggly old willow trees wishing I were somewhere else, anywhere else.

H.P. must have been calling in his chips everywhere, I thought, looking around and taking notes. It must have taken some intense maneuvering to get this bunch to come to the Eastern Shore on a day like this.

I scanned the skies for some sign of clouds, but they

were blue and empty; we were in the midst of a long summer drought.

There were some well-known faces here, slowly burning red in the blazing August sun. I spotted our governor checking his watch and looking impatient. Our congressperson alternately played with her pearls and her beeper, doubtless annoyed that her hair helmet was melting in the heat. Annapolis was represented in force. I noted the speaker of the House of Delegates of the Maryland General Assembly, a good ole boy from up the Shore, mopping his forehead with a handkerchief. The secretary of the Department of Natural Resources glared at me in concert with the state's attorney general. I had the feeling they disliked the media even more than they despised each other.

And of course all the Daughters of Santimoke Lineage were here; when a Wescott dies, they troop the colors. A fluttering flock of blue-haired old ladies more interested in studying the old Wescott tombstones than the services for the more recently departed.

But I knew I wasn't going to escape unscathed when I saw Jason.

State Delegate Jason Hemlock, looking absurdly handsome and absurdly cool, glanced once at me, then quickly fixed his attention firmly on the casket. After that quick, stabbing recognition, I preferred not to look at him again. Too much baggage, you understand, even though almost a year had passed since we'd parted company under less than amicable circumstances, to say the least.

Idly, I picked out several other prominent types, both political and social, some of them breathtakingly famous. None of them looked like they were thrilled to be here, even to pay their respects to the son of the man who owned a good chunk of the state and regional action. In fact, I doubted if many of them even knew Sam, who had left the Eastern Shore more than a decade ago to, as they say, pursue other interests. Like being a boat bum in the Caribbean and the Keys and staying the hell away from the Eastern Shore and his family and the whole worlds of trouble he'd caused from Cape Charles to Havre de Grace and all points in between.

Sam's had not been a useful life, all things considered.

Having made my findings on who was there, I tucked my notebook into my bag and focused on the enormous mahogany coffin about to be lowered into the open grave. The Wescotts were one of the few old families left in Santimoke County who could afford to maintain their own private cemetery on the ancestral estate.

From this lovely point on Mandrake Creek, you could look across Chesapeake Bay all the way to the Western Shore. If Sam and I had stayed married, eventually I too could have been buried here among the historically prominently dead. Postmortem waterfront is not a good reason to stay married.

See, on the Eastern Shore, there are three types of Society with an up *S*. There's old blood and old money, old blood and no money, and then there are the ten-cent millionaires, whom everyone deplores. Their money is welcome; everyone just wishes they'd stay home in Washington or Philadelphia or wherever. The Wescotts are old blood and old money and all the new money H.P. has spent his life accumulating, which is considerable.

Me? I'm neither blood nor money. Look back far enough to the family of Hollis Ball and all you'll see is generation after generation of dirt-poor but church-honest watermen from Beddoe's Island. When I married Sam Wescott, it was the mésalliance from hell, according to both sets of parents.

Well, Sam was dead now. The obituary that had been faxed into the paper from Dreedle's Funeral Home said he'd been back in Santimoke County for thirty-six hours when his propane galley stove had exploded, blowing him and a hundred thousand dollars worth of sailboat very high and quite wide.

The investigating cops I'd spoken to this morning said you could hear the explosion all the way into the next county. What was left, and I understood it wasn't much, was being lowered into the ground in that mahogany and

brass coffin. But I heard that the watermen were still bringing up bits and pieces of boat and Sam from all over
Mandrake Creek. I preferred not to contemplate the improvement in the crabbing in that body of water.

Sam had gone out in a blaze of glory, and there were no
wet eyes here.

I was not surprised that the VIPs were not exactly pros-
trate with grief. They were here to pay honor to H.P.

God help them, if they weren't. Lack of respect for H.P.
could be fatal. Care must be taken, attention should be paid
where H. P. Wescott's ego was concerned.

But it was the Wescotts—my former in-laws—who interested me. None of them seemed to be grieving Sam's unfortunate demise either. And so soon after the prodigal son
had returned, too!

I wasn't terribly surprised. For all of his charm, Sam had
left a trail of careless damage everywhere he went. And
someone else had always cleaned up the mess. Usually it
was his father, wielding his battalion of lawyers, his flotilla
of influential friends, and his fat checkbook. It's amazing
how much damage can be smoothed out with money. It's
always in style, it's always the correct size and the right
color, and it soothes and silences and placates like nothing
else.

Himself sat there with his arms crossed looking like Big
Daddy's evil twin in a bus and truck tour of *Cat on a Hot
Tin Roof*, without so much as a tear marring his once handsome face. He had not aged well. Still, the aura of power
clung to him like an expensive cologne.

And it made him look virile, even though he must have
been about seventy. He was tall and bulky, with sharp blue
eyes beneath bristling brows, eyes that took in everything,
missed nothing, like an old hawk. Truth to tell, I'd always
been slightly afraid of him. Unlike most people, I'd always done my best never to let it show. I could even feel
a grudging amount of sympathy for the Old Man, for his
having lost his only son. Not that Sam had been much of
a son.

All that remained was H.P.'s daughter Claire.

Draped in expensive black, Sam's sister twisted her good Republican pearls and lifted her sunglasses so that I could see the displeasure snapping in her eyes as the service droned on. If she'd been paying attention instead of counting the house, she never would have noticed my humble presence.

Now, Claire is a woman who gives new depth to the word *bitch*. Butter would freeze in her mouth. Money and social position are her twin obsessions, and oh, how she enjoys being a large fish in the Eastern Shore's small social pond. Her face, so much like Sam's, turned up with depressing regularity on the social page of the *Gazette*. The Daughters of Historical Santimoke, of the American Revolution, the Confederacy, Bilitis, it mattered not as long as it was social; country clubs, yacht clubs, garden clubs, the Junior League; they were her natural habitat. She was a leading light in the Daughters of Santimoke, a group dedicated to worshipping their ancient connections to blackbirders, criminals, and Tories, the founders of this county. Historical (read: hysterical) societies, preservations, heritages were all hers. Something known nebulously as the arts (but, God forbid, not any artists, so undependable and unpredictable and likely to be unimpressed by her mighty position) knew her all too well as a one-woman steamrolling committee. The Historical Arts Preservation Benefit Ball for Distressed and Genteel Interior Designers at the Santimoke County Yacht Club was hers to kill, but Habitat For Humanity or Eastern Shore Fuel Fund or Headstart would have gone into shock if she'd as much as peeled a dollar out of her Gucci wallet for them.

If you guessed that I cannot stand my former sister-in-law, you get twenty-five points. The feeling is mutual, fear not.

Unfortunately for both of us, her passion for publicity brought us into more contact than either one of us really wanted. God help the *Gazette* if every single event she graced with her presence failed to show up in our pages with photo, written up in fawning terms worthy of a ball at Versailles.

Unfortunately, Claire's latest fancy was real estate. Here she could parlay her social connections into a series of million-dollar deals, mostly selling her friends' waterfront estates to each other after every successive divorce. Recently she'd been demanding free news space for her latest project, hawking new, badly built, and overpriced waterfront houses to rich retiree Republicans from the Western Shore.

Hey, it's a family tradition.

Alas, Wescott Development Corporation had lately run up against some trouble with a tract of land that the Environmental Protection Agency had declared an official wetland, or so I remembered reading somewhere in the business section. Rumor had it that Delegate Jason Hemlock had worked long and hard to have a special exemption bill passed to drain and fill the marsh, making way for more Victorian Colonial chalets and French Tudor schlosses.

Happily Claire was the business editor's problem on this one. He had my deepest sympathies, since Claire's reaction to unfavorable publicity was a public tantrum in the newsroom, full of threats to sue us until our teeth rattled. Since her understanding of the legalities of libel was limited, it made for exciting guerrilla theater to say the least.

This latest project had led to a new outlet for satiating her desire to see her name in print. Her vociferous, irrational, and book-length letters to the editor detailing how unfair it was that she couldn't buy, drain, and develop every square inch of wetlands on the Eastern Shore had branded her as a full-fledged pest to every news editor in the mid-Atlantic region.

Staring at her back, I felt just like Robespierre contemplating Marie-Antoinette's neck.

Sensing someone staring at her suicide blonde (dyed by her own hand) head, she turned and looked at me. "What are *you* doing here?" her glare asked me. With a little toss of her Gloria Vanderbilt bob, she turned away. I was amazed she didn't stamp her Ferragamo'd foot and demand my removal from the premises.

Her husband, C. J. Cromwell "Skipper" Dupont, patted her hand from time to time. He looked sort of sad and beige, but that was his natural aspect. Skipper had done himself proud by marrying the boss's daughter and done himself wrong by marrying Claire, who had made his life a living hell ever since. Poor Skipper. Old blood and no money, he had that rabbity, inbred look so many of the Eastern Shore aristocracy have after marrying their first cousins for the past three centuries. Poor Skipper. He'd been taking orders from his father-in-law for fifteen years and never once had H.P. expressed the least gratitude or praise for the way Skipper labored for the family firm. As the two in-laws in that family, there had always been a certain terse sympathy between us. I wondered if he had a mistress. I hoped so, and I hoped she was good to him. God knows, the Wescotts, father and daughter, weren't.

Although it was hard to imagine Skipper and Claire actually having sex, I suppose they had because there were the twins Cromwell VI and Wescott, who had been flown in from Groton or Saint Paul's or somewhere to present what passed in the Wescotts for a united family front. I couldn't believe how they'd grown. The nose studs were particularly attractive and would have made Sam proud.

A soft sobbing caught my attention and I glanced at the edge of the crowd where an elderly black couple stood a little apart from the whites. Estelle and Phillips Brooks had worked for the Wescotts since birth, no doubt, slavery being only de facto dead in some sections of Santimoke County. After Miss Rose, H.P.'s long-suffering wife, had (some said) taken an overdose of Seconal, and turned her face to the wall, Estelle and Phillips had pretty much raised Sam and Claire, along with their own daughter Charlotte, whose busy career as a Washington attorney no doubt prevented her return to the old plantation for this event. Smart lady.

H.P. was, of course, too busy making money to pay much attention to his offspring.

Alone of all the people here, Estelle genuinely mourned Samuel Sewall Wescott. Even Phillips didn't look that upset. And why should he? Sam had been a pain in the ass. A charming pain, but a pain nonetheless.

In fact, it may largely have been due to Sam's great charm that no one had killed him. That smile, that sunny personality, you could just about forgive him anything. *Almost* anything, I added to myself.

It was hard to admit that ten years later, I was still smarting over what he'd done to me ... damn Sam!

There was a general stir among the gathered mourners, and I snapped back into the present tense. Apparently, the service was over. The governor's state police boys almost ran me over trying to get him into his limo, and our congressperson stared right through me as she was literally carried away by her entourage.

State Delegate Jason Hemlock looked like he was dying to come over and pick a fight, but Claire looped her hand into his arm and almost jerked him out of his handmade Loafers. I jammed my notebook deeper into my battered old Coach bag and turned to wend my way through the tombstones and boxwood toward my car, waving my hand in front of my face as an ineffectual mosquito repellent.

Dammit, why in hell did Jason have to be here? I wondered angrily. You would have thought that seeing him these days would have produced no more than a mild nausea, but anger, never too far from the surface, was rising fast from his sleazoid presence.

I felt my heart beating a little too fast and turned away. I was sweating. There's nothing quite like an Eastern Shore summer. From June through September, it's like breathing bath water. It's not the heat, it's the humidity, so thick you can touch it. And yet, it had not rained in six weeks. Farmers were complaining as their soybeans dried up, as corn browned and drooped in the fields.

"Hollis?"

I turned to see Phillips coming toward me. He moved a little more slowly these days, as did we all. As usual, he was immaculately attired in a black summer worsted, his graying hair neatly trimmed, his dark eyes impassive. The perfect butler. Ice ran in his veins.

I put my hand out and after a moment's hesitation, he took it with a faint air of lèse-majesté. One simply doesn't shake hands with the servants; they don't want to touch *you*. "How are you, Phillips? Long time, no see," I offered.

Not so much as a smile cracked that glacial exterior. If anything, he was still more elegant than any of the white people he worked for. He certainly had a whole lot more dignity. "Mr. Wescott has requested that you come back to the house for the buffet. He said 'please'."

I stared at him for a moment. "He said '*please*'?" H.P., you understand, never says *please*. He says "jump" and everyone else says "how high?"

Phillips nodded impassively. Prince Charles could have learned a thing or two from him about dignified behavior.

I sighed. "Okay." I guessed I was getting soft in my old age. "Tell him I said thank you, but I—"

"Hollis, I think you should come," Phillips said firmly. "Estelle would like to see you."

Well, in that case.

I couldn't say no to Estelle. No one could. Beneath that motherly exterior, there was a whim of iron. Besides, she makes the best crab cakes in Santimoke County. I genuinely liked Estelle; she had been kind to me in my brief tenure as a Wescott, something no one else had seen fit to do.

Phillips nodded, almost clicked his heels, and turned toward the family, who were clustering around the Mercedes for the ride up the road to the homeplace.

I sighed and walked across the yellow, parched grass toward my beaten-up, decade-old Honda Civic. It was the last car left, all the Beemers, Mercedes, and Land Rovers having taken off for the funeral buffet or parts unknown.

I opened the door and fell into the sweltering pigpen that

is a reporter's car. If you know a journalist with a clean car, chances are excellent that that person is a lousy reporter. I crawled in among the old newspapers, burger wrappings, and diet soda cans, turning on the engine and collapsing against the seat, waiting for the a/c to kick in as I fumbled in my bag for a cigarette. I lit it with trembling hands, letting out a long sigh. As I exhaled smoke, I thought about things I could do to revenge myself on my editor for this assignment. None of them were pleasant, and many are forbidden by the Geneva Convention.

When I felt the tepid air pumping into the car from the air conditioner, I stole a look at myself in the rearview mirror, wondering if there was anything I could do to repair heat damage to my hair and face before making my entrance chez Wescott.

Then I saw my ex-husband's face floating in the rearview mirror.

TWO

·

The Turning Up of
a Bad Penny

Sam's smiling face hung in the mirror for several seconds. Then slowly it faded away.

Just like that. He was there, and then he wasn't there.

I blinked once or twice, then leaned out the window for some fresh air. Evidently the heat was getting to me, and I was hallucinating. "There will be no more of that," I said firmly to myself. "What you need is a diet soda and some food, girlfriend." I hadn't eaten since lunch the day before.

Quickly, I combed my hair, smudged a little lipstick, and dabbed at the little melted welts of mascara beneath my eyes.

It wasn't perfect, but nothing was in this heat. I turned around and guided the Honda down the lane that led to Mandrake House.

"Be it ever so humble, there's no place like home," I hummed under my breath as I caught my first glimpse of stately Wescott Manor as it hove up from the long, long lane through the woods.

There are plenty of grand old houses on the Eastern Shore, but Mandrake is one of the few that are truly beautiful. Ancient red brick shaded russet with age. A Palladian sweep, flanked by two wings, nestled among ancient oaks, boxwoods, magnolias, and crepe myrtle, it has a welcoming feel to it that comes from three centuries of living. Spreading out along a pretty curve in Mandrake Creek, it's a jewel in a perfect setting. Seeing it again after all these years, I felt a faint, nauseating anxiety.

Anyone who had to live there with Claire, Skipper, and H.P. and Sam would have felt the same. Talk about dysfunctional.

And resentful. And covetous. Who wouldn't want a beautiful old waterfront estate of their very own?

Just one big happy family, everyone with their own wing. The place was big enough that you'd have thought that you could go for days without seeing anyone else, but even that didn't seem to lessen the trauma and drama; they all seemed to enjoy going out of their separate ways to make each other miserable.

I eased the Honda up the oystershell drive and parked it well out of the way of the other, more elegant vehicles, down by the kitchen beside a white van marked Greens 'n' Things Catering.

I remembered the first time I had walked up the brick pathway between the ancient boxwoods, how young and shy and how very intimidated I had been by all this grandeur. An awestruck waterman's kid from Beddoe's Island at the other end of the county. Sam *could* have told me that he was one of *those* Wescotts. It really wasn't fair, to just bring me here and throw me to the wolves. . . .

That had happened to another person in another life, I told myself. Mandrake and money had long since lost their ability to awe me. I'd been taught the fine art of cynicism by experts.

And I was whistling past the graveyard. Mandrake still had the power to intimidate.

I walked through the front door into the vast open hall, where the central air, at an arctic temperature, hit me like a slap in the face. From the inner rooms I could hear the sounds of people being social. The bar, it would seem, was open. But, then, the bar is always open on the Eastern Shore.

The familiar lemon-oil-musty smell of old things filled my nose, and I glanced at my own reflection in the pier glass that hung in the great hall. The woman I was, not the girl I had been, looked back at me. Nice haircut, good black dress, string of pearls, not bad for thirty-five, maybe work on those hips a little, get a trim soon, color out those wisps of gray, but—I blinked.

Sam was standing behind me. He was wearing a blue shirt and chino pants and grinning that crooked grin of his, that cat-ate-the-canary grin that used to turn my knees to water and other parts of me into liquid tides of lust.

It was Sam, but I could see *through* him, see the doorway and the Lucien Freud painting of Miss Rose and the Flemish arrangement on the rectory table *through* the misty outline of his body. I spun around, gasping. "If this is one of your damn jokes, I'll—"

There was no one there.

There was no one in the mirror when I turned about, either, except for me, looking slightly pale, with an expression as if I'd been kicked from behind, which maybe I had.

Now I knew that I needed a drink, and something stronger than diet soda, too. Obviously, I was not as in control as I wanted to believe I was, and that irritated me no end. I like to be in control. Control is good. Seeing things is not. It must have been the heat, I thought.

Firmly putting negative thoughts out of my mind, I marched into the fray. And right up to the bar, where I ordered a vodka and tonic, lime twist. I rarely drink, never when I'm working, but I felt as if I deserved this one. If I fell asleep at my desk this afternoon, I deserved that, too.

Le tout Santimoke County was there, at least the fraction of it that counted in the business and social world. Have you ever been to a WASP wake? It's a model of restraint. No one cries or screams or throws themselves on the coffin or gets *too* visibly drunk, although enough alcohol is consumed to deplete a distillery. In fact, a WASP wake is a lot like a WASP cocktail party, except the clothes are in better taste.

I'd like to say I didn't see a soul I knew there. Unfortunately, I saw lots of souls I knew there, but not one of them

I wanted to talk to. Sam was dead; it was a foolish, wasted end to a foolish, wasted life. What else was there to say? As an ex-wife whose brief marriage to the deceased ended badly, I didn't feel that I had much to contribute to the fun. Nor did I feel that my presence would be approved by Miss Manners.

So why the hell was I there? H.P. had evidently wanted my presence badly enough to turn the screws on my editor, not that that was so hard; Rig Riggle has a spine of marshmallow.

Well, one quick drink and I'm out of here, I thought, selecting a handful of crab balls from the tray of a passing waiter and wolfing them down. I recognized Estelle's fine hand at once; backfin crabmeat delicately spiced, lightly rolled in cornmeal, and broiled to perfection.

A county councilperson, whose phone calls I was trying to avoid returning, caught my eye. I waved to him from across the room and positioned myself in such a way as to allow a bevy of Historical (Hysterical to the features department) Daughters of Santimoke to carry me in their wake, out of his line of vision, all the while waving at him sadly. Bye-bye, catch you later.

"What in the world brings *you* here?" Yes, it was the lovely Claire, and she was looking at me as if I were last year's dress. In a polyester knockdown version from Wal-Mart.

"Believe me, I'm not here by choice. Your father called my editor and personally requested my presence," I replied. "If you have a problem with that, why don't you take it up with Daddy Dearest?"

Where are all my clever retorts when I really need them?

Sam had received all the charm in that generation. Claire opened and closed her mouth, but nothing came out for several seconds. Those ice-blue eyes flashed. Then she hissed at me. "It was an accident, Hollis. An *accident*. Don't go dredging up the past, because there's nothing there. *It was an accident!* I don't want to see anything negative in the paper about this." With a final, fishy stare, she marched away to do some serious sucking up to a former president's wife, leaving the heavy scent of her Mitsouko hanging in the air.

I stared after her, popping a crab ball into my mouth.

"Don't mind Claire," Skipper drawled as he came up and pumped my hand in a grip perfected by years of tennis and sailing. "She's pretty upset by this whole thing. It's been tough on all of us. God, what a way to go, even for Sam." He shook his head, pushing his wire-rimmed glasses back up on his nose. He was without a doubt the most colorless human being I'd ever met in my life. I would have been hard pressed to give a height, weight, or hair and eye color if asked. He was beige. "But it was an accident, you know."

Automatically, I glanced out the window toward the creek, where the blackened and twisted dock and boathouse still bore mute witness to the explosion. It must have been a doozy. Iranian terrorists couldn't have done better on twice the budget.

"Of course, our boat was badly damaged, too," Skip added peevishly. "Thank goodness we were insured. But right in the middle of racing season, now that's annoying. Typical of Sam, don't you think?"

I had to agree with him. "That's Sam—that *was* Sam all over," I sighed. "He was a great maker of messes. But I can't understand *why* he came home after all these years. After everything that happened, you would think that he'd have been happy to stay down there in the islands and be a remittance man or whatever he was doing."

Skipper frowned behind his glasses. His colorless eyes blinked, and a line appeared between his eyebrows. "I must say that his death was timely, if nothing else," he said thinly. "If he hadn't killed himself, someone else might have killed him. Sam could make you just that crazy."

"You don't have to tell me that," I replied sotto voce. We exchanged a meaningful look. Both of us, I assumed, were mentally reliving old memories of Sam's more disastrous adventures. Situations into which we had been dragged, sometimes out of bed in the middle of the night, to try to fix things. Skipper was H.P.'s bag man and spin doctor when it came to family damage control.

He looked like he would have liked to elaborate on this theme, but his lawyerly training prohibited it. Awkwardly, he patted me on the shoulder. "Well, I've got to go spread a little joy among the state and federal boys. May as well get some use from this event. You know we're going ahead and developing White Marsh? Going to be quite the project since Claire got the wetlands permits. Houses, a minimall, the works. Great stuff, really upscale. Stop by my office next week, and I'll let you have the exclusive scoop." He winked and eased away from me, gripping and grinning as he worked his way across the room.

"Hollis." I'd have known that deep bass rumbling voice anywhere. A heavy hand fell on my shoulder, and I turned around. Himself Almighty was right behind me. I'd forgotten the power, the overwhelming force of personality that was H. P. Wescott, staring down at me from beneath those bushy brows. "Come with me. We need to talk," the Old Man commanded.

I didn't bother to waste time protesting.

You don't argue with H.P. Besides, I was curious. It took us about five minutes to cross the room. Every few feet, he had to stop and shake a hand, pat a shoulder, compliment an Hysterical Daughter matron, growl a command, receive a condolence, field a question. When he caught Phillips's eye, he muttered something, and the perfect butler nodded.

Eventually, we found ourselves in his office-study where a small fortune in original Audubon prints cavorted over the carved teak paneling. Waterfowl decoys lined the shelves where books should have been. I stopped to admire a pair of canvasbacks, and he lifted the wooden carvings down from the shelf with loving hands. "These are my latest. A pair of Wards. I had to outbid a Japanese cartel for them, but I got 'em." He turned the hen over so that I could see Steve Ward's signature on the bottom, which put their value into the high six figures. I could care less about decoys, but in this region, they're the collector's wet dream, as in: he who dies with the most 'coys wins. "Don't suppose your daddy wants to sell those Eddie Dean old-squaws yet?" he asked me hopefully.

I shook my head. I didn't tell him that even if Daddy had wanted to sell his prized decoys, H.P. would have been the last person on his list, that he would have fed them to the woodstove first. I watched as he lovingly restored the Wards to their place on the shelf and gestured me to a seat in front of the immense mahogany plantation desk before settling himself in the throne behind it. His smile was that of a well-fed crocodile.

As if by magic, Phillips appeared with two fresh drinks on a silver tray, offering them to us without so much as a word. As I took mine, I tried to read the butler's face, but he avoided my eye. No hints there.

As soon as he closed the door behind him, H.P. leaned forward and directed that smile at me. There were no fine aristocratic lines in his expression, just a meanness that could scare the hell out of you. "It's been a while, Holly," he said, sipping at his bourbon. "What, ten, eleven years? You're looking well."

"Your point being?" I asked politely. I tasted my second vodka and tonic. I had no intention of having more than one drink. He actually looked hurt, the old fraud. His skin was as thick as a diamondback's shell. "How you doing? Are you happy being a reporter? I see your byline in the *Gazette* all the time."

"Happy enough. I'm good at what I do. Good enough to win a couple of awards, anyway." I took another sip of my drink, wondering where this was going.

H.P. picked up a brass duck from the desk and turned it over as if it were the most interesting thing in the world. "Ever thought about the *Sun* or the *Post*?"

What small town reporter doesn't? The *Baltimore Sun* and the *Washington Post* are the big leagues, the show. The *Gazette*'s the Triple As. But I would have preferred a hysterectomy with a rusty spoon to admitting a yearning for anything to my former father-in-law.

"I like the Eastern Shore. I know my beat, and my family's here." It sounded churlish, but I didn't care. Carefully, I took a cigarette from my bag and lit it. H.P. stoked up one of his Havana de Coronas, and we filled the air with politically incorrect smoke and silence for a few moments.

"Got a boyfriend?"

"One brush with romance was enough," I replied. Actually, there was that other disaster with Jason Hemlock, but that wasn't any of his business, even though I was pretty certain he knew all about it. Everyone else in Santimoke County did.

"I'm not proud of the way things turned out with you and Sam." Looking at me from beneath his bushy brows, he sighed. "For God's sake, Holly, he's dead."

Did I detect some genuine grief here? Na. Beneath that steel exterior, there was a steel interior. Suddenly, H.P. sagged in his chair. For the first time, he looked old and defeated.

"When you have a son, you hope that he will do better than you, that he'll accomplish great things. Sam was a disappointment. But he was still my son, Holly. My flesh and blood. I always hoped that he'd straighten out." He swung around in his chair so that he was looking out across the water. "When he came home from the islands, I hoped that he meant what he said, that he would settle down. Just when it seemed that everything was going to go the way it should have in the beginning, he was gone. Just like that. One hell of a mess."

I imagined the explosion and shuddered. Not a nice way to go, I thought. Suddenly, and for no reason, an old song ran through my head. " 'Let's go out in a blaze of glory.' "

And it made me want to giggle. It was *so* Sam, I had to smile. A blaze of glory was exactly what he would have wanted. Sam was the least reverent, most iconoclastic person I had ever met in my life. It was a part of his charm.

H.P., oblivious to my irreverence, hunkered down and

looked at me. "I guess you want to know what I want from you," he said, all business, all the time.

"It's a thought that has crossed my mind. My editor rousted me out here in a move that I would hardly consider the best of taste." As if I'm someone to talk about good taste. I sat back and waited for the inevitable orders.

Just then, the French door to the patio slammed back on its hinges. It rattled the decoys on the shelves.

"Murderer!"

We both looked up as the door to the study flew back. A tall, dark-haired man in thick glasses and a T-shirt that announced Save The Bay Kill A Developer stood there, breathing hard and pointing a trembling finger at H.P.

"I know what you're doing to White Marsh, you greedy bastard, and believe me, you won't get away with it! I'll have the Friends of the Bay, the EPA and the Greenheads all over you before you can—"

"Hullo, Frank," H.P. said calmly. "Frank Dartwood, meet my former daughter-in-law, Miz Hollis Ball. She's a reporter for the *Watertown Gazette*." He reached under the desk.

This was getting interesting, I thought, and reached for my notebook. ENVIRONMENTALIST INTRUDER DRILLED AT SON'S FUNERAL BY REAL ESTATE MAGNATE. Maybe Rig Riggle had been on to something after all.

Frank Dartwood seemed singularly unimpressed by the presence of the media. He ignored me. "You know damn well you can't develop wetlands, Wescott! You just try it, and you'll wipe out the habitat of forty thousand different life forms and the biological diversity of the entire Chesapeake Bay region will have suffered another blow! Section 404 *specifically* states tidal wetlands are—"

"Here, now, boy, you can't stand in the way of progress! It's un-American!" H.P. growled. "Ask Delegate Hemlock if you don't believe me! We've got all the permits, it's all perfectly legal. What are you, some kinda Communist?"

Before Dartwood could answer this question, Phillips and two heretofore invisible and very large gentlemen had entered the room and seized the intruder, lifting him by his elbows.

"How do you spell your name, Mr. Dartwood?" I asked, scribbling away madly. "Are you *the* Frank Dartwood, head of the Greenhead Environmental Army?"

Before my questions could be answered, Dartwood had been hustled out the door by the large gentlemen in the lumpy suits.

"The Greenheads will fight you every step of the way on this one!" he shouted as he was dragged away. "You eco-villain!"

"Should I call the police, Mr. Wescott?" Phillips asked.

"Escort the gentleman quietly off the property and have the caterer's people make sure everyone has a double of whatever they're drinking. I'll be out in a minute. And keep Claire from making a scene. If she starts screaming about when bad things happen to good Republicans again, have Skipper take her upstairs at once."

Phillips nodded and shut the door.

"I never knew you could offer a floor show at a funeral," I said. "What was that Dartwood was saying about White Marsh?" I looked up from my note-taking to see that H.P. had turned the color of an old bedsheet. "Are you okay?" I asked in about as close a gesture to compassion as I could muster.

H.P. picked up his drink in a trembling hand and drained most of it off. "Just a little angina," he muttered. He opened a gold pillbox and popped something into his mouth. As I watched, half-fascinated and half-embarrassed, his ruddy color slowly flowed back into his cheeks. "Not as young as I used to be."

"You didn't used to have security guards, H.P. When the hell did you sign on the *Tontons Macoutes*? Have you been hitting Baby Doc's yard sales again?"

"Let us just say that dangerous times call for protective measures. Phillips arranged it. We expected there might be unwelcome guests with so many important people here today," H.P. said tightly. His little smile was frightening. And, amazingly, I had the idea that he was frightened himself.

He sighed, "Well, Hollis, it has been nice to see you again. I wish the circumstances would have been more pleasant. There was a time when I hoped that you and Sam—. You've got cojones, Hollis. I would have liked to have seen those Ball genes in my grandchildren."

The leather checkbook came out of the drawer as in times of old.

H.P. placed it on the desk. I watched, absolutely fascinated, as he filled out the date and my name as *Hollis Ball Wescott*.

"See what you can do about keeping this entire unfortunate tragedy as low-key as possible," he said as he wrote, not looking at me. "Whenever anything like this happens, there's always lots of gossip and speculation. And right now, gossip and speculation about White Marsh is the last thing we need. And poor Sam, of course. Nothing must be in the paper that would reflect badly on the family." He looked right at me when he said that. "Wescott Corporation is about to close a very sensitive deal on White Marsh, and any sort of negative publicity could damage the company." He sketched the numeral *one* on the short line beside my name.

I watched as the line of zeroes behind the one grew longer, and my eyes must have opened very wide indeed. For H.P., it was chump change. For me, it was six months' salary. I sensed something was not right. Call me stupid, but I hadn't really cared, before that checkbook came out, what the hell was going on. Sam, in his vast carelessness, had finally done himself in, end of story. What gossip? A little street theater at the home of a powerful and unpopular family. White Marsh? What innuendo? It was all news to me.

H.P. ripped the check out of the book and slid it across the desk to me. "The last time I wrote you a check, you tore it up and tossed it back at me," he said heavily. "This time, I suggest you keep it. And I suggest you keep a lid on whatever you might hear or think." He sighed, draining his drink. "Sam's dead, Holly. No amount of money in the world can bring him back. But at least I can do some damage control."

The Old Man stubbed out his cigar and rose from his chair. The audience was at an end. "And I'll tell you, gal, I'm mighty impressed with your writing. When I have lunch with Dick Harwood or Jack Carroll, I'll be sure to mention your name. Hollis Ball, Eastern Shore Bureau, has a nice ring to it, don't you think?"

I picked up the check, put it in the pouch of my battered Coach bag.

As soon as he was out the door, H.P. was ambushed by important people. Skipper was waving a cellular phone at him and making faces. Claire had the former president's wife in tow, demanding his attention to soothe her ruffled feelings. People were shaking their heads.

"This sort of thing never used to happen to *nice* people," a ruffled Hysterical Daughter was saying as she took another drink.

I was about to slip out unnoticed when Phillips appeared out of nowhere. "Estelle would like to see you before you go," he said in a voice that brooked no denial. Doubtless security was waiting to back him up if I disobeyed.

So I didn't quite slip out. Instead I went through the warren of old passages that led to the kitchens. The true heart of Mandrake.

Estelle was reigning supreme in her element, busily bossing the caterer's people around the big bright modern kitchen. Greens 'n' Things Catering, their ID buttons proclaimed; bright and healthy-looking college kids doing the job. Under Estelle's vigilant eye, trays of food were smoothly moving up the stairs in a well-rehearsed ballet. Mandrake was famous for its hospitality, and Estelle was famous for her ruthless administration of the domestic end of things. The delicious aromas that wafted through the kitchen brought back my only happy memories in this house, sitting at the table with Estelle, drinking coffee, eating white-potato pie and receiving the benefit of her worldly wisdom in dealing with rich white people, whom she believes to be as crazy as bald-ass coots. If you ask me, she has more class in her little finger than all the people upstairs have had in this and their three previous incarnations.

"There's my girl!" she exclaimed when she saw me, waving me to her side with an imperious gesture. She was still in her black funeral dress, her Sunday church hat pinned firmly over her Sunday wig. "Come here, Holly, and let me get a look at you!"

After surveying me up and down, and giving me a hug, she shook her head. "Too much fast food. You need to get one of those low-fat, high-fiber diets. Just like the one I put Him on." Him being not the deity, but H.P. Belowstairs, the old man was Him. "You need to take some of those Heartsmart cooking classes with me."

So, I needed to shed a couple of pounds. A reporter's life is not always a healthy life. Sue me. Nonetheless, folded against Estelle's elegant black sheath and enveloped in the familiar aura of bergamot hair conditioner and White Shoulders cologne, I felt welcome here for the first time today. "Oh, Lord," she said. "Isn't it just awful? Poor Sammy. Poor thing. And he was going to try to do right this time, too, he told me so. This was the first time he lied to me."

Estelle shed some genuine tears. That finally touched me and I sighed, as much for what could have been, as for her loss. She was the only one of us who really mourned Sam. I felt pretty guilty for not staying in better touch with her over the years. And I felt sorry that I was not ten years younger and knew everything that I know now. I could have avoided a lot of pain.

She dabbed at her eyes. "Oh, Lord! I could just *shake* him for bein' so stupid! He knew those propane stoves go up just like that." She snapped her fingers. "Here, now! Put a doily on that tray before you take it upstairs. Underliners! Always use underliners beneath a service plate! And pile some more of those cheese straws on it! Do you want to have to make two trips?" she called to a pretty young blonde. The girl hopped to. Most people did when Estelle was at the helm. "My poor Sam. It's always the bad ones you love the most," she said to me. She dabbed at her eyes again. Then she looked at me fiercely. "I don't care what anyone tells you, Holly! I knew Sam and you knew Sam, and—it just wasn't his way. So don't you go and write anything like that in that newspaper, you hear me?"

"Estelle, who is Frank Dartwood, and why did he burst in upstairs? Did Sam know him?"

She shook her head. "Oh, honey, Sammy was only here for three days. He didn't know anybody. He'd just come home to make his peace with his daddy and then, boom! he was gone, just like that. The watermen are still pickin' up pieces of him out of the creek. But he wasn't depressed or anything like that. He says to me, 'Estelle, I've come home to do what's right. This time I mean to do the right thing.' That's what he said to me, right here in this kitchen."

She teared up again. "He was just like one of my own, my baby boy. I hand-fed him from the day Miss Rose died. Sometimes, I feel as if he's still alive, as if, if I turned around I would see him standing behind me." She reached out and gripped my arm fiercely, peering into my eyes. "Don't you dare write anything bad about Sam, you hear?"

A faint, thin light was beginning to crack the darkness.

THREE

•

Sam Redux, and It Sux

The newsroom was deserted when I returned to the *Gazette* building that afternoon. On a morning edition, where you start stripping the news wire at six A.M., the reporters clear out by three, either on assignment or pretending to be on assignment. It was as quiet as the grave, only the drone of the photo wire interrupting the crackle of the police and fire scanner in the corner.

I picked up my phone messages, flipped through them without interest, and opened my mail, which was the usual assortment of requests for stories, grip and grin shots, press releases, and junk mail. I glanced through the monthly crime and accident report from the sheriff's department and put it aside. There was a memo from the editor concerning the newsroom's extravagant use of paper clips, which was cutting into the Owner's profits.

In an effort to squeeze every last cent from his chain of small town rags without returning any capital to the business, the Owner frequently faxed the editor from his bunker somewhere in the South of France with his latest ingenious money-saving scheme. From now on, if you needed a paper clip, you would have to requisition one from the editor stating why you needed it and how it would be recycled. Someone had illustrated one of the faxes with a nasty caricature of Rig Riggle performing an obscene act on a deeply personal part of the Owner. What can I say? We're not Guild.

I thought about the *Post* and the *Sun* and sighed.

You get an amazing amount of junk mail at newspapers.

I sorted it into use, reroute, and recycle, and booted up my computer just to see what had come in on the P.M. wire, which was not much that was new.

After all these rituals were completed, I quickly typed in my story.

WATERTOWN—An assortment of well-known faces from the national, state and local political and social scenes were present today at the funeral of Samuel S. Wescott. Mr. Wescott, 36, was the only son of wealthy Santimoke developer and real estate magnate H. P. Wescott, and the last of an old Eastern Shore family.

Monday, Mr. Wescott died in a boating accident. As reported last Wednesday, a police analysis of the accident scene concluded that a defective valve in the propane galley stove caused his sailboat to explode at the dock of Mandrake, the Wescott estate, killing Mr. Wescott and destroying the yawl-rigged Honduras 36. Mr. Wescott had recently returned to the Eastern Shore from the Caribbean, where he had lived for a number of years. His obituary appeared in this paper yesterday.

A string of notables were present to pay tribute to the scion of the old and powerful Wescott family, who have been prominent in local and state affairs for several generations. Both the Governor of Maryland and the wife of former President . . .

And so forth and so on, listing all the big names in the acceptable AP style, adding all the appropriate quotes ("It's a tragedy, a very sad event for us all") from my notebook. I bit my lip and thought for a while. Then I crammed my tongue firmly in my cheek and keyboarded in:

Guests included Frank Dartwood, well-known environmentalist and head of the radical eco-activist organization, the Greenhead Environmental Army. Mr. Dartwood was present to register his strong opposition to the proposed White Marsh Development project currently being planned by Wescott Development and Real Estate Corporation for Santimoke County. Mr. Dartwood was escorted from the premises by Mandrake's private security force. No charges were pressed by H. P. Wescott.

I ran it through spell and grammar checks and moved it into the morning folder where Rig Riggle could edit it (badly) and send it to layout. From layout, it would go to the printing plant. And voilà, your newspaper. Aren't computers great?

Maybe not. Because then I did a bad thing. Instead of waiting for Rig to pass on my story, I sent it out on the Associated Press wire to Baltimore. Move a few things around with the mouse and hit a couple of keys and bye-bye. It was just one of those little demons of impulse that gets into all of us every once in a while. Don't tell me you've never done something for no particular reason, even though you knew you'd catch hell for it later if it blew up in your face.

You see, by sending it out to the wire service, I made the story available to almost every newspaper that subscribes to AP, *without allowing the editor to check it first*. Which means almost every self-respecting newspaper in America could conceivably access it. Are you getting the big picture here?

As soon as I'd done it, I regretted it. I fooled with the computer, trying to retrieve it, then I picked up the phone and dialed the AP voice phone. At least, I thought, I could kill it by talking to my counterpart at the other end. When the phone rang five or six times and no one answered, I replaced the phone in the cradle and crossed my fingers that it would be so insignificant that the Baltimore AP editor wouldn't bother with it.

Besides, at that point, something else was happening.

HOLL   HELP   ME

HOLL my computer typed neatly across the screen in 24-point Helvetica, without any help, all by itself.

HELLO HOLLIS ITS SAM which was scaring the daylights out of me.

At first, I thought it was a joke. As the ancient and overloaded system crashed, I stared at the screen, then wheeled my chair away from the desk and stood up, shaking.

"No. Oh, no," I said. "No."

HOLLIS HELP SAM

I grabbed my stuff and ran. To hell with the damn story. I needed some sleep. I could come in early in the morning and do damage control then, I thought.

Ha.

Chez moi is a considerable way down the food chain from Mandrake. No grand Palladian sweeps here. No fine old antiques, no smell of old family money.

I live in a ramshackle two-over-and-two-under cedar-shake tenant house on a working farm owned by a second cousin of my mother's, a man who'll tell anybody who'll listen how he's spent his whole life doing for others, especially in church. In reality, he's as tight as a tick with lyme disease and twice as mean. I avoid him whenever possible, especially when the rent's due. He's my least favorite kind of Christian, one who loudly proclaims his religion on Sunday and spends the rest of the week figuring how to screw other people over.

I heat with a woodstove and the wind finds its way through the cracks and chinks all winter, while the heat broils the cedar shingle all summer. It's a dump, but it's my dump, and I share it with a cat named Venus who regards me with contempt, as befits a daughter of generations of semiferal barn cats. As a daughter of generations of semiferal watermen, we understand each other perfectly and go our separate ways.

The best thing I can say for my house is that my nearest neighbor is a half mile away across several soybean fields, and Crazy Woman Creek, a sullen little stream, is just a few yards away. I've got to be near the water and far away from humanity to feel good.

After a hard day of dealing with Santimoke County's criminal justice system, that's what I like. There's just something about the relentless stream of human misery passing through the system that makes you happy to come home alone. As you know, my usual reportorial beat is cops 'n' courts. So Sam's funeral was a bit out of my purlieu. But I was still inclined to chalk it up to Rig's usual bad-taste idea of a punishment disguised as a joke. Rig is a major jerk.

I dropped my bag, kicked off my pumps, and started stripping off my funeral attire the minute I walked through the door. I tossed my sweat-soaked clothes into the washing machine in the kitchen and padded up the steps to the bedroom. The unmade bed gaped back at me as I stepped into the bathroom and opened the shower taps, then punched in the air conditioner to full blast, rewarding myself with a breath of tepid air.

By the time I'd scrubbed this day away from my body, the bedroom would be cool. My plan was to towel off, eat a light dinner that required no cooking, turn on the tube, and zone out in air-conditioned bliss, hopefully to fall asleep in the middle of *David Letterman*. I wanted this day behind me.

Maybe, I thought, it was the acid I'd taken in the 70s coming back to haunt me. One thing is for sure, I'm not used to hallucinating the face of my dead ex-husband. I wondered if I were having early symptoms of the malady that caused Great Aunt Tump to believe that the Union army was camped out in her beefsteak tomatoes. I wondered if the company health plan covered this problem. I wondered if I was having heat stroke. Finally, I just gave myself over to the pure bliss of hot water and Verandah shower gel and stopped wondering about anything.

Obviously, I should not drink hard liquor, and more obviously, I should stop smoking, eat properly, get some exercise and take H.P. up on his offer of the *Sun* and the *Post*. Get a cushy PR job, save up some money, find a nice man, have some kids ... get a life. A real life.

It was the usual self-flagellation, and by the time I had rinsed the shampoo out of my hair and stepped out of the shower, I was good and depressed, the sort of depression you get when you're too tired of dealing with things in your life that are beyond your control.

I wrapped a towel around myself and went downstairs again, where the oven-like conditions of the kitchen and living room were akin to those in Death Valley at high noon. After a brief and discouraging survey of the science project that is my refrigerator, I lit a cigarette, popped a diet soda, and opened a bag of Reese's cups, which I carried outside to my porch.

A lifelong ambition to live like white trash was achieved when I moved an old aluminum glider from the county dump to my screen porch. I now collapsed there to contemplate the angry red sun as it slowly sank behind the pines across the creek. Ah, August! Not so much as a breath of air stirred the humidity, and I could feel sweat reinfesting my showered skin. The red sunset did not predict rain for the morrow. Corn drooped in the fields, a thin layer of dust clung to the trumpet vines. The earth was cracked and crazed with thirst, waiting for rain.

Venus, having sensed that her meal ticket was home, crawled out from beneath a drooping hydrangea bush with something dead and repulsive in her mouth. She spit it out as she made her way up the steps and snaked her way through a hole in the screen door. A trip to the vet may have canceled out incestuous activities with Venus's barn-dwelling kinfolk, but she still has a peeled ear and a street fighter's look in her eye. If the ice skater Tonya Harding were a tortoiseshell feline, she would be Venus, the Cat with an Attitude. Plopping herself next to me, she immediately began to alternately cleanse her private parts with her tongue and attempt to eat the Reese's cup I held in the hand that didn't hold the cigarette. I swatted at her ineffectively and she ignored me.

For us, it was a tender moment.

I leaned back on the glider and contemplated the creek where the blue heron was fishing in the shallows. My favorite neighbor. From somewhere in the marsh, I heard the sound of the evening's first knee-deeps, singing their night song. Down in the little copse of trees where the old graveyard lies abandoned, a mockingbird whistled. The sky was stained orange and pink with sunset, and long purple tree shadows moved across the grass. Somewhere near the pine woods, I heard the indignant cry of the bobwhite, and a quail hen scurried across the drive, followed by her chicks.

Evening on the Chesapeake.

Sometimes I wish I were a Santimoke Indian, so I could see what this region looked like before contact. It must have been a magical place. It still is.

Except for the mosquitoes; even drought didn't affect their hunger. I swatted one and it left a streak of my own red blood on my leg. Venus settled down on the cushion and blinked, lifting her nose as if she were being stroked by an invisible hand. She purred and raised her head, as if someone were scratching her chin, just the way she likes it.

I took a hit from my diet soda, watching her curiously as she stretched and reached and preened, digging her claws into the flowery print cushion, purring away in delight.

Venus? Purring?

Now, you have to understand how it was.

Like mist, like smoke. Like a remembered song. In the twilight, I could just see the outline of him, in the same blue shirt and chino pants, the way his dark hair fell just so, over his forehead.

"Sam?" I said out loud, and the idea didn't seem to be so silly.

"I'm here, Holly," he said. It was Sam's voice, all right.

"No, you're not. You're dead," I whispered. The hairs on the back of my neck crawled.

"Well, that, too," Sam admitted. He shifted his weight on the glider, but it made no sound. His hair fell into his eyes, and he pushed it away with a familiar, careless gesture. Slowly, he reached out and put his hand against my arm. The feeling was cool and dry, like a breeze. I watched as his hand passed through my flesh.

"This is not happening," I said, jerking my arm away. I wanted to get up, but I couldn't. I just sat there shaking my head. "Oh, no. Oh, no." Denial wasn't working here.

Sam looked at his own hand with distaste. "You know, Holl, this isn't easy for me, either," he said. "I'll tell you, being dead is a lot of work. It's not all it's cracked up to be, either. Of course, I'm still getting the hang of it, but—"

"You're a ghost!" I exclaimed. It had me so upset that I lit a cigarette.

"That stuff can kill you, Holl," Sam observed distastefully. He waved his hand in the air, and I caught a vague and familiar scent of clean shirts, sunburned skin, and maleness that was essentially Sam. "Those cigarettes are poison."

"You're a fine one to talk," I snapped, inhaling deeply. "I'm still alive."

"Not for long, if you keep that up."

I eyed Sam nastily. "Especially," I continued, ignoring him, "since you blew yourself to hamburger with a propane stove. How could you have *been* so stupid?"

"Is that what happened? I don't remember much about it." He shook his head. "I've spent the past few days trying to get someone, *anyone* to pay attention to me. It's like I'm not there. This dead business is really beat."

"Oh, no, you don't," I hissed. Fear was turning to anger. "Go find another sucker, Sam. You're dead. Now, stay dead. Get off my porch and march your ass back to Mandrake and get into that coffin and stay there."

"It's kind of interesting, being dead," Sam said wistfully. And he probably hadn't been listening to a word I said. He leaned back, drew his legs up beneath himself, and tilted his head back. To my great disgust, Venus, the Cat with an Attitude, snuggled up against him, purring like she never purred for me. He stroked her absently, his hand going through her fur. "There are a lot of things about it that I haven't quite got yet, but it's kind of interesting how animals and kids seem to sense me. You know, Holl, you should be taking notes. There's a great story here."

"I don't work for *Weekly World News*," I snapped. "And you're not Elvis. Therefore, no story. Seeing a ghost is not exactly something you put on your résumé, anyway. Now, scat. It's almost time for *The Simpsons*."

Sam sighed, shook his head. In the fading summer twilight, he looked pretty handsome for a ghost, all that dark hair and those long eyelashes framing those blue eyes. "I'd like to oblige you, Holl, but I can't. You've got to help me."

"Oh, I don't think so, Sam. You get off my porch and do whatever you're supposed to do when you're dead. It took me *years* to get over you, and now that you're dead, I'm not about to start helping you hang around me."

Sam sighed. He shook his head. "No, I can't do that. You've gotta help me, Holl. It's serious this time."

"Sam, you're beyond help now," I pointed out gently. "Go to the light or whatever you're supposed to do. There's a next step. A train out of Dodge. Take it."

"I need you to help me, Holl."

I collapsed against the glider. It creaked a rusty creak. "It's too late, Sam. It's ten years too late. You lost the right to ask me for anything when you left me. We had been married for four days, Sam, four—count them—four days, and you left me. *Literally* left me. We were on our honeymoon, on that damn Honduras 36, in a marina in Fort Lauderdale, Florida, remember? I went to the marina store to buy a six-pack of diet soda, and you just cast off the lines, started up the motor, and when I came back, you were halfway out of the harbor, motoring out to sea. That was the last time I saw you, Sam. At the Bluegill Marina in Lauderdale. I sat on that damn dock all night, waiting for you to come back. I had a dollar and eighty-seven cents to my name. You not only sailed away, you took my clothes, my pocketbook, everything. You were a prick when you were alive, and I'll lay even money you're a prick now you're dead."

He frowned, looking out across the creek, where the sunset had turned the water to the color of blood. He had taken on the reflected light of the evening, and all I could see was his fine boned profile.

"Why, Sam?" I asked. "All I want to know now is why? I thought we loved each other. After everything we'd been through with your family and my family, all the rich boy–poor girl class conflict stuff we put up with just to be together, why?"

"I was afraid, Holl," he said softly. "I was afraid. I'd never loved anyone as much as I loved you, and it frightened me. I was afraid I would smother. I was afraid of commitment and afraid that I might find someone better. I never let anyone get too close to me because I was afraid of being tied down. I never wanted to grow up. The older I got, the more childish I became. Now that I'm dead, you and Estelle are the only ones who mourn me. And she can't see me."

I stubbed my cigarette out in an oystershell ashtray. It lay there and smoldered. "I wish I could say I'm moved. But I'm not. You're dead, Sam. And ten years ago, you killed off a part of me. You're a cashed chip, a bought farm, a checked-out room in Motel Hell. Now, go away. There's nothing left for you here."

"I can't go away. I'd like to, but I can't. I'm supposed to stay earthbound. Holl, someone murdered me."

"Why am I not surprised?" My hands were shaking as I lit another cigarette, as much for something to do as for anything else. The sun had sunk beneath the surface of the pines, and the sky was full of gathering darkness. There would be rain before morning; I could smell it in the air. "So, who did it?" I asked conversationally.

Sam pushed his hand through his hair. The dark forelock fell forward. "That's the trouble, Holl, I don't know. And I've got to find out. Otherwise, I'm trapped here for—forever. And it's not a great place to be, where I am. I'm in the world but not of it."

"We all create our own hells, Sam. Stitch by stitch, drop by drop. I'd say that yours suits you very well."

"No, it's not hell. Hell's a lot worse. This's like limbo."

There was a terrible sadness in Sam's voice. It was something I had never heard there before. Maybe death had been a maturing experience for him.

"Hell would at least be interesting. This nothingness is awful. It's like a TV screen with nothing but static and ghosts, if you'll pardon the expression."

"So what's hell like? How about heaven?"

Sam shook his head. "I can't tell you. Those're the rules."

"The rules? What are the rules? No running by the pool? Lights out at eleven? No ghastly shrieks or rattling chains during the dinner hour?"

"Easy for you to laugh. You don't have to follow them. Following rules was never one of my talents. It's complicated. But if I'm going to go on, I have to clean up some of the stuff I did when I was alive. I have to make up for certain things. And I have to find out who killed me. And why."

I thought he was laughing, but I didn't look to see. Some things I have always felt better off not knowing, and what happens in the afterlife is one of them.

I slid a look at him. He blended nicely with the darkness. A mosquito flew right through him. "You're not kidding, are you? This isn't one of your stupid practical jokes, is it?"

He reached out and gripped my arm again. A chill, damp and dank and awful, ran through my body. The chill of death. I turned all the way around and looked at him, and what I saw in the depths of his eyes I still cannot find the words to describe except to say it scared me.

"Oh," I whispered.

"Exactly," Sam replied with a thin smile. "Help me, Holl. You're the only one who can."

"Your death was an accident. You blew yourself up with a defective propane stove. The cops checked it all out. So, who killed you?"

Sam shrugged. "I don't know. I thought maybe you would. Somebody went aboard my boat and opened the valves on the propane stove. And I blew up. Boom. Never even knew what hit me. But now I can't remember anything about what happened."

I sighed. "Work with me here, Sam. I haven't seen you in ten years. I don't know who else you've managed to offend in the past decade. It could be anyone. And I do mean *anyone*. You were not a nice person, Sam. A charming person, but not a nice person. You were a selfish, manipulative scumbucket."

"Handsome, don't forget handsome," Sam grinned.

"Oh, you were handsome all right. And funny, too. Some of the stuff I used to watch you talk your way out of, the way you could make people laugh—"

"Aw, Holl, I knew you would help me. Believe me, you won't regret it. Look, I've got to go now, but we'll talk soon, all right?" He leaned over and brushed my cheek with his cool, dry lips.

And then, he was gone.

Did I detect a faint odor of sulfur and brimstone where he had been?

FOUR

•

Denial: It's a River in Egypt

I awoke in the morning convinced that last night had been a bad, very bad dream. I resolved never again to drink vodka and eat crab balls on an empty stomach.

Till the next time.

The day had dawned dusty, hot, and even more humid than yesterday, if that was possible. The cicadas were already screeching at seven o'clock, and a thick, nasty scrim of dead air lay across the land. I drank a cup of iced coffee while I dressed and watched the old blue heron on the creek, patiently fishing on the morning tide. I envied him his life from the bottom of my soul. The car was the temperature of a steam bath in Death Valley as I got behind the wheel and turned up the a/c full blast.

Watertown is the county seat of Santimoke, a market town of about twenty-five or thirty thousand souls. The county likes the redbrick colonial look, and while the dogs don't quite sleep in the streets, it's generally a pretty peaceful place. Or at least it looks peaceful on the surface, if you don't know the ins and outs of small town politics, social and civil. It can be quite interesting around here.

When I was in high school, someone spray painted WATERTOWN BLOWS PIGS on the WELCOME TO WATERTOWN sign outside of town. I had graduated from college before the city council got around to having the damage removed. There is such a thing as Eastern Shore Time. It's about two hours later than you think it should be.

The courthouse is red brick, naturally, and sits squat in the middle of town, where the statue of Our Glorious

Confederate Dead is half-obscured by old magnolia trees. If I told you that the Eastern Shore was occupied by Union troops and placed under martial law during the Civil War, it would give you some idea of our character. And yet, Harriet Tubman and Frederick Douglass are two of our favorite Eastern Shore natives, people we're proud to claim. Go figure. Santimoke County is a nice place to live if you don't weaken, but I always get a kick out of reminding people that when they move here, they're living below the Smith & Wesson Line.

The courthouse is the hub of county activity and it's my beat, along with Lawyer's Row, the side street of attorneys' offices that flanks it, and the cop shops and other, more obscure places civilians don't know about. Like the folks I write about, I'm a courthouse barnacle. And I like my beat. It's the most interesting place to be in a small town.

And the most interesting events are the ones I can't print. Little-known facts about well-known people are very useful, especially when these people violate the public trust and rape the taxpayers who voted them into office. Hey, it happens.

I was able to spend most of the morning making my rounds. It's like a mall; everything is conveniently located in one place. I start by poking my head into the sheriff's office to see if they have made any arrests. Then I check the dockets for the district and circuit courts to see what trials are coming up, look at the charging documents that have come in the past twenty-four hours, drop by the Watertown police office to see what they've got, use their phone to call the state police barracks out on Route 50. Go past the clerk of court's office, see what's happening. Drop by the judges' chambers, the state's attorney's offices, say hello. And schmooze. I am very good at schmoozing with people. If you've been on a beat for a while, you start to get to know everyone, their families, their lives, their problems. The fact that Eastern Shore people are constitutionally incapable of greeting without passing the time of day for a while always works in my favor. If there's something going on, someone, somewhere will tell me about it. Besides, I like the people in the courthouse; they're my friends and I'm theirs. And except for some ego-bloated lawyers and rookie cops, everyone understands that business is business, and I have to write about what's going on. Sometimes it's a game of cat-and-mouse where I have to dig in old records and transcripts and sometimes it's Deep Throat time, where I get an anonymous tip from a familiar voice over the phone, late at night. But I nearly always get my story. Getting it into print is sometimes another matter. My editor is not a champion of the people's right to know, especially if the advertisers or those who can do him some personal good are concerned. Rig Riggle is a man of limited vision and venial temperament.

Today, it looked like the pickings were slim. No drug busts, no drunks, no overnight arrests. Usually, if circuit court's not in session, I stop by Judge Franklin Carroll's chambers anyway. If he's not busy, we talk. I really like Judge Carroll; he's given me a lot of good advice over the years. Alas, circuit was hearing preliminaries for a dull civil case, the kind we see so much around here since so many rich retirees moved here. Your new deck blocks my morning sunlight sort of stuff. I skipped it. Unlike the plaintiffs, I do not have too much money and time on my hands. As things turned out, it would have been better for me if I'd gone into the courtroom and watched Judge Carroll's patience wear thin.

Judge Helen Quick of district court was not in chambers either; she was hearing DWIs. We scrape up the drunk driver convictions and publish them as a list at the end of the month. But sometimes I like to hear the excuses people come up with.

No internal warnings went off when I walked down the hall to the state's attorney's office. They should have, but if they did, I wasn't listening. I wish I had.

Kenisha, whose official title is receptionist, but whose real job is keeping the SA's office and the Victim Witness Program organized, grinned at me as she saw me coming down the hall. The beads in her extensions swung from side to side as she shook her head at me.

"Not a thing today," she said. "Elizabeth's having her baby, Tommy's up in Baltimore, and Sev's slipped out for a minute to get some of his health-food tea." She rolled her eyes. Our state's attorney's preoccupation with all things healthy was something of a joke among us lesser mortals.

"Somebody making fun of me again?" Severn Capwell was dragging his sleek Italian bicycle with him through the swinging doors. He rolled it down the floor, carefully placed it on the kickstand, dabbed at a dust speck with his finger, and unclipped the leg of his gray Brooks Brothers suit before advancing on us, tea in hand. He uncapped the paper cup and took a sip. "Delicious," he pronounced. "Raspberry skullcap goldenseal. Good for the kidneys."

"Yuck," Kenisha and I both said at once.

Sev allowed his handsome blond features to assume an expression of great hurt. "You all should try it sometime, instead of polluting yourselves with that sludge they call courthouse coffee. And you could all learn to bike, instead of riding everywhere in your cars." He winked at Kenisha, who laughed, throwing up her hands.

"This from a man with a brand new Range Rover," she sighed in mock exasperation.

"The better to carry my Giacometti in, my dear." He petted the bicycle. "Any messages?"

"*State v. Dimwell*'s been postponed till two. And Mrs. Coldstone's attorney called."

Sev took the slips of pink paper from her, glancing at them. "Mrs. Coldstone," he repeated. "That's a damn shame, that mess," he murmured, looking at a slip. "Her daughter ran away from college. Joined some cult or something. They think she might have headed to the Shore."

As he talked, we walked toward his office.

Sev was about my age, but in much better shape. His handsome looks as well as his obsession with healthy living placed him out of my league, but I personally knew about ten women who would have killed for a date with him.

Several of them had taken up bicycling, since he was an avid biker who could be seen riding up and down the roads of Santimoke County every weekend, a vision of male pulchritude in those skintight biker shorts and tank top. Others joined the health club where he worked out just to be able to see him pumping iron. The word I got back was Adonis in spandex. I could believe it. But so far, no woman seemed to have snagged his interest. It was rumored that he had a sweetie up in Baltimore, but no one ever saw her.

Our semisocial friendship was based on the shared ordeals of court (waiting in the Duck Inn, the bar across the street, for juries to return a verdict, Monday morning quarterbacking the judges), a mutual interest in seeing justice done, and a shared interest in those little-known facts about well-known people, but we rarely traveled on the same social circuits. A single man is about five hundred times more in demand than a single woman.

His office was like he was: neat and well appointed. The Baltimore Museum and Walters Art Gallery posters on the walls always reminded me that Sev had come to us from Charm City, where he'd been an assistant SA for several years before caseload burnout decided that private practice on the Eastern Shore suited him just fine. Judges Quick and Carroll had encouraged him to run for state's attorney when his predecessor, the one and only Jason Hemlock, had won his seat in Annapolis.

As he sank into his place behind the neat-as-a-pin desk, I took my usual seat in the wing chair to his right, settling in for a visit. Sev was well liked on the law and order food chain. Most courthouse types respected his ability to get a conviction, and the cops liked his style, as much as they liked that of any lawyer. I considered him one of the good guys.

"This Coldstone thing," he sighed. "I know the family. Charles Coldstone was a friend of mine, before he killed himself."

"Charles Coldstone was the legislator from the Western Shore who was going to run for governor before Jason smeared his name all over the front page?" It had been a nine days' wonder about six months ago, but since then it had been replaced by other scandals.

Sev winced. He was careful what he said about other people, especially Jason. "That was an ugly episode," he conceded, sipping his tea.

"Guy lives out his life, gets married, has a child, gets into politics, does a good job, speaks up for protecting the Chesapeake, education, jobs, lower taxes, good stuff like that, talks about cleaning up the PACs and the lobbyists with too much influence in the general assembly, and steps on a few toes like your bud Jason's. Hemlock is suddenly under scrutiny by the media for all the special interests he's in bed with, like the real estate people and the developers, two very big, very powerful lobbies. Eats up to the religious right, too. With all the land they own, development is a very big agenda for them, you know. To divert attention from himself, Jason suddenly comes out with these—these *allegations* that Coldstone's gay." I paused, thinking back on it. Since Annapolis wasn't on my beat, I hadn't paid a lot of attention to it at the time.

Sev looked down into his tea, frowning. He remained silent.

"The next thing you know, Coldstone eats his gun. In his own house on Gibson Island, and Jason's some kind of right-wing hero to every Bible-banging developer for ratting him out. Although the allegations were never proved, and you can't sue someone for what they said about a dead man," I recited. "Top ten reasons I don't trust Bible bangers. They always seem to find a biblical interpretation that justifies their particular, personal agendas."

Sev's mouth twisted up. "You have such a nice way of putting things, Hollis," he said dryly.

"Tell me that's not the story in a nutshell! I was out of Jason's loop by then, but I remember the story breaking. It was the sort of nasty mudslinging that Jason has started to refine into an art form. Throw enough and some will stick. It's a trick he learned from his brand new buddies in the religious right. I never saw anyone do such a complete about-face in my life. Once they dangled money and power in front of him, he forgot every promise he ever made."

"You can try as hard as you want, but you know damn well that I am not going to comment on my opinions of Delegate Hemlock."

"Love him? Do nothing. Hate him, give me a sign."

Sev waved his tea in the air.

"My feelings exactly," I said.

Sev picked up the pink message sheet, frowning. "This is about the Coldstone daughter. She walked away from Goucher in the middle of her last semester, and her mother hasn't heard a word from her since then. As I said, Mrs. Coldstone thinks she might have joined some cult or something. She's over twenty-one, so there isn't much you can do, but still ... if you hear of anything, let me know."

"There are a couple of cults around here. Actually, there are people who say the whole Eastern Shore is a kind of cult," I said.

Sev shook his head. "It's a tough place to be a foreigner," he agreed. "I'm still having trouble with the accents of some of these watermen. It's a job of work to understand them."

"Myself, I'm bilingual," I offered. "At home, on the island, we speak the language as we grew up hearing it. Other places, we speak American broadcast English. Television has leveled regional speech. If a waterman's speaking to you in the dialect, he's running you for his own reasons."

"I thought that might be it," Sev admitted. "What do I know? I grew up speaking good Baltimoron in Roland Park. Did you see Franklin today? I could hear him losing his temper all the way down the hall this morning. Gordon must have gone in there unprepared."

"Pity Gordon." Judge Carroll's intolerance of lawyers taking up his court time unprepared is legendary. "Is it true that Sheriff Barlow came over here from Devanau County and got into a hair-pulling contest with the new boy out at the state police over who had jurisdiction over that crack dealer they busted on the Devanau River bridge?"

Sev grinned. "You know I can't comment on that."

"If he didn't, don't do anything, just sit there. If he did, make a move," I suggested.

He wadded up Mrs. Coldstone's pink message slip and tossed it at me.

"Strictly off the record."

"Life is good," I laughed. "But it's better if you're not the new guy out to the state police."

After a while, I pushed on down the hall to my next stop at the clerk of court's office, still smiling.

However, dawdle as I might, and I am mighty good at dawdling, there still came a time when I had to put a wrap on the lack of news and head for the *Gazette* offices across town.

I went as if to my own execution, hoping that Rig Riggle would be gone. Since he is generally only in the office about two hours a day, I hoped that the Merciful Deity was staying with me.

I was wrong.

I knew for sure I was in trouble when I walked into the office.

"He wants to see you," Norma the receptionist told me around her wad of gum, patting her giant bouffant. Norma's hair has a life of its own. Today it looked like it could destroy Tokyo. "Right away," she added, going back to her two-fingered typing.

"Shit," I said under my breath as I made my way to my desk in the newsroom.

Not one of the other reporters met my eye, so I knew I was in for it. I grabbed my mail off my desk and made a hasty retreat toward the door. I would have made it, too, had not Jolene, the office snitch, seen me.

"Oh, there you are! He wants to see you right now, Hollis. Rig, I found her!" Jolene called in the same voice she uses when she's doing her question and answer stint in beauty pageants.

Do I have to tell you that Jolene is boffing Rig? That, and her certificate from Patti's Christian School of Tap and Ballet, qualify her as a journalist. She's the worst reporter to ever win the Most Retractions in One Edition award. Of course, she's community reporter and her specialty is church suppers, quilt raffles, and the sort of social events Claire attends, real heavy-duty stuff that still taxes her tiny intellect. If her brain were a pea on a fork, it would look like a BB rolling down a four-lane highway. Her hobby is spying on everyone in the newsroom and running to Rig with any subversive thoughts anyone might have. Doubtless, she pours them into his shell pink ear during their sessions at the Cocky Locky Motor Inn out on Route 50.

"Ball! In my office! Now!" Rig Riggle shouted. He fancies himself Perry White, I think. But this ain't the *Daily Planet*, and I sure ain't Lois Lane.

"Oooh, Hollis, you are in so much trouble!" she sing-songed at me, shaking one of her long pink Lee Press-On Nails in my direction.

With a glare at Jolene, I trudged into the lair of the beast.

Rig, sitting behind his empty desk, glared at me for several moments. For effect, I think. Since he looks like Maury Povitch without a chin, I usually focus on the wart in the middle of his forehead. I think it's where they connect the feeding tube when he discorporates and goes back to Uranus every night.

"What in the hell is *this* all about?" he demanded, throwing a copy of the morning edition of the *Gazette* across the desk.

I looked.

There was my story, right above the fold, on the left. "And this?"

He then tossed out the *Post*. There it was, hot off the AP wire, in the gossip column in Style.

"And this?"

Maryland section of the *Sun*.

AP had done its job all too well. They'd even kept my byline, bless their pointed little heads.

"How did that happen?" I asked innocently.

"That's what I want to ask you. You're such a hotshot reporter," he sneered. "You tell me. And this bit about Frank Dartwood? What the hell is that all about? You know that Mr. Wescott called me at home this morning, at six A.M.? What the hell made you write that Frank Dartwood was there? Don't you know that H. P. Wescott is one of the most important men on the Eastern Shore? That he's one of our most powerful advertisers?"

Don't I know that the reason they promoted you to editor is that you're a man? I thought. *Come on, Rig. When you were an intern, you couldn't intern, when you were a reporter, you couldn't report, and now that you're an editor, you can't edit.*

Aloud I said: "So what do you want from me? I reported what happened. I was talking to my former father-in-law about my late ex-husband, and Frank Dartwood broke into the office and started yelling about environmental sanctions and White Marsh."

Now, you know and I know that you wouldn't print a word against Wescott Development. How the hell else did you think I could tell the outside world what's going on behind the scenes here at Pravda?

The wart in the middle of Rig's forehead turned bright red as he glared at me. He knows as well as I do that he was promoted by a prick, because he's a prick who's got a prick, and pricks stick together. And according to what Jolene told Norma when she, Jolene, had a really bad case of PMS, well, Rig's personal rig is no eighteen-wheeled, two-ton Peterbilt semi, if you know what I mean and I think you do.

"I'm busting you," he barked. "From now on, you're back on the turd express."

The turd express, pardon the expression, is newspaper slang for stripping the AP wire at ungodly hours of the morning. It's a job from hell if you hate getting up early, and I do.

"Fine," I said through clenched teeth. "That means you

might have to cancel your daily afternoon golf game over at the country club to actually do some work around here. Last I heard the courts and cop shops don't close down for nine holes at your tee-off time, Rig. And don't forget, you've been banned from Judge Carroll's courtroom forever."

"You really think you're smart, don't you?" Rig sneered, flexing a muscle in his jaw. "A couple of awards and you're Brenda Starr."

I leaned forward. "I can write rings around you any day of the week, Rig. And the next time I catch you changing the direct quotes in my stories, I'll tell your wife to stake you and Jolene out at the Cocky Locky."

"You're fired!"

"No, I'm not! I quit!"

It was an old song, and I was about to get up and leave when a heavy hardboard edition of *The Associated Press Stylebook and Libel Manual* lifted itself off a file cabinet behind Rig's head and sailed gracefully through the air. As I watched, fascinated, it dropped at warp speed right on the top of Rig's head.

I winced at the *thunk* it made when five solid pounds of paper and cardboard made contact with his skull. It slid to the floor, falling open on its spine at my feet. The entry that caught my eye was *dead end*.

For a moment, Rig and I stared at each other, nonplussed. This wasn't in the script.

"How did you do that?" he asked. And then the phone rang.

"Riggle, the *Gazette*," he barked, as if this were a bus-and-truck revival of *The Front Page*. He rubbed his head. Suddenly, he sat up at attention. "Yes, sir! Yes, *sir*! She's right here in the office, sir! Yes, I saw it, but she went behind my ba—yes, sir!"

He handed the phone to me and, gentleman that he is, punched the speaker so he could hear it all.

"It's H. P. Wescott," he breathed reverently.

I raised my eyebrows but took the phone. "This is Hollis, H.P. What can I do you for?" I asked crisply.

"Hollis? I want you to come right out here. Right now. Tell that solipsistic fool to send you out here right away!"

While I was talking to H.P., Rig picked up the AP *Stylebook* and placed it back on the file cabinet. When it didn't fall again, he poked at it with a pencil. It remained rock steady.

"What's this all about?" I asked, eyeing Rig curiously as he picked up the stylebook and stared down the spine at the binding.

"I'll tell you when you get here. Just come as soon as you can."

"You heard the man, get out of here! Go, do whatever he wants!" Rig screamed.

I didn't have to be told twice.

When I left the office, Rig was still trying to tip that book off the file cabinet, cursing to himself when it steadfastly refused to fall. A lump was developing nicely on his forehead, right above his wart.

I climbed into the Honda and lit a cigarette. There was nothing I enjoyed so much as hating Rig Riggle, the Editor from Hell.

And then I looked over and saw Sam sitting in the passenger seat. "Oh, no you don't," I said. "You're a dream, an unresolved issue. Go away." I stared at him balefully, but he refused to disappear.

"How'd you like that trick with the book?" he asked, grinning at me.

I blinked. "You did that?"

Sam nodded. "It was really great, wasn't it? But an awful lot of concentration. I've never been real good at concentrating on anything for any length of time. Wow, who *is* that guy? Is that your boss? He's a major asshole, isn't he?"

I started waving my hands at him. "Sam, go away! You're dead! Shoo! Stop it right now! Go haunt someone who deserves it!"

Two pressmen having a cigarette break outside the *Gazette* printing plant stared at me. I collapsed against the seat. "Great! They think the newsroom's full of crazies anyway. The next thing you know, they'll be hauling me off to the state hospital at Cambridge!"

"Speaking of great," Sam continued. "I really enjoyed the way you handled that lawyer guy at the courthouse. That was masterful, Holl. Truly masterful."

"My God, are you *everywhere*?" I asked, horrified. "Have I no privacy?"

"Not until my murderer is found," Sam replied. "Look, Holl, if I were you, I would peel this bomb out of here. Those two printers are starting to come over here, and I don't like the look in their eyes. Let us go see the Old Man."

I turned the key, smiled, waved at Wilmer and Poot and peeled out of the *Gazette* lot. It wasn't even noon, and already this day was spinning out of control.

FIVE

•

Checks (and Balances)

"You know, I am starting to believe that you really are a ghost, Sam. That this isn't a hallucination, a hormone storm, or a manifestation of my unresolved issues. I might just believe that you are really and truly a ghost, and it is scaring the hell out of me." I naturally had to reach for another cigarette.

"I'm glad you are finally starting to see the light." Sam coughed meaningfully. "Now, will you work with me on this?"

"I'm still thinking about that," I replied cautiously. "I can only handle so much at one time, you know." I laughed hollowly. "I always knew I was a slice of cheese short of a reality sandwich, but this is ridiculous."

We were leaving Watertown and driving out into the country on a two-lane blacktop. The fields lay limp and dusty across the flat and endless landscape. Here and there, new houses were going up on barren, treeless lots. Santimoke was getting a lot more crowded than it had been when Sam and I were both kids, growing up on opposite sides of the county.

As we took a corner, the road ahead was clogged with a plague of bicyclists, a road hazard we have come to expect over here during high tourist season. As usual, they were not riding single file, as the law and common sense commanded, but stretched out about a dozen abreast across the road and not about to give an inch. Attired in expensive, if unflattering, unnatural fibers and commanding thousand-dollar pieces of flimsy equipment, they firmly believe they own the road.

Until they encounter some yobbo in a '75 pickup doing about seventy-five who *knows* he does. The carnage makes for great news photos.

I tapped the horn to alert them to the presence of a car behind them, and two of the young urban professionals flipped me the bird. I carefully wove my way through them, ignoring their advice about what I could do with my redneck ass. Charming people. We locals despise them more than any other tourist for their complete lack of manners and their incredible arrogance. Biking, I've decided, is an asshole magnet.

Sam just laughed as the fingerees suddenly veered out of control and into a deep tidal ditch at the side of the road. We left their outraged howls in the distance. If he had something to do with it, I didn't want to know.

"I can't believe how built up everything has become around here," he said, looking out the window. "It was the first thing I noticed when I came back, how all the open land was gone, or going fast. I guess we have the Old Man to thank for that."

"Probably. We had a lot of unrestricted development back in the '70s and '80s. There was a lot of speculation on real estate. A lot of people, farmers and such, were selling off their land for all they could get to developers and real estate brokers. The Eastern Shore was like a real estate Dodge City. All of a sudden, every foreigner within a five state range just *had* to have a piece of the Eastern Shore. Santimoke County has become the land of the newly wed and the nearly dead."

"They still call the non-natives foreigners," Sam said with a smile in his voice. "You know, Holl, the living don't have a clue. You take everything for granted. When you're dead, it's different. You suddenly realize how much you missed, pursuing really stupid stuff that ended up not mattering after all."

"Just what I need. Garbled philosophy from a ghost.

From the ghost of my ex-husband." I stuck out my hand. It went through him. It was like putting my flesh in the vapor from dry ice.

"Hey!" Sam exclaimed. "That's rude, Holl!"

"Just wanted to be sure. You'll forgive me if I am justifiably cynical about your ghosthood. And everything else about you."

"And?"

I glanced down at my hand. "I guess I'm going through the stages. You know, denial, rage, bargaining, something, and acceptance."

"And what stage are you in?"

"Much against my better judgment, acceptance. I don't understand it, and I don't like it, but it seems to be true. All the people in the world you *could* have haunted, though. Why pick on me?"

Sam sighed, ran his translucent fingers through his hair. "One more time, Holl: I was murdered. You've got to help me find out who did it."

"Just double checking. I thought that's what you said, but then again, I thought last night was too many crab balls and a rare shot of vodka. Oh, shit!"

A biker with a small child in a drag seat wove blindly off the shoulder and right into my path. Oblivious to near death and screaming brakes, she continued on down the middle of the road, another clueless tourist inhaling the quaint and rustic scenery.

I turned the car to the gravel shoulder and leaned back in my seat, closing my eyes. "I don't need this. I don't need any of this," I said thickly. I turned and looked at Sam, transparent as tissue paper, iridescent as mother-of-pearl. "Why are you doing this to me? My life was fine until you showed up. Since you've been—whatever—everything that could go wrong *has*. My editor's all over me. H.P.'s about to be all over me. And it's only going to get worse if you start nagging me to play Suzie Detective. I *need* this damn job, Sam. Everything you ever touched turned to trash. You were a royal screw-up when you were alive and you hurt me like nobody else has ever hurt me before or since. For all I could care, you can rot in hell—literally." And suddenly cynical, hard-boiled me, I burst into tears.

Well, it happens. I never said I was made of stone.

"Oh, wow. Oh, dammit, Hollis." Rather ineffectively, Sam tried to put his arms around me. It didn't work too well; he kept passing through my shoulders like a cool breeze. But I didn't care; I was too busy sobbing. A decade's worth of stored-up pain all came gushing out. "Oh, God, I am sorry, Hollis, please believe me."

"I don't care! I just want you to go away and leave me alone," I wailed. "Haven't you hurt me enough?"

"Yes, I have hurt you enough," Sam said softly. I could feel his fingers, soft, like a feather's stroke, touching my cheek. "I wasn't a very nice person, I know that now. God, Holl, I was a total shit. Especially the way I left you. That's a part of all this. I've got to make up to you for what I did."

"I can't forgive you," I sniffled, digging in my purse for a Kleenex. "I'll never forgive you, Sam Wescott. I loved you!"

"Believe it or not, I loved you too. So much it scared me to death," Sam said and then giggled. "Get it? To dea—"

"Oh, shut up!" I snapped, blowing my nose. "*Damn* dead people anyway! Especially you. How do you know *I* didn't kill you?"

"Because you've got an alibi. Because you don't want me to be dead."

"Huh?" I sniffled.

"Because I can feel it. You still feel something for me, Holl. You know, it's different when you're dead. You develop these intensified hunches or something. I can't explain it. I'm still trying to learn how to figure this all out, this dead stuff."

"You never even figured how to be alive," I replied. I looked at my reflection in the rearview mirror and dabbed at my mascara. My eyeballs were the color of sunset.

Great. I really needed to look like hell when I faced the wrath of H.P., the Terror of the Eastern Shore.

I took a deep breath and collected my few remaining wits. "You have to admit that this is all just a bit much, even for a semitough cookie like me," I said shakily.

"Me, too," Sam sighed. "But as long as there's this bond between us, we seem to be stuck to each other. Unresolved issues and all of that good stuff."

"And they say hell happens after you're dead," I muttered.

"Well, that's half-true anyway," Sam agreed. "You feel better now? I know this is a lot to handle, but maybe if we work together, we can get through it. Now, let's go see what my old man has to say. Not that he was ever much help to either one of us in the past."

"If you're gonna be there, you've just got to promise me, no more floating books, Sam. This is tough enough."

"So you'll help me?" he asked eagerly.

"I didn't say that. Let's just see what happens when we get to stately Mandrake House. There's just one thing."

"What's that?"

"I can't believe I'm holding a conversation with a ghost."

"Believe it, sweetcakes. And you always did have the sweetest—hey, what are you doing?"

"Looking for your *off* button."

"This is bad! This is very, very bad!" H.P. rumbled. The Audubons on the study walls shook in their frames.

"Daddy, your blood pressure!" Claire warned. She shot me a dirty look. "Now look what you've done," she snarled at me. "You and that damned article! What do you think people are saying about that—that Dartwood, that damned *Communist*, barging in here and making a scene about White Marsh? It looks bad! We want a retraction and we want it now, do you hear me? All you care about is making this family look bad!"

"You're doing a pretty good job of that yourself without

any help from anyone else," Sam said. He was sitting in the windowsill behind his father's desk. The sunlight poured right through him. H.P. and Claire couldn't see or even sense him, of course. But I could, and he was annoying me. It was hard to concentrate on what they were saying with Sam adding his two cents. I shot him a dirty look.

"Don't you give me that expression! You think you're so clever!" Claire's pearls twitched as she put a hand on her father's shoulder. "Daddy, why don't you let me handle this? We should just demand that that editor fire her!"

"For God's sake, Claire, sit down and shut up!" H.P. bellowed, waving her away from him as if she were a pesky fly. "If I wanted any advice from you, I'd have asked for it, not that it would do me any good." He glared at her from beneath his eyebrows. "If it weren't for you, we wouldn't be in this damn White Marsh thing in the first goddamn place!"

"Well, that's the thanks I get," Claire sniffed, stiffening, "for bringing in a deal that will put us in the Forbes 400! Believe me, if it weren't for me, Wescott Development would be asleep on the side of the road! Don't you care what people will say? Several people at the yacht club are on the board of the Save the Chesapeake Foundation, you know! How will this look to them?"

The old man winced. Like many rich people who like to pretend that they don't care what others say about them, H.P. cared, and cared very deeply about his standing with his peers. "We'll write 'em a goddamn big check. That should stop them from grumbling too much. Now, get out of here, Claire! Don't you have a Daughters charity luncheon or something? I want to talk to Hollis privately."

"I'm not leaving you alone with her! I've got a right to be here, Daddy! I want what's due me! I was the one who *conceived* this whole project!" Angry, Claire flushed a violent red. Hands on hips, she stamped her foot. "I was the one who brought everyone else in! I was the one who thought of using that idiot brother of mine—" She broke off, biting her lip, her eyes sliding uneasily toward me.

"Using Sam for what?" I asked pleasantly.

"Yeah, I want to know that one too," Sam said.

"Don't you have to be somewhere?" H.P. asked in a low, dangerous voice.

Claire opened her mouth, then closed it again. "If I were a boy, things would be different!" she said in a voice of deep bitterness. She slammed the door behind her.

Sam whistled.

H.P. turned back to me, thick fingers crossing over his desktop, glaring at me over the top of his reading glasses. "What do you intend to do about this?" he demanded.

"What, indeed?" Sam asked.

"What do you want me to do, H.P.?" I asked, looking at the newspapers spread on his desk. "I just write up what happens to the best of my ability."

He glowered at me from beneath his big, bushy eyebrows. His cheeks puffed in and out. "I gave you a check for quite a bit of money." He leaned forward. "To make sure that things like this did not appear in the paper." He gestured across the broadsheets. "This is exactly the sort of negative publicity White Marsh is trying to avoid!"

"I thought it was for being a jerk when you were my father-in-law," I said evenly. The truth was, I'd forgotten all about it. I don't get offered bribes often enough, I guess. Oh, there's the occasional lunch, the comp tickets, but—well, you get the idea. A small town reporter's life is poor pickings.

Sam clapped. It was the sound of one hand clapping.

"Stop that," I said to him before I thought about it.

H.P. shrugged. "Well, anyway, what's done can't be undone. But while I was waiting for you to show up, I had another little talk with your editor, and we have decided to take care of this little problem."

"What are you going to do, whack me?" I asked. "You'd have to stand in line."

"Don't put ideas in the old man's head," Sam said. "Like as not, he whacked me, you know. Anyone in the family could be a suspect."

"Is there something going on out there?" H.P. turned to look through Sam, out the window, where there was that magnificent water view. "I had the gardeners ripping out some of the rose garden where the explosion damaged it, but like as not, they're lazing on the job. It's hard to get good help these days. Damn that boy," H.P. fumed, "he's just as much trouble dead as he was alive."

"You can say that again," I murmured sympathetically.

Sam made a particularly ugly face.

"Anyway, I have had a talk with Wig Waggle, is that his name? Obliging sort of fella, always anxious to please, Waggle, and we have decided that you will be working on a special *Gazette* supplement on White Marsh for a while. A supplement that will place the development in a most positive and favored light, I might add." He *did* add, and heavily at that. He lowered his eyelids and looked very pleased with himself. "You will be writing this supplement."

Sam stood up and thrust his hands into his pants pockets. He looked down at his father, grinning.

"Great going, Holl! This will give you an excuse to snoop around and see what's going on," he said.

"What about my usual beat?" I asked. "There's the Grooby trial coming up and a couple of arrests that I need to follow up on—"

H.P. held up a huge hand. "This will only take a few days," he said. "And of course, there are other considerations in it for you—" He reached into the desk for the ubiquitous checkbook.

"That's okay," I said. "We'll talk about that later." You bet we will, I thought.

"Well, I'm glad we seem to have reached an understanding on this, at least, Hollis. Why don't we have a bit of lunch served on the terrace, and then you can drive over to White Marsh so you can take a look at the project. Skipper will be over there."

"Ask him about me, Holl," Sam commanded.

"I can't ask him about you," I said nastily.

"Of course you can," H.P. replied. "You can ask Skipper anything you want to. We want this to be a first-rate story. Lots of pictures, too. Color pictures. Something we can show to our clients and buyers. About five thousand words will do fine."

I looked at Sam and shrugged. He grimaced at his father disrespectfully.

I knew I was backed into a corner. There's no law on small town papers that says reporters don't write puffy, fluffy, buffy supplements for the advertisers. In fact, it's one more insidious way they have of squeezing every last drop of what's left of your creativity out of you while they increase their advertising revenues. And advertising is king, remember. Okay, now that you've got the picture here, back to my lunch with H. P. Wescott.

We ate on the brick terrace overlooking the water, where we were served by Phillips at his frostiest. If Estelle was around, she didn't choose to make an appearance, but her touch of divinity was apparent in the menu.

We feasted on thin fillets of broiled bluefish with a lemon crab sauce, served with a romaine salad and delicate cornbread slices that melted in your mouth. Estelle's healthy cooking didn't preclude taste or the Eastern Shore touch. Because I was working, I declined the wine in favor of iced tea, but H.P. more than made up for my sobriety by quaffing a half bottle of California Chablis. Not that he wouldn't have downed a hogshead without turning a hair. H.P. could drink the devil under the table. Still, I could see by the thin smile and the pink flush that the food and the Chablis softened him up just a tad.

While we ate, I watched out of the corner of my eye as Sam wandered through the grounds. And when I say *through*, that's precisely what I mean. As I was savoring my bluefish and half listening to H.P. brag about White Marsh, I watched Sam walk *through* a boxwood hedge. Pleased with himself, he *backed* through it, then *ran* through it, waving his arms. Not so much as a leaf moved.

He grinned back up the slope at me like a little kid, then disappeared.

"You know," I told H.P., savoring fresh raspberry mousse topped with sugared mint leaves, "this is the first meal I've ever eaten at Mandrake where there wasn't a fight going on, and someone slamming away from the table."

He sighed and shook his head. "All unhappy families are alike," he brooded. "Now, Hollis, you know that I gave those two kids everything they ever wanted. Sent 'em to the best schools, which Sammy got thrown out of every time. They had every advantage money could buy. And they still turned out—" He made a small, sour face. "If their mother had lived, things might have been different. Maybe I should have remarried. Hindsight's always twenty-twenty, isn't it?" He poured more wine. "It's ironic that Claire's more like a son than Sam ever was, you know? She's handling the development permits and the sales for White Marsh, and doing a damn fine job of it. She surprises me, sometimes. There's something heartless about her." He drained his glass and refilled it. "Claire is cold. She's always been ruthless. I really don't know where she gets that from, but it's hell to deal with. I don't understand why Skip married her, or why they stayed married, except for the kids and the business. I've seen people stay together for less. Money can be a powerful cement, Hollis. And Skipper knows this company inside out. I'm not as well as I used to be, and when I step down as CEO—Claire doesn't know how to handle people."

"There's never been any love lost between Claire and me," I said carefully. That was the understatement of the epoch, but I was reluctant to let this unexpected mood of frankness evaporate. Maybe the old man was mellowing now, with so much sorrow, but I doubted it.

He gave me his fleeting, sour smile. "I'm not proud of the way she treated you when you married Sam. I'm not proud of the way *I* treated you when you married Sam. I admit that I'd hoped for someone in our class. A Sewall, a Baldwin. I was too pissed off and too proud to see you for

what you were—and are. You would have been good for
Sam, Hollis. But, as usual, he was too damn selfish and too
dumb to see it."

"That's not what you said at the time," I reminded him.
I couldn't help it. Old wounds don't close as easily as that.
"You said, as I recall, that I was a common, sorry Beddoe's
Island redneck not fit to marry a Wescott of Mandrake. It
was all rather Victorian and melodramatic."

H.P. winced. "Did I? I must have been in one of my
rages. Well, Hollis, I'm sorry I said that. I probably didn't
mean it. But there the two of you were, grinning like idiots
because you'd gone to North Carolina and gotten married,
with no more sense between the two of you than this wine-
glass. And don't tell me your parents were thrilled because
they weren't. I doubt they are to this day. Sam is—*was*—
very few parents' idea of an ideal son-in-law, I'm sure. He
was hardly the ideal son." He tapped his empty glass with
a fingernail. "You hadn't even finished college yet. And
Sam had flunked out of his third or fourth school. To get
him into Watertown, I had to donate a goddamn fortune to
the endowment fund." He glowered at me.

I looked into the depths of my iced tea glass.

"There was never any love lost between you and Sam,"
I ventured. "I think he did things just to get you angry. Like
marry me."

"When a man has a son, he hopes that that son will carry
on his family, take on the tradition and take up the work
he's started. Sam never even showed a glimmer of interest.
All he cared about was boats and cars and parties and
women. You know you weren't the first woman in his life,
nor the last. Do you think he understood the meaning of fi-
delity? When I think about Rose and me, our marriage . . .
There wasn't a serious bone in his body. He's—he was—a
goddamn playboy! A disgrace to the Wescott name. I can't
tell you what he cost me first and last. And not just in
money, either." He glowered at me from beneath his bushy
eyebrows. "I hope you don't think I didn't love my son,
Hollis, because I did. But he was dead to me a long time

before he came back here with his goddamn ideas. I'd done all my grieving a long time past for my son. That was some stranger I laid to rest up there in the family cemetery. When he took off and deserted you, he took off and left the family and the company, too. He betrayed the Wescott name, the Wescott tradition."

"Why did Sam come back to the Shore?" I asked.

Like an old bull, H.P. shook his massive head. "Damned if I know. He just came up the bay in that damned sailboat one day and cast a line at the dock. He wasn't welcome here, I can tell you that. Him and his damned ideas."

"Ideas?" I asked. I looked at H.P. from beneath my lashes. But he leaned back in his chair and crossed his arms over his chest. "Yours wasn't the only heart Sam Wescott broke," the old man said softly. He looked at me, hard. "He only came back here to make more trouble for the family. He's better off dead."

A thin chill ran down my spine when he said that. I felt what my mother called a goose running over her grave.

At that moment, Phillips appeared, carrying the phone. "Excuse me, Mr. Wescott. Your broker is on the line from New York?" He also laid several faxes in front of the old man which presumably required his immediate attention. I saw the letterheads of several well-known brokerage and banking firms before I tastefully looked away toward the view of Mandrake Creek.

I tried to picture the old man climbing aboard a Honduras 36 and opening the valves on a propane stove. It was hard to picture. He was more likely to have a fit of temper, gun Sam down with a .30-.30 Purdy at high noon in the middle of Watertown after inviting everyone in the county to witness the thing. No jury in Santimoke County would have convicted him. Especially if they had known Sam.

Besides, whatever H.P. said, Sam was his son, his flesh and blood, and genetic ties counted for everything with people like the Wescotts. They pay their failures to stay away; they build hospitals to hide their misfits. Murder is for the masses. It's tacky. But possible.

H. P. Wescott was capable of a lot of things, but killing his son? Well, yeah, it's possible, I thought. I could see him murdering someone who stood in the way of what he wanted. But murdering his own son? It could happen. Anything can happen. Ask any reporter, ask any cop.

While I was sitting there thinking these thoughts, H.P. barked orders into the phone and scrawled orders across the bottom of the faxes in a firm, decisive hand. Phillips stared impassively over his head, ever the perfect majordomo. Ah, power.

"You know, Phillips could have done it," Sam said, suddenly materializing by a topiary shrub. He looked at the butler, who flicked an invisible speck of lint from his immaculate lapel. "I don't know why he'd do it, unless he was tired of cleaning up after me. Holl, you wouldn't believe it, but there are security guards behind every shrub around here. This is a whole new development. What the hell is Dad afraid of?"

This was something to think about. I remembered how Frank Dartwood had made an unexpected appearance at the funeral, only to be surrounded by large gentlemen in dark suits. At the time, I assumed they had been put on the payroll for the occasion, so I was surprised that they were still here. No one had stopped me at the gates, and I hadn't seen anything unusual in the house, aside from the expensive alarm system that every big house in these parts had adopted in the past decade. But the idea of those guys lurking in the gazebo and the boathouse was sort of intimidating.

"Phillips, call Mrs. Shively and tell her I'll be a little late for Senator Claiborne's dinner party tonight," H.P. commanded, handing back the sheaf of faxes. He rose, a signal that the audience was over.

"Well, Hollis, I thank you for coming, but we've got a crisis in the market, so I won't be able to go with you this afternoon. Got a software company in danger of a hostile takeover, you understand. Tell you what, girl, you go on over to White Marsh and talk to Skipper. He's hands-on with the project, and he can show you all the nuts and bolts. We'll talk real soon, hear?"

He offered a paw and I shook. I felt as if I ought to curtsy. Was it my imagination or was he smiling?

I waited until we were well out of earshot and halfway down the hall before I ventured a question to Phillips about the security. "I noticed these men hanging around at the funeral. Why in the world?" I asked.

Phillips's jaw tightened. "Things aren't the same around here as they used to be. All kinds of criminals and terrorists out there. A rich man can't be too careful. Especially with those Greenheads."

"Greenheads? The environmental people?"

"They've made some threats," Phillips said shortly. He opened the front door.

"Thank you. And please send my love to Estelle," I said. But the door closed behind me before the words were out of my mouth.

"I think he used to work for the Addams family," Sam said, stepping out of the boxwoods and onto the brick path that led to the driveway.

"Oh, Sam, grow up," I replied. "He's a black man from another generation whose dignity is very, very important to him."

"All I know is he makes the rest of us look like cheap Christmas-trailer trash. The French ambassador once mistook him for James Earl Jones. I think Phillips's idea of relaxing is to loosen his tie."

"True, true," I murmured. "And yet Estelle is so laid back."

"We were chalk and cheese too. You took everything so seriously." Sam thrust his hands into his pockets. "While you and the old man were eating, I went down to the cemetery. Estelle was there. She was putting fresh flowers on my grave. I could almost make her see me. I think she sensed me, just a little." His voice was wistful.

"She's a lovely woman. One of the few genuinely kind people I know."

"So, I don't think she could have killed me. No motive. Nor Phillips, unless he was tired of my slob habits. *That's* a motive."

"In Maryland, you don't need to prove motive, just opportunity and commission," I said absently. "Damn, Sam, now you've got me going."

"Light dawns on the doubting."

"We'll see." I climbed into the Honda and lit a cigarette.

SIX

•

The Plot Heats Up
Somewhat

White Marsh was a long ride spent arguing with Sam over my choice of tapes in the deck. I wanted the Lemonheads; he wanted Jimmy Buffett. We compromised on David Byrne. If I hadn't been arguing with a dead person, it would have been just like old times.

"I'm not dead, I'm living impaired," Sam suggested. He was getting into this ghost thing. We both were.

"You're ectoplasmically challenged."

"Breathing disabled."

It reminded me of why I had fallen in love with him in the first place. One thing about Sam, he was never boring. Maddening, undependable, charming, heartbreaking, handsome and careless, but never, ever boring.

Okay, so he'd crapped out on me in a major way.

He'd broken my heart.

He was dead.

But he was still a lot of fun.

Which, in my experience, is something you can't say about many of those who are among the breathing.

"Okay, I'll try to help you out," I said.

"Holl, you won't be sorry. I promise, sweetcakes."

"But you've gotta help me out, Sam. I mean, if I went to the police right now and said there's been a murder, they'd laugh me right out of the state police barracks."

"True. What we need is evidence."

"What we need is motive, suspects, opportunity, *and*

evidence. And evidence is the most important. Unfortunately, it seems like all that got blown away when you turned on that propane stove. If that's what did it." I stubbed out my cigarette. "God, Sam, why didn't you give me something *hard* to do?"

I turned down a narrow county road that was more gravel and oystershell than asphalt. White Marsh Neck is a long, broad spit of land that sticks out into Chesapeake Bay between Santimoke Bay and the Devanau River. It's about twenty-five thousand acres of empty sky and salt marsh.

Out at the very end of the neck there's a good-sized stand of ground, maybe thirty acres, high enough above high-tide line to support hardwood trees with roots deep enough to keep the water from washing the land away. It's called White Marsh Island, but it's an island surrounded by marshland, not water. In the old days, it was the haunt of pirates and worse.

"When I was growing up," I mused, "my father used to run traplines out here in the winter, and I used to come along with him on Saturdays and Sundays. In those days, you could get a dollar and a half for a muskrat pelt, a dollar for a nutria. These days, I think you can get about thirty cents. No one wants fur coats anymore, I guess. Politically incorrect. Daddy used to say that an acre of marsh was worth about the same as an acre of blue sky. Now, of course, we know better. Or at least some of us do. The rest of you, meaning your family, see it as wasteland waiting for houses, malls, and fast-food franchises."

Sam made no reply.

"They tell me it used to be that you could buy marshland for about a quarter an acre. About the only people who were interested in that wilderness of grass and loblolly pine hammocks were muskrat trappers, hunters, and escapees. They still tell stories about pirates and slaves who escaped into the marshes and Civil War draft evaders who camped out there on the marsh for years. It can be done, but I wouldn't want to be the one to do it. Freeze your ass off all winter, with the wind blowing cold across the water, then it's like hell, hot and thick with mosquitoes and deerflies all summer. No one wants to live out here, so what the hell does your father have in mind? The marshes are lonely places. Good for ghosts. Maybe you should move out here and haunt the marsh. You'd have good company. There's Big Liz, the headless slave, and Captain Josiah Whaley, the Tory pirate, and Levin Harbeson, the Crab Bait Killer. You remember they lived out on White Marsh Island, and Levin killed his brother Daniel with a tong head and chopped him into pieces and salted him down and baited Daniel up on his trotlines—"

"Can't you put that Jimmy Buffett tape in now?"

As we argued and I drove, the scrubwood gave way to pine barrens, which gradually gave way to a vast prairie of marsh grass punctuated here and there with cripples—stands of high ground that support a few scraggly loblolly pines. My daddy used to say that in the battle between land and wind and water, wind and water always win.

By now, we were on the causeway, a narrow gravel road that circuited its way from one stand of high ground to another, crossing over creeks and guts on covered culverts. The tide was rising, and it laid right up on the road in long, creeping pools of salt water. Given a good tide and an east wind, the causeway becomes almost impassable.

Sam and I had grown up around marshlands all our lives; this landscape was familiar to us. Memories of following my father through these marshes while he tended his traps. The cold wind howling across Santimoke Bay, whipping over the yellow grass, cut right through our coats, down to the bone. Threaded with narrow creeks, called guts, that carry the tides through the marshes and out to the bay, these marshes had been trenched, channeled, dug at, ditched, and pooled in an attempt to drain them, but the water always came back. Now, people have begun to realize that wetlands are the primary source of the world's fresh water, and there have been some attempts to preserve them. But not half enough, if you let the Claire Duponts of this world take over.

From out here, at night, you could see the lights of Oysterback across the Devanau River, in the next county. Around the next curve, the lonely ten-second flasher, where Swann's Island had washed away into the Devanau thirty years ago, hove into view. At night it was a landmark for the oil barges going up and down the river to Delaware.

People who don't know any better think marshes are dead places. Far from it; they are abundant with life. A red-wing blackbird perched on a ragweed gave his trilling call, and overhead, in a flash of russet feathers, a hawk circled, casting her shadow across the waving stands of grass. Her tercel perched nearby in the top of a dead pine, scanning the landscape. Suddenly, he flapped his wings and rose, stooping on the currents until he struck and rose again, a field mouse gripped in his talons, moving off across the rippling grasslands toward the nest in the arms of a scrub pine. I caught, from the corner of my eye, the flash of a fox's tail as he headed into a greenbrier thicket.

In the winter, this place is a haven for geese, swans, loons, and ducks. Mallards and blacks live here year around; widgeons, scaups, teals, oldsquaws, canvasbacks, even a merganser or two come up through here. And some winter over: it's on the Atlantic flyway. Blinds dot the landscape; this is good hunting.

About eight or ten long and twisting miles down the road, we crossed a guardrail bridge over a narrow gut where the water lapped at creosote pilings and schools of shiners darted in and out of the shadows. A crab scuttled across the surface of the water and disappeared into the depths. Jenkin's Creek, the widest gut that wound through the marsh.

And we finally came to White Marsh Island. A stand of high ground large enough to support a thick woods, it had once belonged to the Harbesons, an ancient, inbred family who lived out here in lonely and primitive isolation, at least until the unfortunate incident.

That was a trial I would have liked to cover, but it was way before my time. Levin said his brother salted down real good. Daniel was almost all used up by the time some-one noticed he was missing from the liar's bench at the general store over at Oysterback and came to see if something was wrong. Legend has it that Levin said he'd tonged Daniel to death because he got sick of the sound Daniel made when he snored.

"At least they knew who did it," Sam mused disconsolately. "I don't know who killed me."

"We've got all the motive we need," I told him. "Almost everyone who ever knew you is a suspect with a motive. What we need is opportunity and evidence."

We turned down an extended road carved from the woods and passed an enormous wooden sign incised with goldleaf script:

White Marsh Island
Luxury Estates
An Elegant Way of Life on Chesapeake Bay

It looked as out of place here as Queen Victoria shucking oysters. I wondered what the Harbesons would have said, could they see this. Their idea of elegance, or so it was said, was using a Buck knife rather than their fingers to scrape out the baked bean can.

As I turned down the rutted road hacked through the woods, I made gagging sounds. "There has just got to be a place in hell for these damn developers."

"They probably all worked on a newspaper and think real estate is heaven by comparison," Sam said. "This is where I get out, Holl—catch you later." With that, he disappeared. I was getting used to this, but it still startled me a little.

I bounced down the rutted dirt road through the woods for about a quarter mile until I came to something I could have classified as Frank Dartwood's worst nightmare for sure. It looked like a war zone.

Stands of old growth woods had been logged out, leaving

hulking, skeletal rows of brush and stumps behind, flagged with strips of plastic ribbon. Someone had set fire to them; they still smoldered. Thin gray wisps of smoke rose to the cloudless skies. Deep trenches had been dug through stands of marsh grass, allowing tidewater to seep into man-made guts, where it lay stagnant and algae-ridden beneath the boiling sun. The grass looked as if it had been treated with Agent Orange; it was blackened and trampled. High on a dead tree, what was left of an osprey's nest hung limp in the skeletal branches, slowly shredding away in the desultory breeze. Greenhead flies the size of Volkswagens banged angrily against the car windows, thirsting after mammal blood. Mosquitoes about the size of dinner plates with the same craving splattered against the windshield.

Mammoth orange earthmovers shoved mounds of bilious dirt here and there, dredged fill from Baltimore harbor filled with God only knew what toxins. The site was littered with aluminum cans, Styrofoam cups, burger wrappers, and other human debris. Someone had been moving a whole lot of earth here; there were several loaded dump trucks full of the stuff just waiting to be emptied.

I sort of had to gasp. What I remembered from childhood was a forest along sandy beach on the bay. I remembered a thick woods filled with greenbriers, songbirds, and a heron rookery, not this mise-en-scène from a postnuclear holocaust. I felt slightly ill just looking at this mess carved from the middle of White Marsh Island. I remembered the slow rhythm of my father's workboat as he worked up and down his trotlines, scooping crabs into baskets with a dipnet, the cool green water here, the way the clouds moved in shadows across the vast, grassy marshes. This had always been my father's favorite lay, a peaceful stretch on a quiet creek where the crabs were always biting. Well, almost, crabs being creatures of an innate cussedness.

Welcome to Future Hell.

I parked beside some pickups and dump trucks filled with dirt and looked around for the job trailer. It stood in the woods on the other side of a manufactured pond about fifty feet across. The pond appeared to be shallow. I decided this was a place for my rubber boots and pulled them out of the old newspapers and fast-food wrappers in the backseat. You never see Brenda Starr in rubber boots, slushing through construction craters full of sour mud to cover a fire or an accident or a weather disaster, do you? I slipped off my pumps and pulled on my Red Balls. White-trash boots is what my cousin Toby calls them, because they're white rubber and poor people wear them. L. L. Bean doesn't sell them. You have to check out Wal-Mart or Ray Bob's Gas 'N' Go for these babies.

"Check out the babe!" someone called, and I saw two guys taking a smoke break from some nameless job in the shade of the trailer. They were leaning into the side of a pickup truck.

"Hell, that ain't no babe! That's my cousin Holly! Hey, Holly! Over here, gal!"

I discerned my father's cousin's grandson appearing among the T-shirted, sweating hulks. "Hey, Earl Don!" I called, picking my way through the craters around the pond. "How you doin', bunk? What's Crystal up to? You all have that baby yet?" Without even thinking, my voice slid from American broadcast English into my native tongue, the guttural, consonant-swallowing patois of Beddoe's Island. And sweet on the ears of a Shorewoman it is, too.

Earl Don grinned. "Hey, this is my cousin Holly Ball. She writes for the paper. We don't read much of what she writes, but she's a damn good writer, what you do read."

The other two guys smiled and nodded. I have met women who have this thing for working guys, and I can see it. You do see a hunka hunka burning love out there every once in a while, all solid abs, washboard stomach, and those nice tight jeans. But for me, having grown up with the whole thing, it lacks charm. I know those stomachs are going to pooch after the third or fourth thousandth case of Bud, those taut butts are going to sag from too much spread time on an earth mover or an engine house, and a network of lines will appear in that deeply tanned face from too many wives, too many kids, and not enough native intelligence to stop.

Nonetheless, once I had been scanned and identified as one of the Ball tribe, I was in.

"Hey, are you a writer? Boy, you could write the story of my life, it's a good one," one good ole boy, not more than twenty-three or -four said, quite sincerely, scratching the tattoo on his arm. As tribe, I was entitled to be treated like a lady, you see. No flirting. That I would not have minded. Flirting is very Eastern Shore and nine times out of ten, means absolutely nothing serious, something visitors never pick up on around here. The tenth time, you just threaten to call his wife.

"She writes up alla them trials and po-lice articles in the paper," Earl Don said helpfully, tamping a Camel from his pack.

"Oh, where were you when we got into that fight over to Riverside House with those doctors from the Western Shore that night?" the third guy asked me drily. "I woulda remembered seeing *you* in court." High compliment.

"I was there. But you guys were so busy joking around with Judge Quick that you never even saw me."

"Hot damn, them doctors sure could fight," he said admiringly. "We had a regular Six-Day War out there in the parking lot. And they womped us good! We all had a drink together by the time the sheriff got there. Of course, Bubba had to press charges because we broke out the front window. But them doctor fellas put up a good fight!"

"They were good boys," the first said, nodding sagely.

Earl Don sighed. "I tole 'em, next time you come over here, I'll carry you goose shooting for free. That was a damn good fight."

I took up a pickup-truck-leaning stance and fished out a cigarette. We all stared into the flatbed where two or three bushel baskets and a length of polyester rope lay among the dead leaves and mud.

"You on this job?" I asked Earl Don casually. My cousin

owns an excavating business. Don't let the good ole boy act fool you either; he's got a half-million-dollar house on a nice piece of Beddoe's Island waterfront, and Crystal drives a brand new Acura out of the showroom every year. Ball Excavating is a solid gold business in the wake of the great building boom of the '80s.

"This is something, ain't it?" Earl Don asked. "It's not what I would have done, but they had the permits, and I got twenty guys on the payroll with kids to feed. This is gone be something when all's said and done. You seen the model Skip has over to the office in Watertown? You oughta talk to him."

"That's what I was on my way to do. You know, Earl Don, I thought there was laws and stuff about fillin' in wetlands and all that?" What did I know? The environment wasn't my beat; it went to the business reporter who covered all the real estate stuff.

Earl Don looked uncomfortable; he shifted a toothpick. "All I know is the permits are all in order. You'd hafta talk to Skip or Mrs. Dupont about anything else. We oughta get back to work now, boys. You guys are on the clock."

I watched as they walked away, leaving me leaning all alone.

"I'll get you at Mum-Mum's next Christmas," I muttered at my cousin's back.

I was about to pick my way across the site to the job trailer, but I was distracted, looking distastefully at the man-made pond. It was filled with greenish, algae-ridden scum. Charming.

Just when I'd slogged through enough mud to really stick to my boots, the door of the trailer flew open and what should emerge but the lovely and talented Claire.

"I don't give a good goddamn what you do," she snapped over her shoulder in those unmistakable transatlantic accents. "Just keep on going! Every time there's a delay, it's costing me money! We practically financed your whole campaign singlehandedly, and we can fill two seats on the zoning board with our people! I don't care what the hell you have to do, just keep doing it! Just remember, you're in this with us!" Her face was dark with rage, and as she stepped down from the trailer, her heels didn't even sink in the mud. Before she could see me, I moved behind a backhoe, watching from cover as she hopped into her burgundy Mercedes and drove away in a cloud of mud and dust. She did not look happy. But Claire *never* looks happy. She moves in a perennial aura of discontent, in case you hadn't noticed.

"Whoa," I said to myself. "Such language from a lady." I can swear like a drunken waterman on a Saturday night at Toby's myself, of course, but there's a time and place for everything.

I started to pick my way across the mud, skirting the ugly pond, heading for the job trailer. It wasn't the door I was headed for, but the window. Hey, it works for me. I stood on tiptoe and peered through the dusty window.

I was prepared for almost anything but what I saw in the dim light: Skipper and Jason Hemlock, my least favorite state delegate, locked in mortal combat.

Well, it wasn't all that mortal, actually.

In fact, it looked to me like Skip and Jason were indulging in that good old Maryland pastime, trying to gouge each other's eyes out in a fair fight. Well, more or less fair. Compared to Earl Don's crew, these two were definitely flyweights. And neither of them knew how to fight, that was for sure. They were both sort of batting at each other with open hands, like a pair of prep school roommates in a pillow fight.

When Skipper finally got Jason pinned down on the desk and had his hands wrapped pretty seriously around the honorable delegate's neck, I decided maybe it was time for me to knock on the door and put an end to this. I'd seen two Ocean City crack whores fight with more skill outside the Dutch Bar on a slow night.

I slogged around to the door of the job trailer and rapped on it with my knuckles. "Skipper? It's Hollis. The Old Man sent me over to talk to you."

There was some muffled thumping and muttering. I put my ear to the fiberglass but heard nothing more.

After about a minute, Skipper opened the door, still adjusting his tie. His face was a deep purple, an unflattering color for him. Behind him I could see Jason Hemlock combing his hair and dusting himself off. When he saw me, his eyes slid away from my interested gaze like two fried eggs on a greasy plate.

Skipper's smile did not quite reach his eyes. "Sorry, Holl. We just had a meeting, and Delegate Hemlock and I were going over some permits."

Jason was giving his adenoids a real workout, panting heavily. Reluctantly, he glanced at me. His smile was sickly, as well it should have been, I thought. "Oh, yes, I know Ms. Ball," he admitted, as if he had just been reminded that he was under oath.

"We've met," I said dryly. "I understand you have an interest in White Marsh?" Sometimes, if you imply you know more than you do, people will tell you things you didn't know.

Jason gave me a look that should have peeled my paint. I just smiled. "I have no comment on that at this time," he said stiffly, adjusting his seersucker jacket on his broad shoulders.

I laughed. "Come off of it, Jason. I've been enlisted in the cause, too. Rig assigned me to write an advertising supplement on White Marsh. At the Old Man's command, I might add." I gave him a *we're all in this together* sort of grin.

Jason shrugged. He wasn't buying it. He knew me too well. It took him a moment to recover his composure, but he was slick. "Hollis, honey, I wouldn't tell you what time of day it is," he drawled.

"Now, Jason, why do you want to go and act like that?" I asked. "What have I ever done to you?"

"Plenty," he replied thickly. "And not all of it for print."

"Not a damn thing you didn't deserve, you low-rent, knuckle-dragging, common sorry snollygoster. Whyn't you go out and toss around some more libelous allegations and see what happens?"

"Come on, you two," Skipper said uncertainly. "Knock it off."

"I will if she will," Jason replied. A glance in the tiny mirror above the sink told him that he was restored to neat, clean, and put together. And cute, if you like that type, which I did before I found out what he was *really* like, a couple of legislative sessions ago in Annapolis.

I hear they still talk about that fight we had at the Maryland Inn. It was a doozy.

I was not surprised to find Jason here and obviously up to his eyeballs in the Wescott family's business. As Claire had huffed, the old man had contributed heavily to the Hemlock campaign, so the family might reasonably believe that Jason owed them. And one of the things he might owe them was the juice to get them all kinds of permits and variances needed to fill and develop wetlands, which was, last time I heard, illegal without them.

Not that I knew that much about it, but looking around at this mess, I felt slightly ill. "Skip, why in the hell would you put a pricey development all the way out on the end of a marsh?" I asked.

"I can see that you have business to discuss," Jason was saying to Skipper. "So I'll be on my way. I'll talk to you about—Claire—later." He looked at me. "Stay out of this, Hollis, or I'll make sure there's more trouble than you can handle."

"Now, why would you want to say things like that?" I asked sweetly. "That could be taken as a threat."

"Just do as you're told," he snarled, and he was out the door and gone before I could think of any more witty repartee.

Skipper took a white linen handkerchief from his pocket and mopped his head. He sighed, pulling himself together with a visible effort. "You would not believe the problems we have had, just trying to get this far," he said. "You would think Wescott Development Corp. was the Great

Satan or something, the way that Frank Dartwood fellow goes on." He gestured to a table in the center of the room, where an architect's model had been laid out in perfect, miniature detail, like the landscape for a model railroad. Even on that scale, I could see that the houses were going to be huge. The Colonial Victorian turrets and towers and garish colors were fashionable, if not tasteful, examples of twentieth-century *fin de siècle*.

"As you can see," Skipper breezily informed me, "White Marsh Estates will be a first-class residential development. There will be a total of twenty luxurious homes in the latest historical style, each one on its own five-acre lot, each one facing its own glorious waterfront, with anchorage, dock, and boathouse on Santimoke Bay. We're planning the houses in three styles: French Tudor, Plantation Medici, and Victorian Colonial—"

"What is that?" I asked, bending over the board to peer at a large, blue pool by the ornate brick entrance pillars.

"That's our ornamental pond. As you can see, it quite makes the approach from the guardhouse. In ten or twenty years when the Japanese weeping cherries are grown, it will be quite lovely—"

"Yeah, but what are those things floating in the middle?" I asked, squinting at it.

"Oh." Skipper grinned, just as pleased as could be. "Those are going to be islands in the form of the letters *W*, *M*, *I*, the initials of White Marsh Island. Clever, huh? We're going to shove up all the leftover landfill from the dredging we're going to do to deepen the harbor so people can moor their larger sailboats at their own docks. It was Claire's idea."

"Gawd," I muttered, truly appalled for the first, but not, I was sure, last time.

"And of course, here's the gates and the guardhouse. We're offering twenty-four hour security. Plus the natural security allowed by several hundred acres of inaccessible marsh. Natural protection. Security is the thing of the '90s for the affluent."

"You'll need it if you make those islands," I said. "The Bad Taste Squad will be all over you like fleas on a lab."

Skipper looked at me over his glasses. Probably it was a good thing he never gets my jokes. "Claire thinks ponds will be all the rage with the gardening set," he said, as if that settled it. "When you're selling houses in the one-to-two-million-dollar range, you need to think about things like this."

"Target market, the three Rs," I said, making notes furiously.

"Three Rs?"

"Rich, retired, and Republican," I explained again.

Comprehension fired up his expression. "Exactly! That's the kind of people we want in White Marsh!" He beamed at me, rambling on for about twenty minutes about four to six bedrooms, six bathrooms, hot tubs, atriums, swimming pools, maid's quarters, heated garages, waterview kitchens, infrared laser security systems, and other wet-dream stuff poor people like reporters never see. Just as my eyes were beginning to glaze over, he handed me two pounds of glossy color brochures and another pound of classic ivory bond rag stationery with yet more information extolling White Marsh Island Estates. "This will help you make sense of what you're seeing in that mess out there. As soon as we get this marsh filled in, then you'll see something," he promised. "Look, Hollis, I'd really like to talk to you some more about this, but today we're kind of busy. Tell you what. Have your girl call my girl, and we'll do lunch real soon and talk about White Marsh. In a couple of weeks, we should have all the permits straightened out." He winked. "In the meantime, we're just plugging on ahead! When you've got someone like Jason on your side, you know you'll get what you want. Or Claire will," he muttered, looking beige and angry.

"Uh-huh," I said. "Jason wouldn't happen to have any sort of financial interest in this, would he? A silent partnership, a political contribution, an outright bribe?"

But Skipper was already getting ready to hustle me out

the door. "You'll find everything you need to get started in those papers," he said quickly. "Read them and we'll talk some more."

"Just one more thing, Skipper. The other day you said Sam could make someone crazy enough to kill him. Do you think someone did?" I hung on to the doorjamb, watching his features. He turned a sort of purple, a beige purple, at the mere mention of Sam's name.

"What did H.P. tell you?" he hissed.

"Enough," I ventured.

"The old fool. He's losing his grip." Skipper recovered himself, clamping his lips together firmly. "Sorry, Hollis. I really don't have the time to discuss this right now. I'll have my girl call your girl. But I'll give you some advice. Don't go there, okay? Just leave the whole thing alone, and no one will get hurt."

And I was back out in the mud again, the door closed firmly in my face. "Don't go where?" I asked the closed portal.

The distant sound of heavy equipment, bulldozers and earth movers filling in marsh hummed in the air. A mosquito droned in my ear, and I swatted it away, trying to picture this land manicured and filled with overpriced ugly homes for people who came to live on the Eastern Shore behind locked gates and guardhouses and miles of marsh. A bunker mentality on the dwindling undeveloped waterfront.

I slogged through the ugly yellow mud back to my car. There was no sign of Sam, and I found myself wishing he was there to pick it all over with. I felt vaguely ill, out of balance. Something was wrong, but I felt as if, whatever it was, it was so huge and powerful and I was so small and powerless that there was nothing I could do.

Swatting off deerflies and mosquitoes, I climbed into my Honda and tossed the brochures on the seat beside me. I wondered what they planned to do about the bugs, spray with DDT or some other pesticide that would kill all the wildlife while it was at it? Probably. Or maybe they'd only show homes in spring and fall, when the bugs were dormant.

I lit a cigarette and thought for a moment about Jason Hemlock. Seduced by charm again, we'd started an affair when he was Santimoke County's state's attorney. When he'd run for state delegate, I believed that he would do his best to represent all the people, not just the affluent and powerful. Although I was officially forbidden by ethics as well as the bylaws of the Owner to overtly work for any political candidate, I had done some stuff behind the scenes for Jason. He'd promised to be the environmental candidate, to work for limited growth and clean light industry. He'd promised to work for the working man, to get the rich to pay their fair share of the tax burden. He'd promised the watermen and the farmers heaven and earth, and we'd all believed him. When he got to Annapolis, he was seduced by the developers and the lobbyists who dazzled him with flattery and wrote him big campaign checks. Basically, he'd sold out; association with money and power went right to his head. Soon he was moving to the far right, enjoying seeing his name in the news with his public attacks on environmentalists, liberal humanists, and anyone else whose agenda threatened the ultraconservative interests who'd purchased his votes. If he really believed in any of this stuff, I could have accepted that. But he just moved with the way the wind blew. "You gotta go with the trends, ya know?" he said to me once. "I gotta think about me, ya know, and frankly, you just can't do me enough good anymore, Hollis."

So he took up with a blonde bimbo who allegedly did secretarial work for a lobbyist of dubious repute. When I'd caught him, ten toes up and ten toes down with Cinderella Fotney in what was supposed to be "our room" at the Maryland Inn, the hurting I put on him was swift and short. The hurting his betrayal put on me lasted for a much longer time. It had been quite a scene, that last fight. A year later and I was still angry.

I was ruminating over my poor taste in men so hard as

I started up the car and wound my way over the road through the marsh, that I barely noticed the man who emerged from the high grass until he was standing right in front of the car. I was slamming on the brakes before I noticed that he was masked and carrying a gun. I screeched to a stop, suddenly all attention when the gun was leveled right at me.

That was when I noticed the other masked figures easing out of the tall grass. Someone opened the car door and peered in at me through a ski mask. I saw the glint of sunlight on blue steel and realized that it was later than I had thought. It would be dark soon; the long shadows were stretching out across the marsh.

"Hollis Ball?"

I nodded.

"Come with us, please."

"I have a choice?"

"No."

SEVEN

•

In the Hall of the Marshland King

If you've ever been kidnapped at gunpoint from a lonely causeway by crazies, blindfolded, put in a canoe and paddled deep into the creeks and guts of the Great Santimoke Marsh, then you will understand how I was feeling.

Journalists get kidnapped in Lebanon, and whatever other armpit country is killing its taxpayers this week, not the Eastern Shore of Maryland. Normally the most hazardous thing I could expect was an irate call from the Daughters of Santimoke wanting to know why we'd printed the name of a prominent descendant of dead European people in the DWI column. But abducted? This was a new one on me.

My kidnappers were nice enough to bring along my bag and spray me with some kind of organic mosquito repellent that smelled like a citronella candle, but no one was answering my questions.

"Can I have a cigarette?" was naturally the first one I asked.

"Those things will kill you," a woman's voice somewhat behind me said, so I figured out that my abductors had come in two boats. By the difficulty of boarding, the movement and balance, I knew that I was in a canoe. Judging from where I had been abducted, I was pretty sure we were traveling northeast through North Marsh, just under a thousand acres on the northeastern side of White Marsh Neck.

"I'll bet you think I'm someone else," I offered.

Silence. Just the dip and splash of paddles as we moved through water.

"Believe me, the *Gazette* will not pay ransom to get me back. In fact, they'll probably ask you for a twenty-five-dollar return fee, like I'm a newspaper box or something."

Dip and splash. Somewhere in the marsh, I heard the rise-and-fall song of a redwing blackbird.

"I've got it! You're aliens from Uranus! Take me to your leader!" Maybe it was true what they said over in Oysterback about UFOs in the marshes.

Ahead of me, a man snickered then stifled himself. Okay, a man, a woman so far, I thought. What else? I was collecting information, just like I'd seen people do in the movies. I figured if they wanted to kill me, they would have already done it. Besides, the blindfold was a good indication they intended to let me live. Damn, where the hell was Sam when I really needed some supernatural book throwing?

"I'm being taken to see Elvis, right? He's alive and well and living in the marsh, right?"

"Close," another woman's voice said, perhaps from the second boat. Canoes made sense in these waters. No outboard motor noises, they maneuver well in shallow water, and they're easy to hide and portage from one gut to another across the muck.

I sat tight after that and waited to see what would happen.

When nothing did, I started playing with my blindfold, really nothing more than a cotton bandanna. I felt the touch of something cold and hard against the back of my neck. I was more than willing to guess it was a firearm.

"I wouldn't do that, if I were you," the first woman's voice said in matter-of-fact tones.

So I didn't.

"You haven't seen a ghost anywhere around here, have you?" I asked after a while when nothing had happened. "About six feet tall, dark hair, blue eyes, if you touch him you can sort of put your hand through his body? Answers to Sam?"

"I told Frank she was nuts," the first young woman muttered.

Frank Dartwood? I thought. *Hmmm.*

A bit of light was peeking in beneath my bandanna blindfold, and I sensed that we were reaching that late afternoon–early evening part of the summer when the shadows stretch long and purple. When I lifted my head, I could smell the pungent scent of marsh mud and salt water. The tide was going out. They say there's Santimoke Indian blood in the Balls. Maybe so; I could sense the tension of a coming thunderstorm in the air. Maybe we'd finally get some rain.

Somewhere across the bay, a distant rumble of thunder proved me right; a storm was brewing. I settled down and tried not to rock the boat.

After what seemed like about an hour but could have been more or could have been less (it's interesting how easy it is to lose track of time when you can't see) we beached on what I felt was sand bottom.

Someone touched my shoulder. "I'll give you a hand getting out," the man's voice said. "Give me your hand and stand up, easy like."

I am not a small woman, but my escort lifted me up and placed me on solid ground as if I were a rag doll. Unfortunately I was wearing my pumps, and they sank into the sand. "Damn it, I do have boots in the car, if you'd just waited," I said irritably.

"Well, I did bring your purse," he said apologetically and tried to sling it over my shoulder. I took it from him. "We can't take the blindfold off yet, sorry."

"Just as long as Squeaky Fromme doesn't point that damn gun at me again," I said a trifle waspishly.

Before I could protest, my escort had lifted me off my feet and into his arms, carrying me along a bumpy path. I could hear the others dragging the canoes into what sounded like the brush. Leaves and brambles slid along my legs and arms as I was carried up and into the hinterlands. I could smell the composting leaf and pine smell of woods and something else that was awfully like cooking fish. It made me hungry.

"My, I feel just like Fay Wray," I murmured. There's just something about hard muscles.

"Who?" he asked. Good Lord, he wasn't even breathing hard. I wondered if he looked as good as he felt. Too bad he didn't get the *King Kong* reference. Nostalgia for him was probably *The Brady Bunch*. Actually, Fay Wray was way before my time too. My head was obviously spinning in the presence of so much male pulchritude, but then again, so what?

I sort of regretted it when I was gently placed on my feet again and someone fumbled with the knot in the back of the bandanna. "Thanks for the ride, sailor," I said. My carrier was everything I had imagined and then some. Tall, blonde, chiseled with that beautiful, clear skin that is wasted on the gender.

"Hi," he said shyly. "Sorry about all that, but—"

I was about to say I wasn't one bit sorry about it, that he could kidnap me any day of the week, when someone said, "I'll take it from here. Hollis Ball, glad you could make it."

Then I found myself looking up, way up, at Frank Dartwood. He was even taller when I was standing up. His glasses were sliding down his nose, his ponytail was askew, and he had the look of an abstracted college professor. He was wearing a chamois shirt and shorts, which made him look even longer. Since he was holding out his hand, I took it in my own and shook. "Dr. Dartwood, I presume?"

He did grin at that, I'll give him credit. "Ms. Ball, I bid you welcome."

I looked around. I was standing in a clearing in a scrub woods, where a sort of encampment of tents and lean-tos had been thrown up around a one-story cedar shake that looked to me to be a duck camp. I guessed that we were on an island in the marsh. It looked a lot like a Girl Scout camp I had attended every summer in Pennsylvania growing up. In addition to such homely additions as laundry fluttering from lines and a propane stove upon which a large graniteware pot was boiling up, if my nose for Old Bay seasoning did not deceive me, a nice mess of crabs. "I hope you've invited me for dinner, Dartwood," I said.

"We would be honored," Dartwood said. "Ball, I'm really sorry about this, but you understand no one must know where the headquarters of the Greenhead Army is located."

"Well, look, it's all very nice to play Robin Hood and his Merry Men—and Women—but they have planes and choppers these days for aerial surveillance—"

"All you can see from the air in the summer is the canopy of trees." He swatted at the mosquitoes and scratched some bug bites on his arms. "This is a small island in the marsh, inaccessible by land. If you wanted to look on the deeds in the courthouse, you'd see it belongs to the Mallard Busters Gunning Club, with a D.C. address. As a matter of fact, we have certain friends in the Department of Natural Resources who alert us to any incoming."

"In the country long?" I asked, alerted by the buzzword *incoming* that he had been in Vietnam.

"Two tours. Quang Tri, '69 and '70. I was with the 101st."

"The Screaming Eagles. My brother was an interpreter in '67."

We grinned at each other. I was starting to relax a little. So what if I had been kidnapped at gunpoint and dragged several miles deep into the marsh by environmental radicals? There were steamed crabs, and the blond hunk was handing me a cold beer. I was enjoying the way he was spraying me with mosquito repellent too much to care about his body piercing.

"This is a great place," I said, "if you don't mind the bugs, the mosquitoes, the biting flies, and the Lyme ticks too much."

Dartwood nodded. "No one ever comes out here but a few trappers. And believe me, they hate the Wescotts as much as we do. But, that's why we got you here. To hear our side of the story."

"I've already seen theirs," I said. That first sip of Boh hit the back of my throat like ice water in hell. I grappled for a cigarette and my notebook.

"We did what you wanted, Frank," the girl said as she came up alongside me. About twenty, she had long blonde hair under a baseball cap, and a gun, a big old .38, was tucked into the waistband of her jeans. Sheena, Queen of the Marsh. Too cute for words.

I reached out and grabbed the .38 faster than she could pull away. "These things can kill you, too. Just pointing them at someone will get you up to twenty for simple assault. Next time you point a gun at someone, remember that."

She sort of pouted in a femme fatale way, but Dartwood made a stilling gesture. I broke the gun and looked at the chamber. "That's another thing. Never leave the hammer sitting on a loaded chamber. It's a damn good way to blow your boob off." I removed one bullet, closed the gun on the empty chamber, and decided I was now Firearms Queen of the Universe. I dropped it into my bag and handed her the bullet. "Jesus, back in the seventies, when *I* was a radical, we knew the basic rules of gun safety. It was the establishment we wanted to off, not ourselves. And don't laugh about that boob story either; it really happened to my trashy cousin Wanda when she went to the VFD dance looking for her husband Delmar and his new squeeze one Saturday night."

"Thank you, Jennifer," Dartwood said and she stalked off, looking like a thwarted debutante who's just learned Lester Lanin won't be available that night.

"It's so hard to get good help these days," I sighed.

"Jennifer's committed to the movement," Dartwood said defensively. "She really cares about the bay."

"I'm glad someone does. After what I just saw—"

"That's why we brought you here. You can tell our side of the story. We've been getting a bad rap in the media."

"And you think kidnapping me at gunpoint will make me predisposed to like you any better? What part of your budget is going into public relations? You need to fire your press liaison, Dartwood." I exhaled furiously.

Dartwood smiled. "Well, we were sort of hoping you could help us with that."

"Maybe you could sell this as an amusement ride to bored yuppies," I fumed.

"I used to be a yuppie," Dartwood said, leading me by the arm toward the lodge. "I had to give it up for Lent."

I tried to scrape my brain for what I knew about Frank Dartwood, which was not much more than what I'd seen on the AP wire or caught in sound bites on the television. "Eco-activist" was the word most talking heads used to describe him, but people are more than just a label. I recalled that he had been a lawyer for some giant oil corporation, that he had been associated at various times with federal and state governments, that he had joined the private sector at some point and then dropped out, declaring that the various "save the bay" organizations were too soft on the developers and polluters who, to his mind, were ruining the Chesapeake. In fact, he seemed to feel that the two were hand in glove. He became more and more radical and more and more outspoken in his views until he was arrested for vandalism when he was caught spiking ancient trees that were scheduled to be cut down to make way for a strip mall in Onancock.

When next he appeared, about a year ago, it had been to proclaim the existence of the Greenhead Army, following, I seemed to recall, reports of sabotage of Chesapeake Bay polluters. After that the media blamed the Greenheads for sabotaging a petrochemical plant allegedly dumping stuff into the Susquehanna River, the mysterious, if spectacularly explosive, destruction of heavy equipment at the site of some proposed condominiums on Tilghman Island, a really interesting set of damages done to a paint factory in Baltimore, and a fertilizer plant on the Rappahannock, all done in. All said by the media to be the work of the Greenhead Army. However, the environment wasn't sexy enough for the broadcast boys. Five seconds of film on the evening news and gone. And since it didn't have much to do with cops and courts in Santimoke County, not my problem. Til now.

"Yeah," I said, after mentally reviewing all of the above, "it sounds like you need some spin control. Or are you guys *really* the ones who stopped up the slush pipes at Nixon Petroleum in Fort Deering, Pennsylvania?"

Dartwood merely smiled as he held open the screen door to allow me to pass into the building. There were three or four other college age kids in the big main room, all of them bunched up around a solar-powered computer terminal where they seemed to be intent on whatever was on the screen. When we walked in they glanced up, without apparent interest, then went back to the screen again. Curious, I glanced at it. They were not, as I had suspected, plotting the downfall of Exxon on the Internet, but playing Street Fighter. Cool. They looked vaguely familiar to me, but I wrote it off to their transcendent air of tanned WASPishness. Even the token Asian and African-American kids looked preppy.

On the walls were posters extolling earth first and the beauties of the Chesapeake Bay. The furniture was '50s, that twisted twig and bark stuff that decorators always think is so butch and rustic. I noticed a CD player and a healthy stack of discs and a big screen Sony TV, complete with VCR.

"Welcome to Greenhead Central," Dartwood said with a smile. I noted bedrooms off the main room, furnished with bunks and an almost military neatness. But it was the kitchen we walked into, where another young man was shredding field greens into a big wooden bowl and my handsome blonde abductor was seated casually at the table, reading yesterday's *Wall Street Journal*. Out loud. He smiled at me and I smiled back.

"Andy, did you make sure that the canoes were dragged up in the brush and covered?" Dartwood asked him, and he nodded without missing a beat as he continued his narrative about a highly placed Wall Street broker indicted in an insider trading investigation.

"Andy, Charlie, and those were Theresa, Jon, Wade, and Mookie in the living room," Dartwood said absently as he walked me out to the screen porch where a big table had been set for dinner. I hoped there was a place for me; those crabs smelled heavenly. "And, of course, you met Jennifer."

Frank gestured me into a metal porch chair and sat in its opposite number, balancing his beer can on his foot. "We're small in number, as you can see. But our friends are everywhere. In every strata of life. Like us, they think that more can be done to preserve the environment than is being done. Perhaps not all of them agree, in principle, at least, with our methods, but they understand that sometimes extremism is necessary."

"So you have been behind all those things they say?"

Dartwood shrugged. "You know that I can't comment on that." He smiled. "You also know that about ninety percent of what the media says is bullshit. But that's not our concern right now. Our concern is saving White Marsh. Any way we can."

"Nails in trees? Exploding earthmovers? That's my cousin's excavating company out there, you know. And it won't do a damn thing to the Wescotts. What are you planning?"

Dartwood smiled an angelic smile. "I can't tell you that. Let's just say that we have our ways and means. And what you describe sounds a bit primitive." He drained the last of his beer and carefully crushed the can for later recycling. "But that's not why we brought you here, Ball. I understand that you were once married to Sam Wescott?"

"Guilty as charged. But that was a long, long time ago." My surprise must have shown on my face.

"Were you in contact with Sam since the divorce?"

While I searched for a snappy, noncommittal answer that would avoid the delicate question of whether I had last seen him alive or as a ghost, Dartwood got up and got us both another beer. By the time he'd recycled both our cans, dug in the refrigerator (also solar powered, I noted) and produced two more beers, I'd forgotten the question.

Dartwood was happy to remind me. "I was hoping that you had stayed in touch with Sam. He left us with some unfinished business."

I sat up straight. "Unfinished business? You and Sam?"

Dartwood handed me my beer. He crossed one leg over the other and looked at me over the rim of his can. "We were roommates at Groton."

"One of the many prep schools Sam was kicked out of," I responded, still trying to digest the fact that Sam had been connected to Frank Dartwood. "But how, I mean, *what* did he have to do with the bay?"

"He was a Wescott. I had hoped, when I contacted him, that he would have some say with Wescott Development Corp. I thought perhaps he could somehow prevent his family from developing White Marsh. So I tracked him down."

"Tracked him down?"

Dartwood smiled. "It wasn't that hard, you know. I found him living in the Caribbean. On an island called Big Pig Cay. It was about what you would expect from a place called Big Pig Cay."

"Something out of Somerset Maugham, I would imagine. Booze, babes, sleazy bars, heat, bright colors, peeling paint, smell of rotten fruit, remittance men, wanna-be coke dealers always on the verge of the big one, that sort of thing."

Dartwood lifted his beer can in salute. "Like Jimmy Buffett only not one half as interesting." He grimaced. "Sam was living down there on the Honduras."

I looked down into the triangular hole of my can, as if all the answers were floating around in my beer. "What was it like?" I asked.

"About what you would expect. Drank too much, hung out in some low-rent dive, didn't do much of anything." He shrugged. "Hell, who am I trying to kid, he had a great life, if your idea of a great life is doing nothing, having no reason, no *cause* to fuel your life."

"My idea of a great life is a bag of Reese's cups, a Diet Pepsi, a good mystery, and *One Life to Live*," I said. "Unfortunately, I rarely get it."

Dartwood lifted his eyebrows. "I don't believe that," he said. "I think you only need to find your cause, like I found mine."

"Maybe I've burned out on causes," I grumped, thinking about Jason Hemlock. What he did to the county, he'd also done to me. But at least the voters had their pants on. I shook my head. "But let me ask you this: What's a nice boy like you doing in a place like this?"

Dartwood sighed. "Someone has to do it. Look, you may or may not know that I started out as a corporate lawyer. After Nam, I went back into college, back into the life I thought I was supposed to lead. It was in Nam, when I saw what we were doing to what was once a beautiful country that I started to change, started to get the feeling that we were out of balance, that we were driving ourselves to extinction. I'd always loved the outdoors, you know, hunting, fishing, boats, camping. But it wasn't until I worked for Nixon Petroleum that I understood how seriously we are damaging our environment, all the lies people tell each other just to get a few more bucks. Gradually, I grew disillusioned. I saw those with the power abusing it for profit, turning a blind eye to the rape of the planet." Frank Dartwood was the only person I've ever met who could say something like "rape of the planet" and make it sound like real people talk. "So, I went to work for the EPA. And what I saw there didn't make me any happier. The Reagan administration had pretty well castrated the agency. So then I went to work in the private sector. You know, Friends of the Chesapeake. But they were too cautious, too determined not to make waves, not to upset the establishment, to which most of them belong. And making waves is what we need if we're going to survive. So now we have the Greenhead Army."

"This would make a great story," I said.

Dartwood grimaced. "And it's one I'm going to ask you

not to write. At least not now, because I don't think it's fin-ished yet."

You're telling me, I thought, but I said nothing. The idea was forming in the back of my mind that Frank Dartwood, or maybe a member of his children's crusade, might have blown Sam and his Honduras 36 into the next world—and back into my life. I wondered where the hell Sam was right this minute. Could ghosts travel without a car? Or a boat?

"So what about Sam?" I asked, lighting another cigarette. I found an oystershell on the screen ledge and used it for an ashtray. "Was it you who convinced him to come back to the Shore?"

"Yes, I think so. I appealed to his better nature, what bet-ter nature Sam had, which wasn't much, to be honest. I think what finally sold him on it was the idea of sticking a spoke—*any* spoke—into the family wheel. I never met anyone who disliked his blood relations any more than Sam Wescott."

"Ah, but do you know Claire?" I asked.

He grimaced. "Would you believe I went to her debut? That seems like a million years ago in another lifetime. But it's true. And now, she's like an antienvironmental harpy, and we're the worst of enemies."

"So what happened when you went to find Sam?" I asked, gently leading him back to the subject.

"He was ready to come back, I think. Paradise wasn't all it was cracked up to be, and besides, I think there was some trouble about gambling debts and a woman and her husband. It was a good time for him to move on."

I nodded. Typical Sam stuff. I could have guessed that. "Did you sail back up with him?"

"Someone had to." Dartwood shrugged. "He couldn't handle that boat alone on blue water, not in his condition."

"Drunk all the time?"

Dartwood shot me a look over his glasses. "I thought you knew. Sam had cancer. Bad cancer."

The storm, long in coming, broke across the marsh in

rolls of thunder and bolts of lightning. But it was an empty storm; the rain it carried would fall somewhere else.

I looked out across the landscape, absorbing this unexpected news. People like Sam met their ends shot by jealous husbands; as victims of really stupid stunts; maybe even from old age in some remote and primitive village on the other side of the world. AIDS, I thought, given Sam's carelessness and the growing HIV statistics among heterosexuals. But cancer? That seemed somehow rotten and unfair, as if fortune had not given him a sporting chance. Cancer had gotten his mother, too, I had heard. But she had eluded it with a large bottle of Seconal and a bottle of vodka. I felt a sadness, in spite of myself.

"I'm sorry," was all I could say.

Andy was the kind of person who had to use a mallet to open his claws. This told me he was born somewhere other than the Eastern Shore. Turned out he was from northern Virginia where you could expect that kind of behavior from people, but who cared, he was gorgeous.

The crabs, however, were delicious, and not even the news about Sam could totally destroy my appetite. In fact, if anything, I was starving. It had been a long time since that lunch on the veranda at Mandrake. In fact, I had no idea what time it was at all.

Thunder had started rolling in over the marsh just as the crabs had been borne to the table on the screen porch, and as we dug into the steaming, spicy pile, flashes of lightning began to pass over us. A dry storm, heading across the bay to dump its precious rain somewhere in Delaware.

Still, it was cozy on the porch by the light of the single solar battery lantern that hung from the rafters. The conversation was general, but it seemed to me that it was almost deliberately so, as if the Greenheads were avoiding any real issues around a stranger.

I was sucking the meat out of a claw when Jennifer, the pistol-packing debutante, poured more iced tea for herself and said, "I think we should kill 'em."

At first, of course, I thought she meant me, and I looked around to see if anyone was coming after me with a claw mallet. But no, they were all looking at her with great interest, as if she had just suggested that they ought to consider vacationing in Camden, Maine, next year instead of Bar Harbor. It was just that they were all so wholesome and outdoorsy, with that freshly scrubbed look of catalogue models for L. L. Bean, that I instinctively mistrusted them. Even Andy's nose ring didn't quite allay my feeling that they were dangerous.

Dartwood, selecting a crab from the pile, broke off the claws and pried open the apron with his fingers. "No," he said thoughtfully. "I don't think that killing Hemlock would do us any good at all. They'd just go out and buy another politician."

"I just don't like him," Jennifer said, and I suddenly realized where I'd seen them before.

"You were the caterers at Sam's funeral," I said suddenly.

"How do you think we finance our day-to-day operations?" Andy asked me. "It also helps us gather information."

"It was my idea," Jennifer said. "Greens 'n' Things Catering."

"Yeah, it may have been your idea, but I was the one who set up the computers," Theresa said.

"And I was the one who could cook," Mookie put in.

"Hey, this reminds me of a dysfunctional family reunion where everyone brings a covered dish and an unresolved issue," I said. "And believe me, I know whereof I speak." I opened a crab claw with a knife and sucked out the meat. "If you're plotting to kill Jason, you'd have to stand in line, though."

That at least got a laugh. The enemy of my enemy is my friend. Besides, given a choice between someone who wants to bulldoze their initials into islands in a marsh and someone who wants to save a marsh, I know which side I'll always land on.

In spite of myself, I liked them. But I was too old, too tired, and too cynical to trust them. Even if I believed in their mission, I wasn't sure that I approved of their methods. And besides, there was something bone chilling about the way Jennifer casually suggested killing Jason. Not, of course, that I blamed her. To know Claire was to despise her with a vengeance, but still, murder was much too close to home right now.

I wondered again if the Greenheads were the ones who had blown Sam to Kingdom Come. With those canoes it would have been easy enough to sneak across Santimoke Bay, climb aboard the boat, open those propane valves, and get back to base without anyone being the wiser. They'd already penetrated security at Mandrake as caterers. And good caterers, too; smooth and professional and if Estelle had even suspected, she would have had a fit.

"I'd hire you, if I were going to have a party," I said sincerely. "This is a nice spread."

They all beamed at me with appreciation. "We can give you a good discount," Andy said. "You should see our vegetarian menus. We're pretty creative with the dips and spreads. Vegetarian also cuts down on the costs. And it's healthier." He smiled at me, showing me his perfect white WASP teeth.

"Uh-huh," I said. Oh, I was falling in love. Or lust. Hey, when you stop looking, you're dead.

Thunder broke right over our heads. Through the dripping leaves, I could see the marsh illuminated by a bolt of lightning. It was eerie, being out here in the middle of nowhere with most of the comforts of home.

"Starts a lot of fires, lightning," Dartwood remarked. "In a dry season, this grass can go up fast. Burns in waves, as the wind pushes the flames across the grass. It will burn everything, right up to the water, if it's dry enough and windy enough."

"In the spring, trappers burn it off for the muskrat lodges," I said. "I remember watching the smoke from the water, when we used to go out fishing with my daddy."

"One good, uncontrolled burning could destroy everything on this neck. The marsh would grow back, but the woods and the cripples would take years to recoup. And the damage to the fish, the wildlife, and their habitat could be devastating. It's not something you want to see go out of control."

I shuddered. I could imagine the devastation a fire could cause, rippling across these acres, consuming everything in its path. Scary. Very.

"About Sam," Dartwood said when the kids' conversation turned toward kid stuff. He leaned toward me. "Did he tell you anything about his plans? What he intended to do about this White Marsh thing?"

"I hadn't seen him in ten years and more," I said quite truthfully. "And I had no idea what he planned to do. I take it he died before he could let you know?"

Dartwood nodded glumly. "I came up as far as Mandrake with him. The kids picked me up, but not before H.P. and I had a go-around. Oh, he was mad all right. Stood right there on the dock in the middle of the night and damned me to hell." He looked out the screens. The thunder rolled. The storm was passing over us, but it was a heat storm without rain. The humidity was gone, but it would be back by morning with renewed intensity.

I slapped a mosquito that landed on my arm. It left a blob of blood on my skin. I wiped it off with my (cloth, please note) napkin.

"Captain John Smith, when he first came up this way in the 1600s, called this marsh the Mouth of Purgatory. Those Englishmen, they'd never seen anything like this. They thought they *were* in hell," Dartwood observed dryly. "To a lot of people, even today, this marsh is hell. It's a barren place, dead, they think. They don't see the beauty in it or the delicate ecosystem. A marsh supports an astonishingly rich variety of life forms. It acts as a filter, catching pollutants, like farm runoff and heavy metals, that might otherwise run into the bay and out into the oceans and ultimately into the water supply. As I pointed out before, wetlands are the world's major source of fresh water."

"And we're destroying them as fast as we can," Andy pointed out seriously.

"Wescott Development chose White Marsh because they think they can ultimately fill in all of this marshland and develop it," Jennifer said.

"Aren't there laws against this sort of thing? I mean, there's Section 404 and all of that," I said. "You need all kinds of state, local, and federal permits, I thought, just to *look* at a wetlands."

"The laws are broad and vague." Dartwood sighed. "There's a lot of room for manipulating and maneuvering, especially if you have the juice and the money to buy yourself a politician or two, or three, like Jason Hemlock, and pack local planning and zoning boards with your buddies. I'd imagine there are a lot of people in this county who owe him or know him. Imagine that on a state and national level, and you have a pretty good idea what's going on here and a lot of other places. Add the pressure of an ever-increasing population density, all those people clamoring for waterfront houses, and you get a mix for environmental disaster. The bottom line is too many people and a diminishing amount of space to support them."

I thought about seeing Jason Hemlock out there and felt the pieces sliding into place. Nice. The Wescotts had bought a politician all right, but what the hell was he going three rounds with Skip about? I needed to know. There was a lot I needed to know.

So I listened while the Greenheads told me more about wetlands, marshlands, and the health of the Chesapeake Bay. I guess like a lot of people, I was proenvironment but sort of with the idea that as long as I recycled my soda cans, newspaper, and plastic, I was doing my bit for the Chesapeake. I knew we were in trouble, but I sort of hoped someone else would do something about it. Okay, okay, so they were radicals, tree worshippers, and possibly even violent outlaws. But on the other hand, after a look around

White Marsh Island, they were also preaching to the converted.

Why the hell should the bay lose yet more acres of wetlands and wildlife so a handful of Three Rs could move into ugly man-made bunkers? So they could die and take it with them? God, I'd had enough beer to float a boat, the crabs were good, and Andy was handsome and his leg was touching mine. And I was sick and tired of being a literary peon for a co-opted small-town rag on a chain that has the moral integrity of the Borgia popes. Those fine out-of-fashion '70s values were swimming in a haze of Boh and I was feeling little or no pain. For a change.

If it weren't for certain nagging, unanswered questions about who murdered Sam Wescott, I probably would have joined up there and then. But I had a cause of my own: finding Sam's killer.

Hell, he or she might be sitting right here at this table, picking over the crab debris with me in search of one last sliver. Someone who killed, then acted perfectly normal. Well, not perfectly normal. I mean this *was* the Greenhead Army here, but you know what I mean.

Opportunity, yes. Motive? To be determined.

"What did Sam tell *you* about White Marsh?" I asked Dartwood.

He was eating his salad. A tiny piece of field green stuck to his tooth. "He agreed that developing White Marsh was wrong. He said that he would try to use his influence with the family to stop it. And he still had voting rights on the board of directors even though he hadn't used it for years. Apparently, part of the remittance deal was that he assign his vote to the family ticket. You know, vote the way they told him. Some sort of a proxy deal, I assumed. But now that the remittance deal was over and he was dying, he seemed to think it was important to do the right thing." Dartwood used his finger to remove the minuscule bit of leaf from his tooth. He frowned, thinking. "I still can't believe that he blew himself up like that. Whatever Sam was, he was a good sailor. He had lived on that boat for years.

He knew what he had to. And I would know; I sailed up from the Caribbean with him."

"That's a long time to assess someone's skills under less than ideal conditions. Did you motor up through the inland waterway?"

"Part of the way, sure. Wind's against you, coming up the coast. And time was of the essence in more ways than one."

If Dartwood had wanted to kill Sam, being alone on a thirty-six-foot sailboat with him would have offered lots of opportunities. Unless Sam got home and reneged on every promise. But why? Dartwood was pretty ruthless, but he wasn't a fugitive yet.

I lit a postprandial cigarette. "So, what do you think about the theory that Sam was killed?" I asked casually.

Dartwood's eyebrows rose. "What theory?" he asked blankly. "Someone killed Sam? But why? He was going to die anyway. Where did you hear that?"

He was either a good actor or innocent. I couldn't tell. And looking around the table, I saw only mild interest. Apparently no one here was going to leap up and dramatically confess.

"I was at the Santimoke County state's attorney's office on my reporter rounds this morning." I implied, without actually saying anything, that the news had come from there. Neat trick, huh?

"Where do they get that idea?"

"I've got a good source," I replied mysteriously. A real good source, but one in whose existence none of these people would ever believe in a million years. The ghost of the victim himself.

Dartwood shook his head. "Anything is possible," he said, pushing back from the table.

The storm had passed, and thin rays of evening sunlight played across the washed, green island. The world was still arid, with just the distant rumble of thunder moving north to torment us with thoughts of rain.

"Andy, why don't you take Ms. Ball back to her car?

You'll forgive me if I ask your permission to blindfold you again, Ball, but we can't risk your unexpected—or forced—return."

I nodded understandingly. "Is there any way I can get in touch with you if I find out anything? Look, I am not anxious to see this development continue."

"It can be restored, you know," Dartwood said softly. "The fill can be removed, that obscene pond filled in. In a few years, you would never know that it had ever happened at all, if it's stopped now."

"What will you do if it's not?"

"You don't want to know," Dartwood said with a small, thin smile. "But you see what you can discover about Sam's votes and Wescott Development. If there's a peaceful way to stop this soon, it will save a lot of blood and trouble later."

He shook my hand. His grip was firm and dry. Looking into his eyes, I knew that he was serious. Dead serious. "Don't call us, we'll call you," he said.

Gently placing his hand on my shoulder, Andy led me away.

I went without protest.

All in all, it had been one hell of a day.

And, although I didn't know it then, it wasn't over yet.

EIGHT

•

Slow Dancing with the Angel of Death Down to Toby's Bar and Grill

Overhead in the starry sky, a thin crescent moon peered out of the last, ragged clouds. Mosquitoes buzzed angrily around my face as I fumbled in the darkness with the car door. In the distance, I could hear the splash of water as Andy guided the canoe back home through the rising mists.

I fumbled around in my pocketbook for my car keys before I remembered that I'd left them in the ignition. The resounding whine as I opened the car door reminded me of that small fact. I collapsed into the car seat and groped for a cigarette. Land of Pleasant Living, my ass. Land O'Loons, maybe. Your typical open-air insane asylum, the Eastern Shore. Still, Andy was awfully cute. I thought I caught a dim whiff of Mitsouko in the air and wrinkled my nose.

"Well, it took you long enough, Holl. Where have you been?" Sam materialized beside me. The pile of junk literature on the passenger seat never moved as he settled in, looking at me sulkily. The thin moonlight shone through his eyes, making them bluer than ever.

"Oh, I'm just finding out all *kinds* of interesting things, and I've been off in the marshes, kidnapped by eco-loons, fed crabs, and engaged in deep and meaningful conversation with an old friend of yours," I snapped. "Where the hell have *you* been?"

"That kid was no old friend of mine. Boy, you two sure did look friendly. Are you dating trophy studs, Holl? He's young enough to be—"

"My younger brother," I finished quickly. "Sam, why didn't you tell me about the cancer?"

That shut him up fast. He folded his arms across his chest and looked away from me, a mulish expression settling over his features.

"You saw Frank Dartwood somewhere, didn't you?" he asked when he finally decided to speak again.

"Frank Dartwood and the Greenhead Army. Like a bad doo-wop band, only no one was going 'sha-la-la' when they kidnapped me at gunpoint."

I filled him in on my adventures of the past few hours, replete with some of that fine vocabulary of curses I told you about earlier. Most of it was directed at Sam. Somehow I blamed him for my troubles.

"So, why didn't you tell me about the cancer, Sam?" I wound up. "Or was that something you just told Frank because it was convenient at the moment?"

Sam gazed out the window, where the blue moonlight danced on the water. I could not read his expression, too misty in the dark.

"No, that was true," he said at last. "I was dying, Holl. And that was part of the reason why, when Frank found me, I decided to come back."

"So, what happened? Did you have any influence at all on the decision to develop White Marsh? How are you involved in this?"

"Holl, I think we'd better get out of here," Sam said quickly. "Start the car and move."

"Come on, Sam. I want the truth. I want the whole story, and I want it right now," I snarled. "I'm tired and I'm dirty and I'm hot, and I've been through enough for one day—"

"Whatever you do, Holl, don't look in the backseat."

Well, of course, I turned and looked into the backseat. I really wish I hadn't. "Sam, there's something back there," I whined uncertainly.

"Damn right. And if you look closely, you'll see that it's a dead man."

I turned on the overhead light. Jason Hemlock lay sprawled among the old newspapers and Burger King wrappers, looking spiffy and clean except for the nasty bullet hole through his head.

"Oh, shit" was all I could think of to say.

There was no question that he was dead and had been dead for a while. A greenfly was crawling happily around the wound, doing things I didn't want to think about.

"Sam, that's Jason Hemlock in my backseat," I whimpered. "And he's a dead body."

"I know," Sam replied uneasily.

"Where did he come from?"

"How should I know? I'm a ghost."

"Is he? Maybe if he is, he can tell us something."

"No, no ghost for Jason Hemlock. Don't ask me why. It's just the rules."

"W-what do the rules say about what we should do now?"

"Sorry. The rules aren't for living people, just ghosts. And there's nothing I, as a ghost, can do about this."

"Who killed him and put him in my backseat?" I demanded. "What am I supposed to do? He looks awful!"

"And he's gonna start to smell worse in this heat soon," Sam said matter-of-factly. "Damn, Holl, you're hard on your men, aren't you?"

"If you weren't already dead, there would be two corpses in this car right now," I said through my teeth. "If it weren't for you, I'd be home right now, in the a/c watching television and reading the comics page, so think of something."

"If I were you, I'd put him out on the side of the road and keep going," Sam said. "I don't think he was killed here. There's no sense of violence like you get around a murder."

"I should call the cops, I guess," I said.

"From where? The nearest phone is back at the job

trailer, and it's locked up tight. Maybe your woodland pals got sick of his shit and offed him while you were flirting with that muscle-bound moron."

"Yeah, but why stick him in my car? There's a thousand acres of marsh where you could dump him, and no one would ever know. You could weigh him down with something and dump him in a creek, and the crabs and the buzzards would take care of him." I was whining and I knew I was whining, but you'd have whined, too, if you had been me.

"That was a rotten trick, wasn't it? As I recall, he was one of your ex-boyfriends, wasn't he? Maybe someone wanted to make you look bad, real bad. Like so bad you killed him. Did you kill him, Holl?"

"I had my chance last year. Come on, Sam, think!"

"I'm thinking, but it's not gonna do us any good."

"Why?"

"Because the cops are down the road, just about to round the next corner."

I looked out the window. Before I heard the wailing siren, I saw the flashing light curving up the road toward us.

I watched glumly as the body bag containing the last of Jason Hemlock was gurneyed into the waiting ambulance.

"Got an aspirin?" I asked.

The thin edge of a headache that had been building up behind my eyes since I had come back to the car was now exploding. In the glare of the klieg lights, the flashes of the cameras, the spinning gumballs, and the smell of chemicals, it was building to a crescendo like a Mozart opera.

"Never travel without 'em." From the glove compartment of his car, Sev Capwell fished out a bottle. A large bottle. He handed me the rest of his bottle of designer water. It was lukewarm, but I was grateful for any liquid.

I was sitting on the seat of his car with the door open, watching numbly as the state boys did the usual crime scene stuff. I swallowed the pills, then pressed my fingers against my throbbing temples. "I appreciate you coming out here, Sev." I said.

"No problem. I probably would have had to come anyway. When you get a dead man on Hemlock's level, you more or less have to come. Hollis, where were you for the past six hours?"

"Are we back at that again?" I asked.

"You'd better answer him," Sam said. He was leaning against the fender of the car, invisible to everyone save, of course, me. "From what those cops are saying over there, they're thinking they can charge you. Stick to your story. *They* have to prove you're lying."

"I already answered that!" I said, to both of them.

"Where did the .38 come from?" Sev asked. "Hollis, come on, cut me a break. Cut yourself a break. I'm doing my best here to help you."

"I know you are, Sev. And I'm trying my best to help you, but I'm telling the truth and you still won't believe me."

"Try me again."

"Stick to your guns, Holl. You've got everything to gain and nothing to lose." Sam leaned over and looked at me. "Don't implicate Frank and the Greenheads. At least not right now. Tell 'em you met a guy with a boat and took a ride and found the gun someplace."

I looked down at my hands, which were covered with ink and chemicals. They'd tested me for powder burns and then rolled me for prints, right on the site. "I was driving back to town. I met a fisherman with a boat here at the creek, and I asked him to take me around the guts so I could get a better look at White Marsh from the water. We got lost, then it started to thunder and lightning so we came home. Why don't you believe me, Sev?"

He smiled a tired smile. "Because I know you, Hollis. Who was this alleged guy?"

"I don't know. Jimmy or Mike or Steve or something like that. He had a boat, and I gave him a few dollars for gas. He wasn't catching anything so he said what the hell."

"Where did you get the .38?"

"I found it alongside the road," I said.

Sev sighed. He ran his fingers through what was left of his hair. "And why, may one ask, was it on the road?"

"I don't know. I thought it was strange myself. Probably some kids took it from their daddy and went out to target practice and left it there."

"Right," Sev sighed. He was making notes on a legal pad as we were talking. I couldn't read them. "Now, let's go over it again."

"Oh, for God's sake, Sev!" I snapped. "I've got a dead man in my car, and I don't know how the hell he got there! How am I going to get home?"

"If you don't start giving me a straight answer, you're going to sleep at the county detention center tonight," he replied, smiling.

My head felt as if red-hot needles were being poked through my skull. "Sev, cut me a break. Please. How would you feel if you had a dead guy in your car?"

"Hey, I resent that!" Sam said.

"Oh, shut up!" I hissed at him. "You've made enough trouble."

Sev's head jerked up. "What?"

"Never mind," I replied, glaring at Sam, who beamed sadistically back at me. "I'm just sitting here having a nervous breakdown. When do I get my car back? Do I have to clean up the bloodstains? Were there any bloodstains? Do I have to write this up for the paper?" I was about to become a major mess. I'd seen homicides before, but this was the first corpse of someone I'd actually had a personal relationship with, such as it was. And no, Sam doesn't count; he was a ghost, not a cadaver. "What am I gonna do—" I started to wail.

"Excuse me, Sev," a voice said, and I stopped, turning to look at a plainclothes cop. He was tall and blond, wearing a severely rumpled sports coat and a pair of baggy chinos, and he looked a lot like Harrison Ford if Harrison Ford had been ridden hard down nine miles of bad road and put away wet. Real wet. He was wiping his hands with a paper towel and lighting a cigarette at the same time. My kinda man, I thought, as his green eyes swept casually over me. One thing about homicide sites, you don't have to look your best.

"Hollis Ball, Lieutenant Ormand Friendly, Homicide, Maryland State Police," Sev sighed, clearly relieved to be spared. "Hollis owns the car and the gun."

"I own the car. I found the gun," I insisted tightly. "I've also found a Godzilla-sized headache."

Friendly looked at me with an expression that was anything but friendly. I immediately felt like a suspect. It was not a pleasant feeling.

"Boy, are you in trouble now," Sam remarked. "This is one tough cop. He knows you're lying."

I couldn't be sure, but I thought that Friendly threw a glance toward Sam. His expression did not change, and he looked down at a notebook in his hand. We looked like a reporter's convention with all of our notebooks. Some crime techs were going over my car and the area around it on the causeway, stopping to swat and complaining bitterly about the mosquitoes and the biting flies.

The flashing lights from the ambulance fell across us like disco lights as it lurched down the dark causeway into the night. I knew that Jason was being taken across the bridge to the medical examiner's office in Baltimore. All violent or suspicious deaths in Maryland end up on the examining tables up there, under the scalpels of the pathologists.

Poor Jason. Whatever sort of a shit he was, and he had been a major fecal deposit, he didn't deserve to be murdered. Or did he?

Whatever, I surely didn't deserve to have him murdered in my car. Or even murdered somewhere else and stuffed in my car. Jason always hated that shabby red Honda, never wanted to be seen in it. We always went out in his clean new Lexus—

"Where is Jason's car?" I asked suddenly. "He didn't just fly here on his broom. He had a Lexus. It must be around here somewhere. It didn't just disappear off the face of the earth, you know—"

"When did you last see Delegate Hemlock alive?" Friendly asked me wearily.

"At the job site for White Marsh, up the road. He was there with Skipper Dupont. They were having some kind of a fight when I walked in. And the next time I saw him, he was dead in the backseat. Listen, I already told all this to Sev."

"Tell *me*, Ms. Ball," Friendly said with a world-weary smile.

So I told the whole story again. And again. And a third time, with them both grilling me at once. I was about to suggest they get the rubber hose and the desk lamp when Friendly sighed and flipped his notebook closed.

"Son of a bitch," he remarked to no one in particular. He looked at his watch, then at the crime scene crew. A couple of uniforms were hanging around watching the lab boys. I knew I was old because they looked too young to be state police, like they hadn't yet graduated from high school. Both of them looked kind of awed. I suppose it was their first homicide. Friendly abruptly turned away from us and spoke to the group around my car.

Whatever they said, he didn't like it. He swore again, swatted a mosquito, frowned, and looked over at Sev and me as if he'd like to eat me alive. Sam whistled through his teeth.

"You're in trouble now," he said, like I needed him to tell me.

"Are you gonna arrest me?" I asked Sev, and I sounded as frightened as I felt, even in my own ears. "You've already got my prints and my powder burn tests."

Sev shook his head. "Not tonight, anyway. We need the ballistics and the ME's reports. *Then* we arrest you." He smiled to show it was a joke, but I wasn't laughing.

"Ms. Ball, I've seen your byline in the *Gazette*, but I don't think we've met before. I was transferred over here from Internal Affairs," Lieutenant Friendly said quickly.

"Whom did you offend?" I asked, genuinely curious. To be transferred from Internal Affairs to a backwater like Santimoke County must be a low blow for a member of state law enforcement.

Was it my imagination or did Friendly wince? I watched bleakly as yet another set of headlights coming up the road turned out to be a wrecker.

"You're towing my car? How am I supposed to get home?" I whined. Wads of steel wool were stuffed into my sinuses and a tight band of pain was encircling my skull. On the other hand, did I want to ride home in a car where a dead body had been, possibly a car where someone had been killed? My stomach lurched at the thought.

"I'll be happy to drive you," Ormand Friendly said.

"Check out that Friendly guy. He's interested in you," Sam remarked.

"Jealous?" Friendly asked over his shoulder, and I could have sworn he was looking directly at Sam when he said it. But I also had the headache from hell, so what did I know? Maybe he said something else and my brain read it as *jealous*.

"Allow me to escort the lady home," Sev said, stepping quickly back toward our happy band. He beckoned me toward his car. "We're almost finished out here, coupla more minutes to wrap, then we can go. Where do you live, Hollis?"

"On Blackwater Farm. It's right on the Beddoe's Island Road, on the other side of Watertown."

"You'll have to show me," he said.

"Friendly's a foreigner," Sam said, kicking sullenly at the asphalt. His shoe passed through a pebble.

"Well, at least he's not one of my cousins," I said out of the corner of my mouth.

Friendly was staring at me.

"Sometimes talking to myself makes a headache go away," I said lamely.

"Uh-huh," he replied.

I don't think he believed me about that, either.

Mercifully, Sev seemed oblivious to what was going on. He yawned, glanced at his watch, and beckoned me again toward his car. "Ladies and gentlemen, Elvis is leaving the building," he said.

"We'll speak later, Ms. Ball," the homicide detective promised.

"I believe you," I replied, turning to climb into the passenger seat of the state's attorney's automobile.

We stared at each other for a moment through the glass before Sev put the car in gear and hung a U-ie on the causeway.

"Thanks for catching the ball, Sev," I sighed.

"No problem, Hollis. Listen, I've been thinking. The media, as you should know, is going to be all over you like a cheap suit by tomorrow morning. And I'd prefer that you didn't speak to anyone or try to write this story up right now. Is there someplace other than your house I can take you for the next twenty-four hours?"

"My folks, down on the island," I said. "But you know, Sev, Rig Riggle, the editor from hell, will be the first one to be all over me for not filing a story on this. Especially since I'm the Number One Suspect. For a murder I did not commit," I added piously.

"Hollis, I know you well enough to know that you're capable of anything, except murder," Sev sighed. "But I'm asking you, as a personal favor, to pick a place where you can stay and to stay there, out of the way, where I can find you, for twenty-four hours."

I bit my lower lip. Most crimes stand a fair chance of being solved within twenty-four hours of commission, *if they will ever be solved at all*. I also knew Sev probably had enough to tuck me away in the Santimoke County Detention Center overnight. In the morning, if he decided to charge me with first degree murder and a string of lesser charges, which he could probably do, I could count on a high bail. Higher than I could make, even with Snooky, the Twenty-four-hour Bail Bondsman, a personal courthouse friend of mine.

I swallowed.

"Toby," Sam said from the backseat.

For once, Sam had a good idea.

"Well, Sev, I have this cousin Toby who owns this bar, down on the island. . . ."

It was about midnight when our happy crew rolled across the counterweight bridge over Beddoe's Narrows, that thin strip of water that separates Beddoe's Island from the mainland. The bridgetender's house was dark and silent; Mr. Alva, the night tender, would sleep on until dawn unless roused by a boat horn or the radio.

The island was dark and silent now, but in an hour or so, watermen would be rising, getting ready to head out on the dawn tide. Then the Narrows would roar with diesel marine engines starting up. The bridge would open and close like a politician's jaw as a hundred workboats headed out into the Chesapeake waters to begin the day's crabbing.

Toby's Bar looked like four A.M. in hell. It can be a fine May morning, and in Toby's it still looks like it's four A.M., and it's raining outside. His customers like it that way.

The only light came from the neon glare of a couple of beer signs, a perennial string of Christmas lights, and a jukebox that is genetically programmed to play only somebody-done-me-wrong country dirges. The only customer there had probably passed out right after the Orioles game went off the TV on the wall. He sat, head down in a puddle of beer, unconscious. The place smelled of stale cigarettes, flat beer, and mildew from the stuffed ducks and geese that pass for decorator accents at Toby's. A sign over the back of the bar announced WE DO NOT SERVE UNPLEAS-ANT PEOPLE.

Judging by the broken pool cues and chairs piled up in the middle of the floor, there had been some unpleasant people having a disagreement in here recently. Toby's is that kind of a place.

There was a brief intake of breath as Sev had his first

good look at Toby Ball. Sev's a tall man, but he had to look up.

Toby was in Vietnam, along with about half our mutual relations. The other half stayed home and marched against the war.

Unlike some of our cousins, Toby came back.

Some people on the island wish he hadn't.

I love him dearly.

I didn't blame Sev for staring, though; most people are a little taken aback by Toby until they get to know him. He's had offers from professional wrestling, and he looks like he's crazier than a bald-ass coot, which he is.

Nonetheless, he cracked a smile through his thick black beard when he saw me and immediately started to build me a vodka and tonic. I bellied up to the bar and gestured Sev onto the stool beside me. Still looking a little stunned, he sat down and was amazed when Toby placed a Dewar's and water in front of him.

"How did you know—" he started to ask, but Toby just shrugged.

"You just look like a Dewar's an' water kind of guy," Toby rumbled, his voice coming somewhere from deep within the wiry black hair that covers most of his head and face.

"Sev, this is my cousin Toby Ball. Toby, this is Severn Capwell, state's attorney for Santimoke County."

I sipped my Stoli and tonic. It felt smooth going down. Toby, however, was not taking the introduction to Sev too well. He frowned, and Sev looked dubious. "I don't like the po-lice, and I don't like lawyers," Toby told him flatly. His big hands opened and closed around his side of the bar, and he leaned forward so you could see his eyes deep beneath his baseball cap.

"Relax, he's a friendly," I said quickly. "I'm in one hell of a mess, and Sev is trying to do his best to clean it up for me." Briefly, I gave him an edited version of the facts, or as much of it as I wanted to discuss in front of Sev.

"So," I concluded, "Sev thinks I should be unavailable

for comment for a while, and I hoped you could help me out."

"Basically, I need her frozen for twenty-four hours," Sev explained. "I'm afraid whoever killed Hemlock may try to come after Hollis next."

"Hey!" I cried, outraged, but no one was paying any attention.

Toby reached under the counter and brought up a sawed-off 12-gauge Remington, which he placed on the bar. "I've got an AK-47 on my boat," he remarked conversationally. "Took it off a dead ARVN when I was in the Nam. You'd be amazed how many little guys, they get a bag on and think they need to fight a big bartender." He patted the sawed-off affectionately. "This usually ends the dispute."

"Personally, I like the German semis," Sev said, and the two of them were off and running on a detailed discussion of firearms, which may have bonded *them* but made *my* eyes glaze.

While they were talking, I noticed out of the corner of my eye that Sam was walking around the bar. He looked at all the stuffed geese and ducks, fooled around the pool table, and stopped to examine the selections on the jukebox. I couldn't read his expression in the dim neon glow, but I sensed a certain nostalgia. Sam had always liked Toby's bar, even after Toby had banned him forever.

Forever had turned out to be a week; Sam's charm won even tough Tobias Bradshaw Ball over in the end, and the two of them celebrated their reconciliation so hard that special guests included a sheriff's deputy. And she got pretty looped too, if I remember right.

Sev was draining his scotch and refusing another. Evidently he and Toby had found a common testosterone ground in firearms in spite of their philosophical differences on law enforcement. "I've got someone at home waiting," he said with a wink at Toby. "Hell of a night to be dragged out of bed for a homicide."

Toby nodded solemn agreement.

Pulling on his jacket, Sev gave me a stern look. "Look,

I want to be able to reach you any time within the next twenty-four hours. Is there a number here?"

Toby slid a bar matchbook across the counter to him. Sev pocketed it. He looked at me wearily. "Jesus, Hollis. I'm going to do my best. Try to stay out of trouble for twenty-four hours, okay? This time it's my ass on the line."

"What about mine?" I asked. "And when do I get my car back? And do I want it back?"

He reached out and punched my arm, like I was just one of the guys. "I'll call you, okay? Toby, good to meet you. Try to keep an eye on her, okay?"

"I've been keeping an eye on her since she was knee-high to a grasshopper," Toby said. He held out one of his hands, the size of a tackle block, and Sev shook it.

"Somebody might be after me?" I squeaked again, looking down the bar at the passed-out drunk as if he might be a hit man.

"Relax. That's just Bobby Buck," Toby said. Bobby Buck's Beddoe's Island's town drunk, but at that moment, I didn't feel like trusting anybody.

Sam waited until Sev was out the door and then came over and sat down on the vacant stool.

"How ya doin', Sam?" Toby asked.

"I'm okay, for a dead man," Sam replied.

I looked from one to the other. "You can see him?" I asked Toby.

He nodded. "Of course I can. I didn't know if you could. And I was pretty sure your lawyer friend couldn't."

"You can see ghosts, too?" I asked, stunned.

Toby nodded. "Our grandmother Russell could, too. She used to see the ghost of Miss Louisa Harmon walkin' down Chicken Bridge Road all the time." That out of the way, he turned to Sam. "So, what'll ya have? The usual?"

"Sounds good to me," Sam said. "Bein' dead is thirsty work."

"We don't get many ghosts in here," Toby remarked as he set a shot glass and bottle of Mount Gay on the bar.

"And at these prices, you won't get many more either,"

Sam said, and the pair of them roared as if it were absolutely hilarious.

Men. Go figure.

Sam leaned over the rum and sort of inhaled from it. I watched, fascinated. He seemed to be absorbing the essence of rum. Whatever, it seemed to do him some good. He sighed and smiled. "There's a pal, Tobe," he sighed. "That's good stuff."

"It's on the house, bunk," Toby replied gravely. From some interior pocket, he withdrew a joint the size of a Havana de Corona, and, striking a kitchen match on the bar, fired it up, passing it over to Sam. He held it under Sam's nose, and the ghost snorked it up gratefully.

I even took a couple of hits, although I sort of gave that stuff up years ago.

"Thanks," Sam said, and Toby did it again. Sam leaned back in his chair and sighed. "Man, that feels good." He threw back his head and closed his eyes. The thin outline of his profile shone in the dim light, handsome and fine. The All-American Boy as ghost. I took a couple of strong hits. My headache relaxed slightly. Toby set me up again.

As I watched, Sam seemed to absorb the rest of the rum. "Oh, I'd forgotten what this is like, I'd forgotten how this feels," he breathed. "It makes me feel like I'm alive again."

"Well, I'm glad it does, because you and I have a few things we need to iron out, Sam. Like this cancer thing. Why in the hell didn't you *tell* me—"

The jukebox kicked on at that moment, and the smoky room was filled with the sound of Patsy Cline. "Crazy." God, it's the saddest somebody-done-me-wrong anthem in a whole sad world of somebody-done-me-wrong songs.

"Dance with me, Holl," Sam said, sliding off the bar stool and holding out his arms to me. "Come and dance with the Angel of Death." Oh, he was stoned all right. And so was I. And Toby, like a master wizard, looked on with what could have been a smile beneath his beard, giving us his blessing.

Like the fool I foolishly believed I no longer was, I slid

off the stool and floated into his ghostly arms. I was feeling no pain, just a tired euphoria.

And there in the four A.M. world of Toby's bar, magic kicked in.

" 'Crazy for feeling this way,' " Sam sung softly in my ear, and I could finally feel his body, sense his arms around me, just as if he were real and it was ten years ago and we were young, dumb, and in what we thought was love as we shuffled slowly around the room. I closed my eyes and I could smell the essence of Sam, of clean shirts and soap and sunlight and maleness. He nuzzled my neck, and I felt his breath, soft as a whisper, on my skin. And when I put my arms around him, I could feel his skin and muscle and bone, the texture of his cotton shirt, as if he were flesh and blood again.

He breathed into my skin, and I held on to him tightly, as if, for a moment, he were real again. I think we both knew it was just a moment, and that it was just the smoky magic of Toby's, a busted-up bar at the jumping-off place, but I hung on to him as long as I could, shutting my eyes tightly and allowing him to move me around the room.

When he kissed me, lifting my chin up with his thumb, it wasn't cold at all, but his tears were wet on my cheeks.

Or maybe they were mine.

And Patsy sang on.

Just another somebody-done-me-wrong song in a somebody-done-me-wrong place at the end of the world in the middle of the night, but at that moment, it was everything to us, just to be able to touch again, two people trapped between two worlds, shuffling around a dirty old floor in each other's arms for one moment in time.

"I always loved you, Holl, you know that," Sam said. "And I always will."

"I can almost believe you."

" 'And crazy for feeling this way.' "

Sam might have been dead, but he still knew how to push my buttons.

Toby was gathering up the empties, as if we were the

most natural couple in the world, a live woman and a dead man.

Down at the end of the bar, the drunk looked up, bleary-eyed. Slowly, he focused on us, and then he jumped up. His hair was standing on end. Unsteadily, he rocked back and forth, his eyes as big as saucers.

"Wuzza matta, bunk? You never seen a ghost before?" Toby asked him matter-of-factly, loading longnecks into the cooler.

"Shit," Bob Buck said after a moment, lurching toward the door. "I'm outta here, man." At the portal, he turned, pulling himself into enormous, drunken dignity. "I don't drink in no bars that serves no goddamn *ghosts*, man," he said.

The door closed behind him.

"Dance with me, Holl," Sam whispered. "Just dance with me and let me be alive for a while."

So I did.

NINE

•

The Clot Sickens

A white-hot beam of light cut through my eyelids and seared into my brain. I woke up.

I was in Toby's apartment above the bar, lying on the foldout couch in the full glare of sunlight streaming in through the window. Another hot, humid day of drought, except this time I was in really big trouble. The hangover had mated with the headache to produce a nuclear blast. It was all I could do to open my eyes.

My mouth felt as if it was stuffed with cotton; even my hair hurt, which seemed totally unnecessary, considering that my innards were rebelling to the point where I had to lurch off the couch and roll into the bathroom.

As I rested my cheek against the nice cool porcelain, bits and pieces of the previous day and night drifted back to me, and I moaned. I had sort of hoped it was all a dream, but it wasn't.

A tattooed hand snaked through the door, and I screamed. My nerves were just a little on edge.

"It's just me," Toby said from around the corner. "Here. Drink this and take a hot shower. There're clean towels in the closet. Then come downstairs and eat some breakfast."

The word *breakfast* made me queasy, but I took the glass from his huge hand. It was filled with some kind of orange liquid. I closed my eyes and swallowed. It might have tasted like sewage or it might have tasted like the nectar of the gods; I couldn't have told the difference, since my tastebuds were numb. All I knew was my headache began subsiding into a faint whine.

I turned on the shower taps, peeled off the clothes I had slept in, and stepped into the steaming water as if I could wash away everything that had happened in the past twenty-four hours. I felt soiled by the idea that I might even now be a suspect in a murder case. Thinking still hurt too much.

I wished I could feel bad about Jason Hemlock. I was sort of sorry he was dead, of course; very few people deserve to be murdered. Jason was a sellout, not a child molester or a rapist, at least not that I knew of. An eternity trapped in a room with nothing to do but watch reruns of *The Brady Bunch* would have been an adequate punishment for being such a prick. Murder seemed a trifle extreme, even for a two-timing, double-dealing, low-rent politician who whored on all levels. Who had only incidentally, I reminded myself as I started to get all moral, treated me pretty badly.

As far as men went, I was hopeless, I thought darkly. Maybe it was time to give it all up and take the veil, sew it up, pack it in, and lead a life of nonemotional involvement. Was there a convent for lapsed Methodists? If so, I needed to join it at once.

I found Toby's good-shepherd-at-the-Christmas-Pageant bathrobe and wrapped it around myself. I'm a healthy girl, but it went around me about twice. Obviously, my dress from yesterday needed to soak in the sink. My pantyhose were in shreds, and my shoes looked beyond repair.

In the bright and sunny kitchen, Toby was chopping something on the cutting board, and Sam was floating over the couch, watching TV.

I looked at the clock on the stove. It was approaching noon. I walked over and squinted at it just to be sure. Yup, noon all right.

"We thought we'd let you sleep," Toby rumbled. "Your friend the lawyer hasn't called." He pointed to the coffeepot. "Breakfast coming right up," he said. "Have some caffeine."

I poured a cup and sat down at the table. One sip of El

Pico and I felt more human. "Turn on the news, Sam," I asked.

"Aw, *All My Children* is just coming on and Erica's about to—"

"The news, Sam," I said. Since I could, and Sam couldn't, I picked up the remote and changed the channel, then wished I hadn't.

"—don't know what's going on. I wish we did. Holly's always been a good girl, but that Hemlock fella, well, most of us down here on the island don't think too highly of him. He came down here and made all kindsa promises to the watermen before the election and never kept none of 'em. . . ."

Both Sam and Toby looked up at the sound of that familiar voice extruding the thick consonants of the Eastern Shore. "Say, isn't that your father?" Sam asked. "He's really gotten gray, what's left of his hair. . . ."

I choked on my coffee. My father, in his Patamoke Seafood Company baseball cap, was talking to a cute young brunette holding a microphone, while video cameras and boom mikes and reporters surrounded him, catching every word live as it was happening. Right on my folks' front porch, not a quarter mile down the road.

"They're on the island!" I cried indignantly. "The whole damn pack of them! There's channels 2, 13, and 11, and 47 and 16, and there's Willis from the *Sun* and Meyer from the *Post*! Is that that girl from AP? How could they do this to one of their own?"

"They all sure know your daddy," Toby remarked, greatly interested. "Man, Uncle Perk oughta run for office, the way he likes that news coverage. They all knew just where to come, din' they?"

When Dad had become president of the Waterman's Association, we had discovered he was a closet publicity hound. With an audience like that, he could run on about the watermen's problems for as long as someone was listening and never run out of opinions.

"There you have it," a vapid brunette was saying to the

camera, while my father kept right on talking. "*Watertown Gazette* reporter Hollis Ball's father, president of the Beddoe's Island Waterman's Association, on his daughter's involvement with the late delegate Jason Hemlock, whose body was found in Ms. Ball's car on an isolated Eastern Shore road last night. Back to you, Chip."

"Turn back to *All My Children*," Sam pleaded. "Yesterday, Erica was gonna—"

But Channel 13 had footage of the causeway and my red Honda being towed away into the night. Channel 54 featured a tight-lipped Ormand Friendly saying he had no comment at this time as he came out of the ME's office. Channel 16 was live at the crime scene where a baby-faced newsman in a checked sports coat fingered the yellow police tape. Channel 2 flashed my high school year book picture on the screen. I gasped in horror. But it wasn't over yet.

Toby slid the *Gazette* under my nose. I stared at a quarter-page photo of Jason and a smaller, blurry photo of me, taken last year at the company softball game, looking guilty as hell, especially after I'd just stolen second base. I could almost hear Judge Carroll asking the jury to disregard the shackles on the defendant, namely, me. From the headline, employee support was not a *Gazette* priority:

DELEGATE'S BODY FOUND IN
GAZETTE REPORTER'S CAR
Editor Assures Advertisers GAZETTE Not Involved

Judging from the byline, Rig Riggle had left his golf game long enough to write the story himself, if you want to call a sloppy mix of incomprehensible writing, garbled syntax, and libelous statements reporting. He did everything but finger me as the killer, I noted. He did have the grace to credit AP, where he had gotten most of the information that wasn't office gossip. God forbid anyone should make him actually go outside the office and gather the news.

For a minute I considered calling in, then decided against it. My behind was more important to me than any job, and I had a feeling that if I surfaced without Sev's permission, it would be in a very big sling indeed. Let Rig figure this one out for himself.

Channel 11 was doing a recap of Jason's life and career. The word *controversial* was used frequently. I was beginning to wish that some famous film star or ex-president had died, that a war had erupted somewhere, anything to take the spotlight off me. Unfortunately it was a slow day. A messy death for a big-mouthed delegate made for big news.

Toby set a plate on the table. A beautifully prepared Jarlsberg and chive omelet, homemade wheat toast, strawberry preserves, and freshly squeezed orange juice were placed before me. Toby is a world-class cook.

I ate and realized that I was starving. Not even a disaster can dull this girl's appetite.

"You really oughta call Aunt Doll and Uncle Perk. Your father looked right worried about you," Toby said.

I snorted. "Ma may be worried, but Dad knows better. Besides, he *loves* the media. Ever since he became president of the Waterman's Association, he holds court every chance he gets. No oysters? Dad's got a comment. Plenty of oysters? Dad's got a comment. Crabs? No crabs? Dad's got a comment. The DNR farts through silk? They all come to Dad for a comment because my father *loves* the media and will always talk to them. Who would have thought?"

Toby snorted. "Uncle Perk does like them TV cameras," he allowed.

"What? Perk?" Sam asked. "The man who wouldn't stand still to have his picture taken at our wedding because he hates having his picture taken?"

"Has become the biggest media hog on the Shore," I sighed. "Except for your sister."

"Your father never said more than ten words in a row in his whole life," Sam replied. A shaft of sunlight passed through his body.

"That was before he became famous," I answered

gloomily. "Now he keeps a scrapbook of all his interviews. There was a stringer down from the *New York Times* who wrote a whole piece on him for the *Times* Sunday Magazine. The tourists come looking for him. *He holds court*, Sam. You wouldn't believe it, he's the last of the red-hot watermen."

"You're right, I wouldn't, but there he is talking to—oh my God! Is that Diane Sawyer?"

"Eat your breakfast, Holl, you're safe here," Toby murmured soothingly.

I obeyed while Sam contemplated these changes. "What's your mother up to, then?" he asked carefully. No love lost there.

"She's still the Rummage Sale Queen of Beddoe's Island," I sighed. "And now that Robbie and Callie have two kids, she's also Grandmother Queen of Beddoe's Island."

"Your brother and his wife have two kids?" Sam asked incredulously.

"One more on the way. And they're still married. And will be married forever," I added. I didn't tell him that the question most frequently asked in my family was when I intended to get married again and have some more grandchildren for Me-Mom and Pop-Pop to spoil. The answer never varied: when hell freezes over.

"Does Dolly still make those wonderful crab cakes?" Sam asked wistfully.

"On birthdays and high holy days. Most of the time she's too busy with Methodist Women, Sunshine Sisters, Senior Citizens, Community Center, Ladies' Auxiliary, T-Ball, the PTA. . . ."

"Huh?"

"They all have rummage sales, you know," I explained. "And where there's a rummage sale, you will find my mother running the show."

"Amen," Toby said reverently.

Just then, the phone rang.

I almost jumped out of my skin. Nervous? Who, me?

"Toby's," my cousin barked into the receiver. He listened a second then handed me the phone.

"Have you seen the news?" Severn Capwell said without preamble.

"Yes," I replied. "What the hell is—"

"There's no way I can keep a lid on this. The governor's been on the phone twenty times today, pressuring us to find the killer. He all but told me to arrest you. What did you do to offend him? The media's all over us up here. Look, Hollis, be careful. Ormand Friendly's on his way. He figured out you're on the island, and he means to find you."

"He's gonna arrest me, isn't he?" I asked.

"I've done all I can, but I can't hold them off any longer. It looks bad."

I swallowed, hard. "Bad? How bad?" I asked.

"Initial ballistics tests say a .38 was used to kill Hemlock."

"But they haven't even had time to autopsy Jason or retrieve the bullet! And then the ballistics tests take days!"

I felt like I had fallen down a rabbit hole into Anti-Wonderland. This was not happening to me.

Sev sighed. "When the victim's a state delegate, everyone hops to. Friendly thinks you shot Hemlock, then dragged him into your car to dispose of the body somewhere in the wetlands. They found Hemlock's Lexus down the road, near White Marsh. It had been driven off Jenkin's Creek Bridge. It was half underwater. They sent divers down there this morning to recover it. Look, if I didn't know you, I'd think Friendly was right. But I know you, Hollis, and I know whatever you said about killing Hemlock, you couldn't kill anyone."

"S-said?" I quavered. What trouble had my big mouth gotten me into now? "What did I say?"

"Friendly found a couple of employees of the Maryland Inn who distinctly remember you screaming that you would kill Jason Hemlock."

"That was a year ago! I'd just found him in bed with another woman. I said a lot of awful stuff!"

"It must have been one hell of a battle," Sev sighed. "They said you were shouting that you'd kill him if it took you a lifetime to do it."

"I was angry. You would have been angry, too, if you'd caught your boyfriend in bed with Cinderella Fotney. Insult to injury." I lit a cigarette, my first of the day, and coughed. "Anyway, what about Skipper? When I walked into the job trailer at White Marsh, he and Jason were about to kill each other. What about Skipper? Claire? The whole construction crew? I mean there were enough people up there to kill an entire platoon of politicians!"

"Skipper has an alibi. He was watching the crew the whole time, until he left at four-thirty. Five people saw Jason alive when he left; Earl Don, three of his boys, you, and Skipper. The last Skipper saw of Hemlock was when he left the job trailer. Nobody passed his car on the causeway when they left. But they all saw your car sitting on the shoulder. The next time anyone sees Delegate Hemlock, he's dead in your Honda. Now what the hell does this all look like to you, Hollis? If you were Friendly, you'd be suspicious too."

"Why are they trying to pin this on me?" I asked, and then all of a sudden, I understood.

The Greenheads had done this, I thought. In their own warped, pinhead way, they had murdered Jason in a sort of environmental jihad and then, after dragging me off into the marsh, rigged it to pin the whole mess on me. And I'd thought they were my friends. I'd lied about their very existence. Well, not *lied*, precisely, just omitted mention of them, I decided conveniently. While I was trying to save their green behinds, they were busily frying mine. Jason Hemlock was no friend to the environment, but was that a reason to kill him? If you were radical enough, it was. They had set me up, and I was pissed.

"If you can give me the truth, Hollis, I can get this mess straightened out. Where were you last night?"

"I told you—"

"You're a damn good liar, Hollis. But not good enough.

There's something you're not telling me. And you've got to tell me the truth. I can't hold Friendly off forever. He's pressuring me to open the files on your ex-husband."

"I see." I felt nauseated.

"Hollis, be careful. I can't shake the feeling that the real murderer is out to get you, if he or she can find you. Let me help you. Just tell me where you were last night. What do you know about this?"

"I already told you," I said stubbornly. "I didn't kill Jason. And believe me, I didn't kill Sam either."

Then I hung up.

"It looks bad, real bad," I said. "Friendly the homicide cop is on his way to the island with a warrant. He thinks I killed Jason. And he's looking at the files on Sam's case. I think I've been set up by the Greenheads."

"At last!" Sam cried happily. "Maybe now I can find out who killed me."

I pitched him a look that should have disintegrated his toes. "The way things are going, I may end up in Jessup, convicted of murdering you and Jason. And then where would you be?"

"Holly's got a point, man," Toby said. "If she didn't do it and they pin it on her, chances of catching the real killer are nil."

Sam nodded thoughtfully. "Yeah, I knew that," he said. He rose from the table and paced back and forth, his hands in his pockets. He sighed. "We're in deep shit."

"Give the man the prize," I snapped. "Meanwhile, what do I do? Sit here and wait for Officer Friendly to arrest me? One hell of a lot of good that will do you then, Sam."

"Make up your minds," Toby said. "I've got to open the bar in a couple of minutes." He cleared his throat and leaned back in his chair, folding his massive hands over his belly and gazing soulfully skyward. "Seems to me, if I was in your place, I'd be off looking for a killer. I'd be paying a call on these Greenheads to see if they have a damn good excuse."

"I don't even have a car, and in about two minutes this

island is going to be swarming with cops. It's already swarming with reporters."

"It's also swarming with your kinfolk who know you didn't do it. And even if you did, there's a lot of folks down here who believe you performed a public service getting rid of Jason Hemlock."

His chances of reelection had probably been slim, anyway.

"Thanks for the vote of confidence," I sighed. "Dammit, when am I gonna learn that no good deed goes unpunished?"

A procession of workboats, some ten or a dozen strong, moved slowly through Beddoe's Narrows. As they approached the drawbridge, the watermen sounded their horns.

Miss Wilsie Crump, who had been the day bridgetender as long as anyone could remember, thrust her head out of the bridge house and waved to the watermen, her rhinestone glasses flashing in the sunlight.

As the state police cruiser approached from the mainland, she pushed down the lever that set the bells ringing, the red lights flashing, and the black-and-white striped gates descending slowly across the road. Then she hauled back on the Johnson bar that raised the counterweights.

Slowly, the bridge jerked upward. In a cacophony of flashing lights, bells, and whistles, traffic coming on or going off the island was halted as the span slowly and majestically raised up against the sky.

Miss Wilsie, my father's first cousin, waved as the boats passed under the open draw. The watermen waved back, slowly sliding through the narrow passage out into Santimoke Bay.

Stuck on the mainland side, a uniform beside him, his state issue Chevy Cavalier engine overheating, Lieutenant Ormand Friendly watched the bridge rise slowly, very slowly, cutting him off from the island and his intended quarry.

He threw a disinterested glance at the workboats, then looked again. He turned to say something to the uniform.

The uniform squinted at the workboats as they passed slowly beneath the bridge. They both looked hard at one boat in particular.

From the deck of *Miss Callie*, my brother Robbie's workboat, I stared right back up at them as we passed under the span. Although I couldn't hear what Friendly was saying, I imagined he was turning the air blue with some select cursing that probably involved the innate cussedness of Eastern Shore people and Beddoe's Island people in particular. Just a guess, you understand, but a good one.

From the tender's house, Miss Wilsie waved and smiled at him. Friendly smiled back through gritted teeth.

She waited until the last boat was out of sight and well into Santimoke Bay before slowly releasing the gear that would drop the span back into the cradle. The lights clanged and the gates rose as the concrete wing dropped back into the bridge. Slowly, the black-and-white gates were raised, the bells and whistles silenced.

Miss Wilsie waved the cruiser onto the bridge. Sweet, blue-haired, and grandmotherly, she has a whim of iron, as anyone who wants the bridge lowered before she's good and ready to drop it knows.

Friendly picked up his mike and started to talk.

I saw him and he saw me as I headed through the Narrows with Toby, surrounded by my father's and my brother's uncles' and my cousins' big white workboats, all moving slowly out toward Santimoke Bay in flotilla. I'm still not totally sure if Friendly recognized me in my waterman drag—T-shirt, baseball cap, jeans, sneakers, flannel shirt, all purloined from Mom's rummage sale stash—but I know there were a lot of other island folks watching as we made for the Santimoke River. One thing folks on the island don't like is outsiders; another thing they don't like is cops.

As soon as we were around the bend in the narrows, the

flotilla began to break apart as the men turned and headed back to the island. I waved at them as they departed.

"You hang in there, honey!" my cousin Leonard called across the roar of his engine, flashing me a V-for-Victory sign as he pulled away.

Pop pulled his throttle up and leaned across the washboards, shaking his fist at me. "Dammit, Hollis, whyn'n hell don't you get married again and quit doin' this shit?" he called.

He then spat in the water, shook his head, pushed his cap down over his eyes, and pushed the throttle all the way down, leaving us behind, rocking in his wake as he hung a U-ie and headed *Miss Jenny* back toward the island.

"You're making your mother crazy!" Dad yelled as he passed us in *Miss Doll Baby*, following Robbie back to the harbor. But he winked as he circled around.

"I don't know how the hell you get yourself into these messes," Toby griped at me over the roar of the engine as he pushed the throttle forward and the big old Mercury Marine engine picked up the boat and tore her through the water. Land fell behind us as he headed her toward the Swann's Island light.

"I don't either," I replied.

"You've got Aunt Doll in an uproar and Uncle Perk all over the damn TV, talking his head off. Your brother's having a goddamn fit."

"Been there, done that," I shouted. I knew my family was upset with and for me, and I didn't blame them. There they were, a hardworking lot with mortgages on their houses and their boats, my brother with two kids and a working wife getting ready to whelp a third, the pair of them struggling to make ends meet, Dad doing his damnedest to represent the watermen of Beddoe's Island, Mom probably sitting home smoking Kools and praying to a Methodist God to keep me safe. They all go to church every Sunday and Robbie coaches T-ball. What the hell they ever did to deserve me I don't know. I'm more like Toby,

I guess; a natural born misfit, a genetic throwback to our pirate ancestors.

Even when I was a kid, Toby was pulling me out of jams and rescuing me from the consequences of my own stupidity. And I was damn grateful that he was coming through for me again when I needed him. I tried to tell him all of this over the engine, but Toby just shrugged.

"We're blood, Holly. You'd do the same for me if I needed it," he said. He reached out and gave me a rough, one-armed hug. He kept the other hand on the wheel. "Just try to stay out of trouble from now on, okay?"

The way he said it made me feel like a reform school girl on the lam. My cousin's faith in my ability to extricate myself from this mess touched me. I wished I felt the same way. We hugged.

Out of the corner of my eye, I saw Sam materializing in the cuddy, huddling into himself, watching us. I could have sworn his expression was wistful. He seemed to be fading into the afternoon light on the outgoing tide.

My family might be crazy, but we love each other and stick together. The Wescotts, on the other hand, well, you could suspect any of them of killing Sam, not to mention Jason, just to add to the day's enjoyment.

After about fifteen minutes, we veered sharp to starboard, up into the mouth of the Santimoke River. "I just hope you know what you're doing," Toby said to me as he cut the throttle down, swinging us toward a decrepit shingle boathouse facing the river. It belonged to the estate of some weekend people who were never there and didn't have a boat. Toby cut the engine and let the current carry us under the roofed enclosure. A pair of swallows who lived there were roused from their nest and swooped, chirping angrily at us. It was dark and cool inside.

"We'll be all right," Sam said. He looked at Toby. "Straightest shooting son of a bitch I ever met in my life. I don't get it. Toby's so straight and you're so—" he made a gesture in the air toward me, grinning.

"Get bent," I snarled at him. "I will be all right," I re-assured Toby. "I know what I'm doing, I really do."

That's what they'll write on my tombstone.

"Well, I thought about it and decided I could raise about five thousand for bail on the bar. We can get Uncle Hulk to defend you—"

I shuddered. Our Uncle Hulk is about the worst lawyer in Santimoke County. "I'm fine, Toby, honest. Besides, I really didn't kill anybody, I swear."

My cousin turned his dark eyes on me, so much like mine that there was no mistaking that we were blood.

"I just hope you know what the hell you're doing," he growled at Sam. "You know, every once in a while, I run into the ghost of someone I used to know, and none of them know the first goddamn thing about anything any-more."

"Believe me, Toby, this will work, if anything will."

"I really should come with you," Toby said.

Sam shook his head. "If we go down, we go down alone. You've got a business to run. If you get tangled up in this, they can take your liquor license away. We can't let you run that risk, Toby. But thank you anyway—for every-thing."

They shook hands as best they could, and Toby tried to clap Sam on the arm. "Take care, yourself," he said.

A distant rumble grew louder, and we watched silently as a DNR whaler roared up the creek past us. The two uni-forms on board never even looked our way. We were hid-den in the cool, green shadows.

"They're looking for you," Toby said matter-of-factly. "You ought to wait for a while before you take off."

"I will," I promised, gathering up my knapsack and shift-ing over the washboards into the small aluminum skiff con-veniently tied up to the dock.

Just like someone had left it there for me, like my father. There was a Johnson outboard, two tanks of gas, and a Playmate cooler filled with survival goodies from my mother's kitchen. A knapsack with a change of clothes and a set of foul weather gear.

Sliding down into the skiff, I turned to hold out my hand to Toby.

"Whatever happens, I just want everyone to know I didn't kill anyone," I said.

Toby's lips quivered beneath his mustache. "Hell, Holl, we all know that. Just be careful. Those people are dangerous."

"Not as dangerous as I am," I replied with far more bravado than I was feeling.

Sam materialized beside me. He seated himself in the bow of the boat. Weightless, he did not even cause her to dip in the water. We watched from the shade of the boathouse as Toby's big fiberglass boat disappeared around the bend. *Bad Attitude* was painted on the sternboard.

"Come on, Holl, the game is afoot!"

TEN

•

Up the Creek, with Paddle

The sun was low on the horizon, spreading dancing diamonds across the waves as we made landfall on the shore of White Marsh Neck. A storm of triangle-wing flies swarmed around me, biting like they were starved for reporter blood. I swatted at them, but they came right back. They were followed by their old friends, the mosquitoes, the state bird of Maryland.

"Watch it, you'll run us aground!"

Sam was floating in the bow, bouncing as it rose and fell against the waves. The hell flies skimmed right through him, of course. I dug into my knapsack for bug repellent and sprayed myself all over, including my hair. It depressed the mosquitoes but only briefly discouraged the flies, which continued to light on my hands and face. They were attracted by the smell of my sweat; the humidity made me feel as if I were breathing Jell-O. The sullen red end of a sweltering August day cast the smell of rotten fish and rancid mud across the tide. And yet not a drop of rain was in sight, just blue and cloudless skies.

The closer we hove into shore, the more shoal the water became until I could see the shells lying in the mud as we skimmed not more than six inches over the flats. The tide was, thankfully, coming in. Before us lay the marshy savannas, marked here and there by a cripple of pines.

I cut the motor back until we were barely moving, cruising along the shoreline until I saw the thin mouth of Muskrat Canal. The marsh is networked like a leaf with old drainage canals and channels, shape-shifting creeks, and narrow guts; I just hoped I could remember enough from my childhood days to navigate my way through here to sneak up on those damned Greenheads. I had a pretty good idea where they might be found, but it had been twenty years since I'd been on these marshes with my father, running his muskrat traplines. Wind and water and humanity could have created a lot of changes. But I'd have to take my chances.

Slowly, I turned the skiff up into the creek and cut the motor. The sudden silence, after its steady roar pounding at my ears for hours, was creepy. I looked at Sam and he looked at me.

A diamondback turtle slid from the mud and disappeared into the water with a small splash. A redwing blackbird took off from its perch on a half-submerged snag, flashing scarlet shoulders as it fluttered away, complaining about our intrusion. A colony of fiddler crabs climbed up the mud bank, burrowing into the soft ooze against the coming tides and somewhere, far away, an osprey shrieked.

"We're here," Sam said. "Let's go for it."

Which meant I'd have to paddle from here; it was too shallow, even with the incoming tide, to try to power into the marsh. And of course, I wasn't about to get any help from Sam; a ghost conveniently can't hold a paddle, can he? At least that's how I read Sam's grin as he lay down on the seat and stretched out, admiring the open sky above us.

I pulled the outboard up and fetched the paddle out from beneath the seats. I would use it to guide us deeper into the narrow, twisting creek; an oar would have been too ungainly. Fortunately, the current carried us along, or I would have been working a lot harder. The grass on either side of us spread out in endless waves that touched the sky. We were at sea level here.

"Hush," Sam said, and I paused to listen, turning to watch as a DNR boat, moving at slow speed, pushed down the bay shore, heading out toward the Chesapeake. I hoped they couldn't spot us, hidden by a bend in the creek. I held my breath and stayed very still, as if I could be invisible, until the sound of their motor faded into the distance.

"I wonder," Sam whispered, "I wonder how many fugitives have hidden in this marsh like this. I can almost, like, you know, *feel* other ghosts around here."

"Ask them how we can find those damned Greenheads," I grumbled, squashing a triangle-wing fly on my arm. I would have started up the outboard and made a run inland, but it was shoal in here, and besides, there were so many submerged snags that I could have torn out the bottom of the skiff if I'd been traveling with any kind of speed.

"You know, this place has got quite a history," Sam remarked. "This ole marsh must be just packed with revenants. All those old pirates, escaped slaves, Civil War draft dodgers, they must be hangin' around here somewhere. Not to mention the Harbeson brothers. Remember the Crab Bait Killer? Levin and Daniel are probably both out here someplace, wouldn't you think? Maybe Levin is still baiting crab lines with Daniel."

"Maybe you should scout around and see if you can find them. They sound like your kind of people," I suggested nastily.

Sam quieted down after that.

I paddled in the hot sun, with biting flies and swarming mosquitoes for company. My shirt was stuck to my body with sweat, but if I took it off, our insect friends would have been all over me. It seemed like hours, but probably wasn't, before we came to a fork in the creek. The larger branch moved west, while a smaller gut wended its way to the northeast. Of course, it could turn and double back on itself or go any which way; I was going by guess now.

The fork was marked by a cripple where three dying pines scraped at the cloudless sky, their roots in a mud bank slowly eroding from endless water, endless wind.

Sam made a small motion, pointing upward into the branches. I looked up and caught my breath.

A hawk glared down at us from yellow eyes. Small,

russet-headed, and brown-shouldered, it was a hawk like no bird I'd ever seen before.

A sullen prince of the air, it shifted uneasily on the branch, watching us watch it. After a few seconds, it glared, lifted its wings, rose on its shaggy legs, then spread those sharp wings slowly and magnificently outward, rising to catch the air, hanging in the sky for a moment before it soared away over the marsh. It cast a long, spreading shadow across the yellow grass. We watched as it chose a distant dead tree, where it settled at the edge of a thatch nest. From that vantage point, it ignored us warily. "Follow that bird!" Sam suddenly commanded. Maybe he had a hunch.

"Seeing that bird was like getting a sign from God," I offered. "I never saw a hawk with a red head like that before, did you?"

"Not me."

I dipped the paddle in the water and chose the direction in which the red-headed hawk had flown, down the narrow gut whose name I didn't even know, couldn't remember if I ever did.

I was able to occupy myself with scrounging my memory for the name of that gut for the next forty-five minutes as I paddled slowly along, sweating and feeling the blisters rising on my palms.

Sam had been quiet ever since we had seen the hawk. He sat facing the bow, his shoulders slumped, his head bowed. He looked heavy and mortal, as if he were flesh and bone, gravity weighing him down against the earth's surface. "The living," he said slowly, "the living don't appreciate life when they have it."

I watched the setting sun cast his revenant shade in red and gold, and swatted at the flies that stung at my back and arms. They just buzzed through him as if he weren't there. We were so low in the marsh, all I could see was the bay laurel on either side of the gut.

"There's another branch ahead, around the next bend. Turn to starboard," Sam said. "We're almost there."

"How do you know?" I asked.

He shrugged. "I just know." He threw a smile over his shoulder at me. "Maybe the marsh ghosts told me. Can't you hear them whispering in the wind?"

"It's flat calm here," I said. To keep myself from getting too much imagination, I stood up on the seat and looked around. Plains of marsh grass, veined with water, stretched in all directions, broken here and there with low cripples and, more distantly, little islands of hardwood old growth. Islands of solid ground. "One of them has got to be the Greenhead camp," I said, poling us into the branch on the right.

"That's it up yonder," Sam said, pointing ahead. "That good size island there in the scrub trees."

About a half mile away, as the crow flies, I saw what he was pointing at, around a bend in the gut. From here it looked like no more than a quarter acre of high ground in the marsh, deeply wooded with old trees, undergrown with brambles and greenbrier, wound around with a thin strip of shallow creek, a sort of marshy oasis. There was just a glimpse of an old cedar shake house. It looked like the site of an abandoned duck camp. If anyone lived there, you could have fooled me.

It was the perfect place for the hideout of the Greenhead Army. "Lemme at 'em," I hissed. "Just lemme at 'em."

It was so shallow up there that I had to continue to pole. Places were so narrow the baybush scraped the skiff on either side. We were just lucky we were riding a high tide in; if we needed to get out of there fast, we were in a whole world of shit, as the watermen say; the weight of the outboard was almost dragging our stern along muddy bottom. But I pressed on, fired by what I intended to say and do to Frank Dartwood and his eco-loons when I got there.

We came up on the island just as long shadows were turning purple and the sun was sinking behind us, tingeing the horizon pink.

It was as still as death.

"I don't like this," I said.

Sam frowned. "Sure is quiet here. Too quiet. Want me to look around?"

"You go ahead and reconnoiter," I agreed. "Since no one can see you, you can spy to your heart's content and report back to me."

"Okay. You sit here and don't move. See ya later." Sam disappeared, and I squatted in the boat, trying to figure out what my best move would be.

I smacked flies and dabbed at mosquitoes, flicking the corpses off my skin. Yuck. Those bites really hurt. Somewhere deep in the thicket, a fish crow cawed hoarsely and was answered by another. A slight breeze, lifted from the bay, stirred though the canopy of trees like a sigh. Shadows lengthened, and the sun hung low behind me, beating down on my back. Time crawled and so did the flies.

I was soaked in sweat. The mosquitoes and biting flies were beginning to drive me crazy. They're always worse at first twilight; they were swarming all over me. I brushed them away, thinking about the stories I'd heard about people who took to the marsh and were eventually driven mad by the incessant pestering of bugs so that their screams filled the night, drifting across the water. If the flies and skeeters didn't get you then the ticks and the chiggers would.

Just then, something about the size of a dinner plate buzzed angrily out of nowhere and landed on my neck. Before I could get it, it got me, a pain like someone had sunk a red-hot needle into my flesh. I yelped and flailed at my neck, jumping out of the boat and tipping overboard into the water.

Not a great feeling, being sucked down into infinite depths of rancid marsh mud, with something biting you like fire. I did the only sensible thing: I dunked myself. Whatever it was, it loosened its bite, but I was soaked through with mud and slime when I sat up, and someone was hauling me to the bank.

"Boy, Hollis, you sure are funny," said Andy, big and

blond and full of grins. "I never saw anyone move so fast in my life."

"*Very* funny," I replied stiffly. I tell you, life is one humiliation after another.

"I've been watching you for miles, girl." Andy grinned. "You came in the long way."

"We've got to stop meeting like this," I managed to say, spitting mud.

ELEVEN

•

Greenheads Revisited

"Well, that took you long enough," Frank Dartwood said mildly, looking up from his computer. He didn't seem surprised to see me, covered with mud and mad as fire. "We expected you here earlier."

I had seen myself storming Greenhead Central and raising all kinds of hell, but the Greenhead reaction left me momentarily nonplussed. No one seemed particularly startled to see me, even me covered with muddy goop, when Andy walked me into camp. The kids were all in the kitchen, doing something with food that smelled heavenly. If they had guilty consciences, they were very good at concealing it. They barely glanced up as Andy and I trooped into Dartwood's presence.

"You look like you could use a cold drink. Beer? Iced tea? You name it." To Andy, he said, "Did you see anyone following her?"

"No. She's clear. I'll have to hide that skiff though, Frank. You don't think anyone would think to look out here for her, do you?"

"Probably not. What idiot could possibly try to hide out in the marsh?" Frank grinned at me.

"I bet you'd like a beer," Andy suggested, shoving off in a skiff-hiding and beer-fetching direction.

"What the hell do you know about Jason Hemlock?" I asked Dartwood, pointing a muddy finger at him. "Did you idiots kill him?"

"You mean you didn't kill him?" Dartwood looked at me over his glasses, as if I'd used the wrong fork. He frowned at the terminal, as if it had told him a politically incorrect joke. Or maybe the terminal had used the wrong fork, I don't know.

"How could I kill him if I was out here with Peter Pan and the Lost Boys when he was being shot?" I demanded. "Do you have any idea *what* I've been through in the past twenty-four hours?"

Dartwood typed something into the keyboard, then looked at me again. "The Greenhead Army does not advocate the use of violence against human beings," he said primly.

"Well, *someone* sure as hell shot Jason with a .38, and a .38 was what I took away from Miss Jennifer last night. Where is she? I just want five minutes alone with her."

"Oh, we're catering a party tonight," Dartwood replied, airily gesturing toward the kitchen, where the activity had slowed a little. They might have been making trays of hors d'oeuvres, but they were sure listening to us. Jennifer glared at me through the doorway, then tossed her head, turning away.

"A party? How the hell can you cater a party at a time like this?" I yelled. I knew I was about out of control, but I really thought I had a right. "You bozos killed Jason and set me up for it! What the pluperfect hell have I ever done to you? To any of you?" I added, glaring at the happy campers in the kitchen. They all of a sudden seemed to find rolling artichokes into pastry dough really fascinating. Jennifer was doing her best to disappear behind a big stainless steel bowl.

"There she is! Hey, you, Jennifer what's-your-name, I want a word with you," I said when I spotted her doing something with a big package of sun-dried tomatoes.

She glanced at me, all innocence, a "who me?" look that made me lunge toward the kitchen. "You and that damn .38 of yours," I growled. "Just let me get my hands on you—"

"Frank, call her off, will you? I have to get this antipasto ready or the dressing will curdle!" Jennifer sighed, as if I were an annoying puppy. "She's too dirty to come anywhere near the food!" She tossed her head again, which would have been effective if she weren't wearing a cafeteria-lady hairnet. The Greenhead Army obeyed all the health department rules, at least; that kitchen was immaculate.

"Back down, Ball," Dartwood said, restraining me with a hand. "You're safe here."

"How can you all be so calm?" I sputtered. "What are you doing out here, in the middle of nowhere, catering a party?"

"Well, we have to support ourselves somehow. Believe me, we don't get any soft money. The Greenhead Army is supported entirely by our own efforts." He sounded so reasonable that I choked. "Greens 'n' Things is quite the fashionable caterer on the Shore this year, you know; we cook Heartsmart: low fat, low cholesterol, and everything is fresh."

"That's your first mistake. You ought to serve 'em everything full of fat and sugar and hope they all die off of heart attacks. The kind of people who can afford a caterer are usually the same people who are busting up White Marsh Island."

"Your prejudices are showing," Dartwood sighed. He slumped back into his chair and pushed his glasses up on the bridge of his nose. The terminal flickered with tiny bytes of information.

Andy returned with three bottles, handing me one. "We've been following your adventures on the news," he said, raising his beer to salute me. "They've got an APB out on you. Did you really shoot Hemlock?"

"He was dead when you all left me back at the car! We—I found him in the backseat, with a small hole in the middle of his head. Is that what they're saying? That I shot Jason?"

"We've been listening to the updates on the news all day. You're wanted for questioning. No one has actually *said* that you did it yet. Libel laws and all of that. You're a likely suspect, however. Especially since you ran." Frank looked at me meaningfully over his glasses. I hoped that he wasn't leading a band of Mansonoid killers who were planning to make me the main course for someone's dinner party tonight.

"I *had* to run. How could I prove I didn't do it if they've got me in jail?" I asked in what I hoped was a reasonable voice.

"Good point. On the other hand, if you did it, it would be wise to avoid arrest," Frank pointed out. "Obviously, you didn't use us as an alibi, for which I thank you. A raid out here would have been very inconvenient at this moment in time. Rising sourdough phyllo is so delicate, the least tremor can make it fall."

I wasn't in the mood to discuss nouvelle cuisine. "Did you kill Jason?" I demanded. "Did the Greenheads kill Jason?"

"Wow," Andy said. "You think *we* did it?" Either he was an incredible actor, or he was genuinely stunned by this idea.

Action in the kitchen came to a stop. There was no pretense of working now; all eyes were on us.

"Actually, our name was bandied about on the Web, Andrew," Dartwood informed him casually. He unscrewed the top of his Boh and took a deep swallow. "But the smart money seems to be on you, Ms. Ball. To answer your question, no, the Greenheads did not kill Jason Hemlock. Did you?"

I took a deep breath. "I did not kill Jason Hemlock," I said for about the hundredth time in twenty-four hours. "But I'm inclined to think that you, or some of your disciples, did. Look, you dragged me out here, and when I get back to my car, there Jason is, dead in the backseat with a hole in his head. Then Sev Capwell, our state's attorney, tells me this morning that Jason was shot with a .38, just like the gun I took away from Jennifer last night, and the officer in charge thought he had sufficient cause to arrest me. What the hell am I supposed to think? You people had a good reason to kill him. He betrayed every pro-environmental stand he was elected on."

"But we didn't kill him," Dartwood said reasonably. "Hemlock was worth more to us alive than dead. You can't reason with a dead man."

Tell me about it, I thought. Aloud I said, "But you guys must have called the police, because I wasn't back in the car five minutes before they came roaring up the causeway, sirens blasting. Didn't you hear the sirens?"

"No, actually, noise from the causeway doesn't travel back up here. We heard about it on the scanner." Dartwood sat there looking calm. Of course, he would. No one was after him for murder. He was so laid back that I wanted to dump him out of his seat, though, just to get a rise from him. "We decided that coming forward would have created more problems for us than staying put. It's not our asses at stake, it's saving White Marsh that matters."

"How do I know you're telling me the truth?" I asked, unscrewing the cap off my beer and taking a long, cold swallow. It was bliss.

"Maybe you ought to sit down," Frank suggested. "You look like you're over a healthy stress level."

"I am. I wouldn't be in this mess if it weren't for you guys. I'm on the run and wanted for a murder I didn't do." I did take a chair, though. Andy leaned against the desk, obviously in no hurry to return to lookout duty. The kids in the kitchen, having decided that I wasn't going to make the pastry fall, went back to work. But they were listening.

"You had motive and opportunity," Dartwood pointed out.

"You don't have to prove motive to get a conviction in Maryland," I said wearily. "Besides, you guys had motive and opportunity too. How do you know the Lost Boys and Girls didn't do it when you weren't looking?"

Andy flushed. "Hey, we were all together last night. No one was ever alone. Jennifer and me and Theresa went out after you. We were never out of each other's sight.

Everyone else was back here. No one had a chance to act alone. Even if we'd wanted to kill Hemlock, which we didn't."

"While you were waiting for Ms. Ball to come down the causeway from White Marsh, did you see anyone else?"

Andy shrugged. "We weren't there more than ten, fifteen minutes. It was low tide, and it took us a while to get there. The red Honda was the only car we saw coming down the causeway. And nothing went back up."

Frank looked at me. I looked at him. "No workmen's trucks, no cars, no heavy equipment, no nothing?" he asked.

Andy shook his head. "Believe me, we would have noticed. We were trying not to be spotted ourselves, hiding in the phragmites."

"Who was on the island when you left?" Frank asked. He made a tent out of his fingers, looking at me over his glasses.

"The workmen, my cousin, Skipper Dupont, and Jason," I said. "But they all have alibis, Sev Capwell says. And without you guys, I don't have anything that even *looks* like an alibi. I lied for you." I bit my lower lip. I wished Sam were around, but as usual, when the going got tough, the ectoplasm disappeared. "If it wasn't you, and it wasn't me, who was it?"

"That's what I'm trying to figure out." Dartwood gestured toward the computer. "Do you have any ideas?"

I drank the rest of my beer, thinking. Andy leaned back in his chair, looping his fingers behind his head. I had a nice view of his washboard stomach as his T-shirt rode up.

"Why did you lie for us?" Dartwood asked me. "A pretty flimsy lie at that."

"Hey, it was the best I could do on short notice," I said gruffly. "Besides, I don't want to believe you all killed Jason. Believe it or not, I like you guys. I like what you stand for. I like the fact that you stand for something I believe in, too."

There was, I finally decided, nothing to lose in telling the truth, or at least as much of it as I judged they needed to know. No way in hell was I going to mention I was being haunted by the late Sam Wescott. People already thought I was crazy. If I casually informed them that I was running around with the ghost of my ex-husband, they'd know for sure.

Being as how I'm a good editor, I worked around Sam, starting with the funeral and working my way up to the present moment. It must have been quite a tale; Frank closed his eyes and seemed to go off to sleep; Andy examined his navel ring.

When I had finished, Dartwood opened one eye. "Very interesting," he said, and closed his eye again.

Overhead, the ceiling fans circled lazily, moving the sullen, humid air listlessly through the heat. I pressed the cold bottle against my forehead; it felt good.

I drank my beer and contemplated Andy's navel some more. It was a nice navel, made for contemplation, and, under other circumstances, could have kept me entertained for hours on end, situated as it was in a tanned washboard tummy with golden hairs disappearing into the waistband of his jeans.

"What do you know about the tests? Have they come back?" Frank finally asked.

"This ballistics testing stuff takes a while, even when the corpse is a delegate. But Sev Capwell, our state's attorney, told me they dug a .38 slug out of Jason. And I took Jennifer's .38 away from her," I answered grimly. "So . . ."

"That can't be!" Jennifer cried, coming in from the kitchen. She was pale as a, excuse the expression, ghost. "That gun was never out of my possession since I took it from my father's collection. I hated Jason, but I never would have killed him!"

We all looked at her.

Her lower lip trembled. "Frank, you know that we—"

Andy walked across the room and put his arm around her slim waist, dammit. "There's no way. None of us were ever alone, all day and all night last night," he said. "You don't have to say anything, Jen."

"She's just trying to pin the blame on someone else," Jennifer said, looking very young, very pretty, and very helpless as she took a *J'accuse* stance, finger pointed right at me. "She did it, and now she's trying to get me involved in it."

"What's *your* history with Jason?" I asked.

She drew herself up to her full height. "All right, so I *knew* him! You weren't the only one he hurt!" She suddenly burst into tears, putting her hands against her cheeks, shaking her head from side to side. "Hemlock killed my father! If you *did* kill him, you deserve a medal!"

"Hey, hey, calm down," Andy soothed her. The others clustered solidly around her, as if to protect her from the likes of evil me. If looks could kill, I would have been dead on the floor with a stake through my heart. Hollis Ball, Vampire Woman.

"My father was Charles Coldstone," she sobbed.

"*You're* Jennifer Coldstone? This is the cult you quit Goucher for?" I asked, unbelieving. "Look, your mother is frantic. She's looking all over the Eastern Shore for you! She's even got Sev Capwell looking for you!"

"None of the things Hemlock said against my father were true! I would have *known* if they were. His lies drove my father to kill himself!" Jennifer said earnestly. "I would have liked to kill Hemlock, but I didn't! You know I didn't kill him!"

"It's true," dark-eyed Theresa told me, wiping her hands on her apron. "I mean, there's no way any of us could have gotten away from the others yesterday long enough to go to the bathroom, let alone get out of here to shoot someone! We were busy making the seviche all yesterday. Jen was never out of my sight! Besides, we all heard the news. *You* took Jen's gun. It was a stupid idea to even have it around here in the first place."

"I don't even know how to use it," Jennifer admitted and burst into tears. "I've never even shot the thing."

I was inclined to believe that. She sure as hell didn't know anything about gun safety.

"I just thought we might need a gun someday, so when I went home to tell Mother I was leaving college to join the Greenheads, I took it. My mother wouldn't miss it; she's so out of it since Daddy died, she doesn't even know what day it is. Daddy had so many damn guns." Jennifer leaned against Andy, limp. He hugged her protectively. "I *hate* guns," she added.

Frank Dartwood sighed, rose, and started to pace the floor. "It's my fault. We should have voted on a rule about firearms." His glasses slid down his nose, and he pushed them back up again, looking at Jennifer sadly. "I wish you had told me this before. Now two men are dead. And you must call your mother and tell her you're all right. I feel like I'm running the Moonies or something."

Everyone looked as if they felt bad about that, even though one of the dead men was Jason Hemlock, a common sorry snollygoster if ever there was one. If I had my way, all the Hemlock politicians would be rounded up in a pen and kept there under close observation, if not shot on sight. Poor choice of words, but there you have it: the man was pond scum.

A faint aroma of burning bread drifted through the room. "The cheese straws!" Mookie cried, running to the oven. And then we had a real tragedy on our hands.

The mood was broken, and Dartwood and I were left looking at each other. "It could have been another .38. It's a popular caliber, .38," Frank said thoughtfully.

"It's a possibility," I admitted. "But a thin one. We won't know till we hear about the tests."

"But there's another thing that's bothering me," he said, poking idly at the keyboard. "Do you think someone might have killed Sam?"

"It's about time someone asked that question," Sam muttered, doing one of his materializations in the doorway. He looked like he'd been through a dogfight.

TWELVE

·

Where There's a Will . . .

"What happened to you?" I asked Sam before I could
stop myself.

"I had a run-in with the Harbeson brothers," he said rue-
fully. "Just because some people are dead doesn't mean
they're polite." He pushed a hand over his hair and floated
up to rest on the bookcase, where he lay down comfortably,
like a cat who's enjoyed a good prowl. From there he surveyed us.

Dartwood looked at me over his glasses. "What happened to *me*?" he asked, puzzled.

"I mean, what makes you think Sam was murdered?" I
asked quickly.

"Indeed, Frank, what?" Sam asked. He rolled over on his
stomach and propped his chin up in his hand, looking very
interested. "Boy, this is some setup Frank's got out here.
Solar-powered, battery-generated *everything*! It's so envi-
ronmentally correct, it makes me nervous."

I tried to ignore him, focusing on Dartwood, but ignoring
Sam was like ignoring a small child. He ogled the girls in
the kitchen. "If I'd been killed by Jennifer, I would not
only have remembered it, I would have died happy," he
sighed. "That girl is a stone fox."

"Young enough to be your daughter," I muttered.

"Younger sister," Sam said with a big smile. "Touché!"

Apparently, seeing ghosts was not one of Dartwood's talents. He was lost in his own thoughts. "That explosion was
not necessarily an accident. You know, someone could have
gone aboard while Sam was up at the house and opened the

151

gas valves on the stove. Given enough time, the place would have been a huge bomb waiting for a spark by the time he boarded again. If he tried the lights and they didn't work, he might have lit a match to see before he smelled the gas and—*boom*! It's just a thought, but I can't seem to shake it."

I considered this. "It *could* have happened that way," I conceded. "But who would have killed Sam, a dying man?"

"Who wouldn't?" He looked at me over his glasses, then pushed them back up on his nose again. "Okay, okay," he sighed. "As long as we're confessing every ugly suspicion, I could see reasons why people would have wanted Sam out of the way. Aside from his, ah, more annoying habits."

"Hey!" Sam cried, aggrieved. "Frankie, is that any way to talk about an old friend?"

"Tell me about it," I said to the Lord High Greenhead.

"You know, of course, that Sam bought White Marsh Island years ago?" If Dartwood had lobbed a pipe bomb into the middle of the room, my reaction would have been the same.

"Huh?" I said, ever the brilliant conversationalist.

"I did?" Sam asked, genuinely interested. "So that's why the Harbesons were so pissed off at me."

"You—Sam—must have been stoned! *Sam* bought White Marsh? When?"

"About ten years ago. Don't ask me why. You know the story about the Harbeson brothers, don't you?"

"I know more than I want to know about the Crab Bait Killer," I told him truthfully. "But how did Sam buy the island? That was about the time I married and divorced him, more fool I."

"After they put Levin Harbeson in the gas chamber, the land was tied up for years in an estate battle among some cousins from Marydel. When the lawyers ran through their money, the island was put up for sale to pay the legal bills. No one wanted a piece of high ground in a marsh back in the '60s. The real estate market still hadn't gone sky high on the Shore. Besides, no one was real anxious to own a piece of land where someone had chopped up his brother and used him to bait up his lines. Stuff like that takes a while to die down."

"Not for Sam. He was never known as a man with taste," I observed nastily.

"I resent that," Sam cried. "I married *you*, didn't I?"

"Well, it was dirt cheap at the time, and he was still looking for ways to spend his trust fund," Dartwood recalled.

"I vaguely remember thinking I could grow dope out there," Sam sighed. "But it was too much like work, being a farmer. And besides, right after I signed the papers, I remember that was when I got out of Dodge."

"An acre of marsh is worth the same as an acre of blue sky." I leaned back in my chair, trying to avoid glaring at Sam, who certainly could have told me all of this before, if he remembered it from his new position as a living-impaired person.

"I guess when Claire got into the real estate business, she found out that Sam owned that island and decided that it would be a fabulous place for a twenty-million-dollar housing development. I doubt she knew a wetland from a Disneyland at that point. In her new role as developer-slash-real-estate agent, she just saw the last damn piece of undeveloped land in Santimoke County and knew it could make her a nickel, so she went after it."

"Since the family had been paying Sam a remittance to stay away from Santimoke County, it would seem to her that that island was all in the family," I suggested, getting into the spirit of things. If you want to bash Claire, call me first. I'll bring the beer.

"And wetlands laws be damned. All their lives the Wescotts have been throwing money and the family name at their problems. A substantial campaign contribution to Jason Hemlock and whoever else and there's the possibility of getting a private bill passed or whatever to get them an exemption to drain every damned wetland in Santimoke County and build a strip mall every five feet."

"Except this wasn't quite as easy as all of that."

"The wetlands laws are complex and frequently don't make much sense across the board, local, state, and federal. During the Reagan-Bush years, the laws were so diluted and confused that we've lost nearly fifty percent of our existing wetlands. There's a lot of room for improvement. We can all agree on that, developers and environmentalists both," Dartwood sighed. He waved his hand in the air and frowned. "I won't bore you with what you already know, how much wetland we lose on the Shore, across the country, and around the world every year. There are, believe it or not, developers out there who are responsible, who are trying to work with conservationists and environmentalists. Then there are the people like Claire, who are only interested in making money at any cost, including the future of a troubled planet." He was in his professorial mode now and probably would have rambled on forever, if we had allowed him.

"Cut to the chase," Sam said impatiently. "Tell her about why you came down to Big Pig."

"When I found out that Wescott Development ultimately planned to own and control all of White Marsh Neck," Frank said, just as if he had heard Sam, "starting with White Marsh Island, I had a title search done on the island and found out it belonged to Sam. When I went to Big Pig Cay, I was going to get him to sell White Marsh Island to me or to a conservation group that would leave it undeveloped in perpetuity. That would have been far more effective than spiking a hundred acres of trees." He grinned at me, enjoying his joke.

"True," I agreed. "So, what did Sam do?"

"What indeed?" Sam asked, fascinated.

"He agreed with me," Frank continued, idly playing with the computer. "I think there were two factors at work. Sam knew he didn't have a lot of time left, and he wanted to do the right thing, for once in his life. And he also saw a chance to thrust a spoke into the family's, particularly Claire's, wheel. No love ever lost there."

"Look in the dictionary under 'dysfunctional family' and you'd find a picture of the Wescotts," I agreed.

"I had all the papers together; Sam could have made a transfer of deed right there in Big Pig Cay. But he wanted to come home, he said he wanted to set things right in person."

"And you think that one of the Wescott contingent took that opportunity to blow him out of the water and off the payroll? Without a will, the family would inherit—"

"A will!" Sam exclaimed, sitting up. He really shouldn't have; his head went right through the ceiling.

"White Marsh Island, plus, and this is a big plus, Sam would be out of the way for good and ever, something else that must have been a factor, if someone killed him," Dartwood said.

"Did he say anything to you about having a will?" I asked. My attention was definitely hooked now.

"He mentioned that he was thinking of drawing one up," Frank told me, "once he got home."

"He would have needed a lawyer for that," I said, thinking out loud. "Did he have a lawyer?"

Sam pulled his head out of the ceiling, running a hand over his hair. "That hurt," he said. "Damn insulation. What did I miss?"

I gave him a filthy look. Then suddenly, something was triggering an old memory. I stood up. Mud flaked off me, falling on the floor. "Ever since he was a kid, Sam had a place in his bedroom where he hid things at Mandrake," I remembered. "His dope, papers, whatever he didn't want Claire to find. If he had something like a will, I bet it would be there. Unless it was blown to shreds on the boat," I added, my spirits, pardon the expression, sinking as I collapsed in a chair. "Was it?" I hissed at Sam, trying to be casual.

"How would I know? I can't remember my own name half the time," he grinned, enjoying this so much I wanted to kick him. "Come on, come on, this is more important: who killed me?"

"Claire," I replied automatically.

"Claire?" Frank repeated blankly. "What about her?"

"Claire is a likely suspect," I said quickly.

"She is in *my* book," Sam agreed. "I never *did* like Sister Dearest. But there's Dad, too, not to mention the irrepressible Skipper, although it's more like a marvel that *he* hasn't killed Claire—or the Old Man by now."

"If there is a will, and a lawyer drew it up, he or she would be obligated to come forward with it."

"Unless there was no lawyer. You can draw up a will with two witnesses to your signature, and it'll hold up in court, you know."

Silence. The fan circled overhead, click-click, click-click, click-click. The heat grew more oppressive as the sun threw long shadows across the bare floorboards.

"I sure wouldn't have left my family anything," Sam teased me.

"There's one way to find out," Frank said. "We have to go to Mandrake and look."

"What do you mean, *we*?" I asked. "I'm wanted for murder. I'm a marsh fugitive! I claim sanctuary! You can't make me leave here!"

Dartwood looked over his glasses at me. "You don't have to leave here," he said slowly, with a grin that reminded me much too much of Sam's. "However, Greens 'n' Things Catering does. In one of those coincidences so beloved of bad novelists, Mandrake is the place we're catering tonight!"

As if to make it so, he picked up the phone and punched in a number, talking rapidly to the person on the other end.

"I don't believe this," I said.

"Believe it," Sam grinned.

"You didn't cause this, did you?" I whispered to him.

He studied his fingernails modestly.

Frank thought the question was directed at him. "Thoreau would be proud," he said, gazing at me fondly. "You're going to make a wonderful caterer's assistant."

"Who, me?" I squawked.

"You could stay here all alone," Sam suggested cheerfully. "But you may not be lonely. I've got Levin Harbeson pretty riled up, and he's looking for me or anyone else he can find. And he's got his tongheads."

"I'll try anything," I said. "If it can prove I didn't kill anyone."

"Relax," Andy told me, punching my arm. "No one ever looks at the caterer's assistants. How do you think Frank got in here during that funeral? He was disguised as the bartender."

"I don't want to know. What I don't know they can't torture out of me," I grumbled. Showered up and dressed in borrowed black pants, a bow tie, and a white shirt, my hair slicked back into a knot, I felt and looked like a dork. Especially after being ridden around for miles and miles in the back of a van stuffed with tray racks. "I don't know nothing about no catering, Miz Scarlett. Besides, Estelle and Phillips will surely recognize me."

Phillips was out in front, supervising the parking of many Lincolns, Mercedes, BMWs, and Volvos. The guests were arriving; their voices carried on the hot evening air back around the side of the house to us.

"You won't have to serve; we'll keep you in the background," Dartwood said as we unloaded covered trays from the back of the white van with GREENS 'N' THINGS CATERERS painted in elaborate script on its sides. No one would have recognized him in his bartender drag. In a blond wig and goatee, complemented with contact lenses, he looked like an out-of-work actor.

We were in the back regions of Mandrake, hidden from the front by a tall hedge. (How we got from Greenhead Island to Mandrake with all that food is a trade secret I have sworn not to reveal. Anyway, I had used the time to have a nap in the back of the van. That's my story, and I'm sticking to it.) The tradesman's entrance opened directly into the kitchen, leaving me with a straight shot to relative safety. Or, from the frying pan to the fire, take your choice.

I treasured the gathering as a good diversion. It would, I thought, help me to slip up the old servant's stairway in the kitchen to Sam's bedroom without being discovered. The family and the guests would be fully occupied on the ground floor. Dartwood and I had reassured each other that this would be a piece of cake.

Wrong again.

When I strolled into the kitchen and took a sharp right, the first thing I saw was a hulking man in Ray-Bans and a conservative gray suit with a bulge in the armpit, standing right in front of the steps. "Security, ma'am. No one can go upstairs," he rumbled.

"Oh, gee, sorry," I replied and backed away. *Damn, now what?* I thought and tried to look busy.

He was looking at me as if I were a presidential assassin and he were the Secret Service. Greenheads, too busy to pay him much attention, were unwrapping the stainless steel trays of hors d'oeuvres and arranging bits of carved cauliflower around a hollowed-out cabbage head filled with dill yogurt dip. Bread was baking in the big oven, filling the room with delicious smells, and Greenheads were busily going about the business of setting up a buffet dinner for thirty.

"You're running late," Claire was snarling, teetering through the kitchen on her high heels, resplendent in Oscar de la Renta and hot rollers. In spite of the central air, the kitchen was starting to heat up with the ovens and the six-burner Wolfe stove all going at once.

"When I say I want you here at five-thirty, I mean five-thirty sharp, not quarter of six," she hissed. "Do you know how important I am? Do you know how many very important, very socially prominent people are here tonight? Snap to it, people, now! Estelle, I am holding you responsible for this! Where's the damn bartender?"

"He's tending the bar, just where he should be," Estelle said, coming right along behind her, literally pushing her out of the room. "You go on and get ready, you hear? You got people right now!"

I watched as Claire tossed her head, all but stomped her foot, and lurched toward the liquor cabinet. She poured herself a large tumbler of straight Jack Daniel's and, with an unrefined "Get outta my way, you lout," she pushed the security guard aside and rushed up the back stairs. Lout. God, what a class act my former sister-in-law had turned out to be. Lout. When was the last time anyone used the word *lout*?

But even Claire didn't dare countermand Estelle; no one in their right mind would. Neither one of them had even glanced in my direction.

Andy placed a foil-covered tray on the counter in front of me. "See?" he murmured. "I told you so. No one looks. Put these artichoke pastries on this plate so I can pass them around."

Shaking her head, Estelle walked into the big pantry and removed a package of crabmeat. She opened it as she talked to Theresa and Mookie, and I eavesdropped. "Those guards are *her* idea," she was saying, and there was no doubt in anyone's mind who *her* was. The Greenheads had worked here before. "The media people have been all over this place like ducks on a June bug since that Jason Hemlock turned up dead. Phone ringing off the hook, people at the door asking questions, well! Mr. Wescott found a photographer with a telephoto lens hiding under the boxwoods this morning!" She clucked. "Well, of course, they're all fit to be tied! But especially her. Here she is, finally getting the Daughters of Santimoke to hold their dinner buffet and annual elections here, and she wasn't about to cancel that for anything. This year, she's convinced they'll elect her Queen President. Huh! She's only been trying for years, and no one's ever even put her name in the hat. Some people just never catch on, that's all I've got to say—Honey, get me down that big yellow bowl over there. I'm gonna show you gals how to make crabmeat stuffing."

I turned my back to her and looked smack at Sam, who had chosen to materialize on the counter right below the china cabinet.

"Nice to see you doing honest work," he remarked as I removed the foil from a tray of cold rice salad.

"Yeah, yeah, yeah," I muttered. "Why don't you go scare King Kong over there so I can sneak upstairs and snoop around your old room for your stash."

"There may still be a joint or a hit of Owsley acid in there," Sam said hopefully. "I must say, Frank is doing real well with his catering business. This salad looks very good." He leaned over and inhaled the essence of it. "Needs a little more salt, don't you think?"

"I never eat this stuff. Too healthy for me."

I looked around. The guests should be coming in and heading for the bar, I thought. Since most of the Daughters of Santimoke were genteel, blue-headed ladies who liked a nice strong whiskey sour, the ceremony of greeting them and pointing them toward the bar should keep the home folks busy for about an hour.

But that guard was still standing by the stairs, looking like he had nothing else to do but make sure that the hired help didn't go up there and loot the family jewels, or worse.

Phillips would be outside supervising the car parking for a while yet. Dartwood was tending bar, cleverly disguised, so he could keep an eye on the ladies of exalted lineage as they tippled and admired the legendary eighteenth-century accoutrements of Mandrake. Jennifer and Andy picked up trays of hors d'oeuvres and went to do their circulation thing. Wade, Mookie, Theresa, and Jon were busily prepping salads, heating nibbles, and rolling crabmeat stuffing into rockfish fillets to go under the broiler. Meanwhile, with nothing better to do, I arranged little blobs of green peppercorn low-fat cream cheese on crackers, decorated them with stars cut from red bell peppers, and placed them artfully around piles of cheese straws. While I worked, Sam did his ghostly tasting. Since it didn't affect the way things looked, I didn't fuss at him too much; I was just amazed how many trays of stuff twenty-seven little old ladies could inhale before eating a five-course dinner.

"Keep it up," Andy advised me as he took two full trays and replaced them with two empties. "See if you can get these filled up before I get back."

"We need more hot artichoke pastries," Jennifer said as she slid a tray under my fingers while at the same time removing another. "Those old ladies are just scarfin' 'em up!"

I gazed yearningly at the staircase, but it remained guarded by King Kong and out of reach. So near and yet so far.

"Better step it up, Holl," Sam sighed. "Those hot artichokes are waiting. Boy, I wish I were still alive whenever I see *her*. She's a real honey."

"A classic case. Go haunt that guy so I can get upstairs."

To my great surprise, Sam actually tried. He walked across the room and stood before the stolid guard. "Boo!" he cried.

The man didn't even move.

Sam stuck two fingers into Kong's gut; his hand came out of the man's back, fingers wriggling. Kong yawned behind his hand.

Riding up on his feet and spreading his arms above his head, Sam started moving back and forth like a crane in a mating dance. "Ya-woo! Save your Confederate money, boys, the South shall rise again!" he screamed, inches from the man's face.

The guard shifted from one foot to the other and fingered his walkie-talkie earphone. "Humpfog," he muttered into the mike on his lapel. "Dibbertumger ten-eighty."

"I'm not getting anywhere here," Sam advised, stepping in and out of the big man's body several times. "This is like trying to scare a dead rock. I need the Harbeson brothers."

"Well, why don't you go get the Harbeson—"

A heavy hand landed on my shoulder, and I nearly jumped out of my skin.

"Here, now, you're not serving that up right," Estelle said briskly as she took the spoon from my hands. "You want to make it look attractive, not like come-and-get-it at some sharecropper's table." Under her breath she hissed, "Just what do you think you're doing, young lady? We've had the po-lice here looking for you and those awful television people too. He's already had two of his spells today and doesn't need another."

"I didn't do it, Estelle, I promise I didn't," I hissed back. "Don't turn me in."

She shot me a sideways look. "You need to add some nutmeg to this," she said aloud. "Come back into the pantry, and I'll show you where I keep the spices."

Dutifully, I followed her into the giant walk-in closet where enough gourmet dry and canned goods were stored to sustain the Russian army through a famine. She closed the door behind us and turned on me.

"The best thing to do is turn yourself in," she told me briskly. "I'll call my daughter right away. Charlotte can be planning your defense while your family—"

"Estelle, I swear to you I didn't do it!" I pleaded. Somehow, after what I'd been through in the past twenty-four hours, I wasn't entirely surprised that she thought I did. "I don't care what they're saying on TV, I didn't kill Jason Hemlock."

"Huh." She shook her head. "That Lieutenant Friendly was around here, asking a lot of questions, like he thought you did. And that state's attorney, he's been here, too. Talking to the Old Man and getting him all riled up." She glared at me suspiciously. "That Hemlock boy did you dirty, it says on the TV."

"Yeah, he did. But I didn't kill him, Estelle. And I've got to find out who did, because otherwise my next relationship is gonna be with a large woman named Steve at the Women's House of Corrections up in Jessup."

"Maybe *she* won't do you dirt," Estelle suggested helpfully. She shook her finger in my face. "Here I am with a houseload of Daughters and you turn up! You ought to know better than to come around here when I've got to entertain for That One." She scowled at me. "Don't you have enough common sense to stay away from here? If Claire sees you, the first thing she'll do is call the po-lice! She's been on the phone all day telling everyone she always knew you were a murderer. Did you kill that Hemlock?" She glared at me in that way she had that made you believe you'd better tell the truth.

"No, Estelle, I swear I didn't," I pleaded. "You've got to believe me, Estelle! Look, I can't explain now, but I've got to prove I didn't kill him. It's all tied into White Marsh, somehow, and Sam's will. And—" I trailed off, watching her expression. It was clear she had her doubts.

"Give me one good reason why I shouldn't be calling the po-lice," she demanded, reaching out for the wall phone. "I could lose my job here and so could Phillips and then where would we be?"

"Comfortably retired in Florida," I replied. "And shut of Wescotts for good and all."

"Don't get smart with me, young lady! Now you tell me what is going on here and tell it fast!" She was mad as fire and not going to take any halfway stories off me. Her hand was on the phone.

"Tell her the truth, Holl. Tell her all of it," Sam said quietly, appearing between us as a thin bleached outline. He turned to her, holding out his hands. "Estelle, I'm here, can't you see me? Please, Estelle, hear me, Estelle, please."

"She can't see you, Sam," I said.

Estelle glared at me. "Who are you talking to? You smoking drugs?"

"Estelle, you asked me to tell you the truth and I am," I said in a rush. "Only you're not gonna believe me, but Sam's ghost is right here between us, and he's been telling me he's been murdered—" I could tell by her expression that she wasn't buying this. "Sam, help me, please!" I begged him. "You've got to try to make her see you!"

He trembled, closing his eyes and rolling up his fists. "I've got to concentrate," he said. "It's not the easiest thing to do—"

Slowly, he pulled into sharp focus. I could tell it was

taking him a giant effort; he was shaking, all his muscles taut as he manifested right there, almost solid, almost real.

"Now look here, Hollis Ball, what you do you—oh, sweet Jesus," Estelle breathed, taking a step back and putting a hand against her black silk breast. "Sammy? Is that really you, honey?"

Tears shone in her eyes.

"You can see him?" I whispered, surprised.

"Estelle, I—" Sam put out his hands, choking.

"I can *see* you! Oh, my Lord, I can see you, Sammy," Estelle said. "It is you! My baby boy." Her hand passed through him, and she drew back, then slowly extended her hand forward. It passed through him again. She looked at it, then at him. "But you're not there!" Then she felt at the shape of him, her hands trembling. "But that's you, I know it is. What—how?"

"I can't hold this for very long," Sam breathed tensely. "It takes a lot of strength. I just wanted you to know that I'm here and that I love you. You were the only person who ever loved me."

"Oh, child, Hollis loved you too," Estelle murmured, touching what she could not feel, pale beneath her blusher. Tears glittered up in her eyes; she was shaking like a leaf. "Why did you do it, Sammy?" she sobbed. "Whyever did you kill yourself like that?"

THIRTEEN

•

... There's a Way

"You killed yourself?" I asked Sam, incredulous.

"There's no time for that right now," Sam whispered. He could barely speak and materialize at the same time.

Estelle sat down heavily on the kitchen stool. She continued to stare at Sam, shaking her head. "You're a ghost." She put a hand out and touched him. "Sweet Jesus. All my life, I've heard stories and I never thought . . ."

"I've only got a short time, Estelle, and there's so much I need to tell you and I can't," Sam rushed. "I need to tell you I'm sorry, and I need to tell you that I love you, and I'm already fading." He held out his hands to her, and she touched him, and they looked at each other for what seemed like a long time. It was probably only a few seconds, but that few seconds had to last a long time. Sam was already starting to blur. "You've got to help Hollis, Estelle. Please do this one last thing for me. I'm sorry. . . ." He was fading, the shreds of his voice hanging in the still air. "I love you, Estelle. Good-bye, Holl . . . it's just til . . . later . . ."

"Sammy?" she asked softly, tears coursing down her cheeks, her empty arms closing on air. "Sammy, come back, just let me hold you for one more minute, child. Just one more minute. . . ."

"He's gone."

Sam had faded into nothingness.

"Will he come back?" she asked, looking around, dazed. "Was he really here?"

"You know he was. And no, I don't know if he'll come back, ever. Estelle, did Sam kill himself?"

She looked at me blankly. "Too many secrets in this house. Always too many secrets," she muttered. Then, with an effort, she pulled herself together, drying her eyes with her handkerchief. She straightened her spine and stuffed her handkerchief into her sleeve. She was one tough lady, and it would have taken more than this to knock her off balance. "You need to get upstairs?" she said, rising from the stool. "I can take care of that guard. Come on out of here."

I followed behind her as she squared her shoulders, briskly marching out of the pantry. Estelle was back in charge.

"Hey you, security man!" she rapped sharply. "We just saw a man sneaking around the back of the house with a camera! Go get him!"

King Kong didn't need to have Estelle tell him twice. He shouted something into his little microphone and lurched out the kitchen door.

"Go on," Estelle commanded, pushing me toward the unguarded staircase. "Go and save Sam's poor soul!"

I didn't need to be told twice.

I was up the stairs before anyone noticed I was gone.

Sam's room was in the far wing, at the other end of the hallway. At the top of the steps where two hundred years of weary servants had fetched and carried, I looked up and down the long hallway, past the famous double hanging staircase written up so often in books on grand old houses of Maryland. The sound of old women's voices, like the rustling of dry winter leaves, drifted up from below. They would be finishing their second drink now.

The hallway was deserted. Down the corridor to my right was Estelle and Phillips's wing. To the left, in the main house, Claire and Skipper had a suite overlooking the portico. Opposite them, the Old Man's suite opened off the hall and looked down over the water. Sam's room was all the way down at the end of the far wing, past a series of guest rooms. All the doors were closed. This was a house of closed doors, angry whispers, deadly secrets. As if to remind me that I was a once and future trespasser in this place, a Copley portrait of Henrietta Maria Chase Wescott stared at me with disapproval. Claire had inherited her beady little eyes, I thought. That painted gaze followed me down the hall.

As I passed the open stairwell, Claire's voice drifted up to me. "I'm just so thrilled to be hostessing the Daughters this year. You know, my mother was president for five years in a row.... Isn't that the most gorgeous pin you've got on there, Miz Baldwin! A family piece?"

I hustled past the open stairwell, holding my breath until I made it down the steps into the far wing. Nothing had changed very much. No time for nostalgia, I thought, although I noticed that the old smell of ancient wood and lemon oil still lingered in the air. My hand was shaking a little when I tried the knob on Sam's door.

The room still smelled of Sam, of clean shirts and soap and sunburned skin, and it made me pause for a moment before I could step inside. Here was the old cherry spindle bed we'd made love in, laughed in, fought in; the same blue curtains, the same heavy mahogany furniture. No one had bothered to remove Sam's stuff. His docksiders stood neatly paired under the fringes of the spread. When I opened the closet door, his clothes were still hung in the closet, as if he would come back any moment.

Funny, I thought, how he seemed more real to me as a ghost. I scanned the books, the paintings of old Newport-Bermuda races, the remnants of his blighted schooling; a lacrosse stick, a tennis racket, group photographs on the chest of drawers of some long-forgotten log canoe crews.

I turned toward the plantation desk. Like the other furnishings in the room, it was a solid old piece that had probably sat in that corner since time began. Carefully, I opened the top and ran my hand over the tiny drawers. The last one on the right slid out easily. If you didn't know it was there, you would never look behind it for the narrow, unfinished box that was concealed behind the frame.

It slid out into my hand.

I turned it over on the desk blotter.

A plastic bag containing about a teaspoon of marijuana seeds fell out on the desk. I stared at it blankly. It must have been there for a decade. Nothing else.

Typical Sam stuff, I thought bitterly, almost choking with disappointment.

The clock on the landing chimed seven, and I started as if I'd been struck with the pendulum. Frantically, I started to pull out the rest of the drawers, but they were all empty of everything but the smell of old wood and must. Nothing.

"Oh, shit," I sighed, so frustrated that I was almost ready to cry. I put my head in my hands and closed my eyes. All this for nothing; I was back where I started. Now what?

I put the seeds back in the secret box and returned the box to its hiding place. Then I picked up the long thin drawer and tried to slide it back into its slot. It didn't want to go in, so I turned it over. That was when I saw the thin blue folio hidden in the drawer's underside, thrust up between the chamfers.

With shaking hands, I drew it out.

Last Will and Testament, it said in that Old English script so beloved of lawyers' offices. And beneath that, some legal secretary in the long-defunct partnership of Bracken, MacKenzie, and Fayette had neatly typed "Will of Samuel Sewall Wescott, 'Mandrake,' Route 1, Box 208, Watertown, Maryland. J. C. L. MacKenzie, Esq., Attorney-at-Law."

"Hot damn," I exclaimed, almost feeling the beat of my heart slow down. I opened it up, spreading it flat on the desk. It took me a moment to focus on the old-fashioned pica font of a typewriter.

"I, Samuel Sewall Wescott, on this 3rd day of February, 1984, devise and make this as my last will and testament, hereby revoking and rescinding any and all previous wills and codicils. . . ."

My hands were shaking when I spread it out on the desk. The clock on the landing chimed the half hour before I finished reading; it was a simple document, but with all the legal gobbledygook and predeceases and theretofores, it was hard reading. And I wanted to be absolutely certain that I knew what I was reading was really what I was reading.

Then I started to laugh.

The sound was eerie; it echoed in the empty room like memory. Or maybe it was the ghosts of all those old Wescotts enjoying the joke with me. For the first time in hours, I wanted a cigarette, so I lit one, sat back, and inhaled. It was all starting to make sense now, or so I thought.

I picked up the phone and punched in Sev Capwell's home number. God knows I'd called him after hours looking for quotes enough times to know it by heart. I inhaled and exhaled as I listened to the phone ring somewhere deep in downtown Watertown.

When I heard his voice, I said, "Sev, this is Hollis. You're not gonna believe where I am or what's going on, but I think I just figured out who killed Jason and possibly Sam Wescott."

"Hollis? Where are you?" Sev's voice crackled over the line. "Where are you? People are looking for you everywhere! What are you doing?"

"Lots, and I'll explain it all to you, but right now, I've got to go confront a suspect. Can you be at Mandrake in fifteen minutes?"

I heard him take a deep breath. "Is that where you are right now? What's happening over there?"

"I can't explain all that right now," I said. "Just get out here."

I replaced the phone in the cradle.

Downstairs, all the old ladies were stoking up second helpings from the buffet table in the dining room. Bless their hearts, I hope I can be a little old lady with an iron digestion, good pearls, and whim of steel when *I'm* seventy.

"Oh, look, there's Holly Ball," said Mrs. Baldwin, not missing a beat as she loaded up on seviche. "Are you working for a caterer now, dear? What happened to your nice newspaper job?"

"Oh, Hollis, how are you?" Mrs. Claret greeted me, waving a fork laden with crabmeat-stuffed rockfish in my direction. "I'm so glad to see you being friends with the Wescotts again, dear."

"Holly, are you going to the bar? Can you get Miz Godfrey another drink? I know it's a trouble, but she's in her wheelchair and it's hard for her to get around on these orientals. . . ."

"That's Holly Ball, innit? She murdered that oily politician, didn't she, the one with all the hair?" Mrs. Godfrey bellowed. Dowager Empress of Santimoke society, she tapped her hearing aid with a beringed finger.

"Hush, Martha, ladies don't talk about things like that," Mrs. Claret reminded her. She hissed at me in a stage whisper. "I'm so sorry, Holly, you know that she had that stroke last year—"

"That's all right," I assured her. "Except I didn't murder him, Mrs. Godfrey!" I shouted so she could hear me.

She beamed, a mass of tanned, leathery wrinkles, the legacy of years of leisure for golf and sailing. "I'm so glad to hear that, dear," she reassured me. She held up the beautiful Blue Canton bowl of seviche. "This tastes like raw fish!"

The room had come to a dead standstill. Even Wade and Jon, serving behind the buffet, looked up. I could have been Charles Manson, but the Daughters would have been too polite to mention it in public. It's just not done on the Shore, where insanity, criminal behavior, alcoholism, abuse, incest, and other sins simply aren't acknowledged. If pride were a fire, Santimoke County's oldest families would outshine the sun.

Claire, hearing a voice raised to a high decibel level, came in from the drawing room, a smile on her lips, the scent of Mitsouko preceding her. She saw me, then stopped dead in her tracks. The blood and the smile both drained from her face, which then took on a most interesting expression. "What are you doing here?" she asked between clenched jaws.

"There you are!" I said gaily. "I came anyway, even though I guess you forgot my invitation." I waved the will back and forth in the air. "Look what I found! It's Sam's will!"

"Where the hell are those damn security people!" she muttered, almost knocking Mrs. Claret over as she made for me.

I took a step back, but it was too late. I guess there is something to be said for playing a lot of tennis and working out regularly and eating healthy. Claire got me in a flying tackle, knocked me down, and before I could get my balance, snatched the will out of my hands and was dodging little old ladies as she made for the front hall at a gallop.

"Hey!" I yelled. I scrambled to my feet and went after but it was too late; she slammed the door to the downstairs bathroom in my face. I heard the lock turn even as I grabbed the doorknob and shook it. It didn't even rattle in the frame. I threw my shoulder against the wood.

"Hey! Claire, don't!" I yelled. "Don't do anything with that will!" I kicked at the door and pounded. "Claire! Damn it! *Open the door!*"

I heard the sounds of paper tearing and the gurgle of the flushing toilet.

"Claire! That's illegal!" I threw myself against the door again. "Stop! Stop that right now!"

The toilet flushed again.

"You know, dear," Mrs. Claret said mildly, "That's not the only bathroom in the house. Why don't you try one of the ones upstairs?"

I pounded on the door. "Claire, come out of there so I can kill you!" I yelled, which may not have been the most fortuitous statement, but hey, I was mad, listening to all my hard snooping going down the literal tubes.

The only response was the flush of the toilet.

Skipper emerged from the drawing room, looking beige and befuddled. He looked at the bathroom door, then at me, then just looked resigned as he put his plate down on a console table. "Hello, Hollis, what are you doing now?" he asked reasonably, as if wanted criminals showed up at Mandrake regularly, which for all I knew, they did.

"Trying to find a killer, Skip," I panted. I kicked at the door. "Your lovely and talented wife just snatched Sam's will out of my hands, locked herself in the bathroom, and flushed it down the toilet! Where's the Old Man? I think we need to talk. Get her to come out of there, willya?"

"Yes, yes, of course," he said calmly, as if Claire flushed wills down toilets all the time. "I rather thought that you would come here, Hollis. Step into the study." He knocked on the bathroom door. "Claire, come out of there, please."

"And bring the bartender, too," I added.

His eyebrows rose slightly, but he turned around and beckoned into the drawing room. In a moment, Dartwood emerged, still in disguise, wiping his hands on his apron. He looked at me, and I shook my head.

"Sam's will," I growled, "just got flushed down the toilet by my former sister-in-law."

As if on cue, Claire emerged triumphantly from the bathroom.

"Damn!" Dartwood pulled off his wig, exposing his dark rumpled hair to the interested little old ladies, who were not missing a bite or a beat as they watched this drama unfold.

"Innit that Bunny Dartwood's boy?" Mrs. Godfrey asked loudly. "Why is he wearing a wig? Does he have cancer?"

"Young man, young man, could you fix Miz Godfrey another gin and tonic?" Mrs. Claret called.

"The study," I said, gesturing in that direction.

"I can't leave my guests," Claire said. "Good Lord, Frank, is that you? What happened to your hair?"

"We'll get this all straightened out," Skipper said. "This way, please."

"Excuse me, please, ladies," Claire called as I pushed her down the hall in front of me. "I'll be right back just as soon as we get this—just a silly little misunderstanding, don't you know?"

"Take your time, dear," Mrs. Wilmot said politely. "Young man, young man! Is there any more rockfish?"

H.P., who had obviously sought refuge from the Daughters in his sanctuary, looked up as we trooped in. He barked something into the phone, then replaced it in the cradle. His bushy white eyebrows rose halfway up his forehead. "What the pluperfect hell is going on now?" he asked in the voice of a man whose patience is being sorely tried by small children and animals.

"Are you all right, sir?" Two security guards, finally having gotten the idea that something was amiss, poked their heads in the door.

"Here they are! Get those two and call the police! She's wanted for murder!" Claire, jumping up and down, pointed at me. "You did this on purpose, I know you did," she accused me. *"Just to Make Me Look Bad in Front of the Daughters!"*

H.P. made a small, sweeping motion with the side of one hand. When you've got that much power, even a small movement like that is enough. "You two can go," he said, nodding to the guards. "Keep everyone else away from here. When I need you, I'll call for you."

"Daddy, for God's sake—" Claire cried. "They may be armed!"

"Claire, please calm down. This is not how Wescotts act," the Old Man sighed. His voice was soft and weary, but it was enough to silence her. But she still swallowed, bounced up and down, and steamed, like a pressure cooker about to blow.

The two guards, having received their marching orders, retreated hastily, closing the door behind themselves.

I leaned over the desk so that I was eye to eye with H.P. "For your information, your daughter just flushed your late son's will down the toilet. In front of witnesses. That's a felony."

"I had to do it! Who knows what foolishness Hollis has created this time? She could have ruined everything we've done with White Marsh!" Claire cried angrily. "Besides, how do we know it was Sam's will and not some fake she cooked up?"

I sighed. "Ever since you forced me to come to Sam's funeral, H.P., my life has gone steadily downhill. I've been threatened, bribed, blackmailed, lied to, kidnapped by eco-loons, found Jason Hemlock dead in my car, been finger-printed, questioned, tested for powder burn residue, and become a murder suspect. I've had to run for my life and lie my way out of hairy situations. I've been eaten alive by bugs and slandered by the media, of which I am a card-carrying member, which makes it hurt even more! I'm pretty damn mad and frankly, folks, I think I have a right to be." I drew an indignant breath. "Then, I find Sam's 1984 will, which could connect all of this mess together, and Sister Dearest flushes it down the toilet!"

I looked at all of them, H.P., Claire, Skipper, Dartwood, and saw that no one was going to argue with me on any of these points. "First of all, I didn't kill Jason Hemlock. While Jason was being shot, I was being kidnapped at gunpoint by Mr. Dartwood and his happy crew of environmental outlaw caterers. The Lost Boys and Girls are right this minute serving the Daughters of Santimoke their Happy Meals."

"What?" Claire breathed. She made to bolt for the door, but Skipper gripped her arm. "You're poisoning the Daughters! I'll *never* be president now," she whined.

"Sit down!" Skipper commanded, and she collapsed into an armchair, probably in shock that he was actually raising his voice. "It's probably the healthiest meal most of them have had in years!" He inclined his head toward me. "I for one, am very curious to hear what Hollis has to say."

"Continue," H.P. glowered. He looked like he was going to blow at any minute, but I was too angry to care; I was not even half finished with my tantrum.

"Everything keeps going back to White Marsh," I said. "I'm no expert on wetlands, but I agree with Dartwood that there's something awful damn peculiar with the way you people have been dredging out White Marsh Island. I am not quite sure that what you're doing with those wetlands is legal, or how you circumvented all the Section 404 stuff and the local law. Dartwood tried to explain all that, and I didn't understand it. I don't think anyone could. That's why it's so easy to step around all these rules and regulations if you've got money and a powerful lobby financed by gargoyles. Jason took money from Wescott Development and used his influence in the general assembly to get White Marsh over. By doing this, Jason also offended a lot of people. You're not in the clear on this one, either, Dartwood," I added. "When I found out Sam owned White Marsh Island, things started to fall out of place."

"But, if one of the Wescotts did kill Jason Hemlock, it was because he knew a Wescott family secret," Dartwood suggested.

Claire and Skipper exchanged a look.

H.P.'s massive hands clenched on the desktop. Had we hit them where they lived? "Get to the point," he said heavily. "What is this nonsense all about, Hollis?"

"It's about the Wescotts trying to keep their private scandals private, H.P. It's about the Wescotts using their money and power to bribe and bully other people into doing what they want. Everyone has a price. All problems can be solved with a blank check. You saw that I was having some problems with what was going down, so you wrote me a big check. I thought what you wanted was my cooperation on your big puff advertisement for White Marsh Estates. But then I finally figured out that what you wanted to buy was my silence on Sam's suicide. At first I thought he was killed in an accident, then after Jason was murdered, I thought maybe Sam was murdered. Then I ... well, tonight, I realized that Sam killed himself. His big chance to create one last, ugly scandal for the family he despised, who despised him. It's just so Sam, and I was stupid not to have seen it from the first."

"You can't prove that." H.P.'s eyebrows slowly lowered until he was glowering at me with those fierce eyes. "What do you want, more money to keep quiet? How much more do you need?" he asked.

"I don't need anything except to prove that I didn't kill Jason Hemlock," I said. "I don't think anyone needs to know Sam killed himself either. He had a terminal disease, he made a decision, and he chose his own death. He was a suicide, wasn't he?"

"Don't answer her, Daddy," Claire said fiercely. "We don't owe her any explanations."

H.P. sighed. "What difference does it make? Sam's dead. There's nothing even left to prove. Accident, suicide, what difference does it make now? He's still dead. He had terminal cancer, just like his mother. He was going to die anyway."

"So he was a suicide."

"Yes," the old man muttered. "My son killed himself. And left another damn mess for me to clean up. Argh!" Contempt curdled his voice. "What a man my son was! My *daughter* has more testosterone!"

Claire looked at her father as if she wanted to cry. All her life she'd been trying to be the son Sam wasn't, as if that would make the Old Man love her, trying to please a man who could not be pleased. But I think at that moment she understood that he was incapable of loving anyone. Saturn had devoured his children. Nothing was ever enough, nothing would ever be enough to satisfy that all-consuming ego.

Skipper put his hand on Claire's shoulder. She looked up at him and put her hand over his. It was the first affectionate gesture I had ever seen them share. He shook his head at H.P. "Claire does what she does," he said softly. "And I love her, often in spite of it. She is what she is."

Claire's grip tightened on his hand.

Dartwood turned around. He looked at me, his expression like that of a man who has been kicked from behind. "Is this for real?" he asked. "Sam suicided?"

"It looks like it to me," I said dryly. "And H.P. just confirmed it."

"You can't prove it. No one can," H.P. grumbled.

"No, I can't. But I needed to know. Don't you see? If someone murdered Sam, then maybe they murdered Jason, too. This changes the whole picture. That's why I needed to know. That's why I needed to sneak in here and find out if Sam had a will."

"So, I destroyed some piece of paper!" Claire screeched. "If you'd gotten it all, I'd have killed you," she hissed at me in an aside.

"Promises, promises," I snapped. "The will you destroyed was made in 1984, before Sam blew out of Santimoke County. He left everything he owned to Estelle. *Estelle* owns White Marsh Island. You, me, Jason, Dartwood, we all are trespassers."

There was a silence, then Dartwood laughed. "Boy, if that's not Sam all over," he said. He sat down in a vacant chair, chuckling. I like a man who can recognize irony when he sees it.

H.P. frowned at Claire. "Do you realize what you've done?" he charged.

"Daddy, your heart! I had to have White Marsh! I've sunk millions into that project! All the work we put into getting those variances, those stupid permits! It was just sitting there, not doing anything, a wasteland! I couldn't let this—this—redneck slut take it all away!"

"Claire, that is no way to talk!" Skipper shouted. "Do you realize what you've done? You could go to jail for this! We could all go to jail for this!"

"What difference can it make? It was just an old piece of paper! We could have lost millions! It's all your fault! The Daughters will never make me president now!"

"Both of you shut up while I call my lawyers!"

"Estelle wouldn't know what to do with it! As far as I'm concerned, we all already owned it! All the money we've dished out to my feeble brother over the years, and then he had to come back here! We owned that land; we certainly paid for it over the years by doling out money to Sam!"

"Be that as it may, don't you understand that—"

"Now listen, you two, I want to know now if those permits are legally obtained or did you—"

While the Wescotts were fighting among themselves, something they've always done well without any outside help, I wandered around the room, looking at the Audubons, as much to distract myself as anything else. I'd never paid much attention to them before. One in particular caught my eye. It depicted a hawk perched on a dead tree branch, a mouse hanging out of its beak by the tail. It surveyed the world with a beady yellow eye in a russet head. The background was a low, swampy plain. Audubon's bird looked just like the hawk I had seen in the marsh.

"Dartwood, what's the name of that hawk?" I asked under the din. "I saw one just like that when I was paddling up the gut."

He had lowered his head into his hands, being a man who hated people and loved causes, but he glanced in the direction I was pointing and squinted. "That's a female redheaded hawk," he sighed. *"Accipter testarossa.* They're extinct. DDT got 'em all years ago. They were always elusive and rare—"

I shook my head before I got a lecture. "No, you must be wrong, I saw one out in the marsh this afternoon."

Dartwood laughed and shook his head at my lack of birding literacy. "No, you couldn't have, Hollis. The last one was found down at Dames Quarter in 1973. You must have seen something else."

"No, I saw that hawk. I *know* it's that hawk," I said irritably. "She was about ten inches long, and she was a hawk, and she had that russet head. I saw her sitting in a dead tree at the fork in Muskrat Gut. Then she flew off to her nest in a dead tree, where her mate was. I may not know beans about birds, but I know my hawks, Dartwood. I did a big feature piece on local falconers last year. I saw *that* hawk, not a chicken hawk, not an osprey, not a bald eagle, not a sharpshin, not a redtail, not a red-shouldered, but a *red-headed hawk.*"

Dartwood rose slowly from his chair and walked over to

the painting. He squinted at it, then looked at me. "Are you sure?" he demanded, gripping my shoulders. "Hollis, think."

I stared at him. "As sure as I am of anything. I never saw a hawk like that before. Ever."

"And you saw one out in White Marsh Neck?"

"She had a nest."

"Hollis, could you find it again? The nest, I mean?"

"I think so. I know so. Why?"

"Hollis, I am going to kiss you." Much to my amazement, he did just that, his false goatee scraping my cheek. "If you turn out to be right, I'll name my firstborn child after you! Look at that painting again—Audubon was not always noted for his accuracy."

I looked at it again. It was my russet head hawk all right. Red, russet, what's the difference? It was my hawk. "Yes, that's the one I saw. I'd bet my computer on it."

"Hollis, I love you!" Frank cried so loud that the Wescotts all stopped bickering and looked at us as he planted a big kiss smack on my cheek.

"Folks, I'm awful sorry—hell no, I'm not sorry at all, to have to tell you this, but I am going to get a restraining order on your development until we can get the ornithologists and the EPA in here to verify this!" Dartwood grinned triumphantly. "White Marsh Neck may be, may just possibly be, the last breeding ground of a hawk thought to be extinct!" He pointed triumphantly to the Audubon. "Behold, the red-headed hawk!"

"Who cares about some stupid bird when there's millions at stake here?" Claire leveled a finger at him. "Don't you try anything funny, or I'll sue you all the way up to the Supreme Court, do you hear, Frank?"

"That's all right with me," Dartwood replied. "You won't be able to move as much as a leaf out there till this is checked out. If what Ball tells me is confirmed by the ornithologists, White Marsh may be the last breeding ground of the red-headed hawk." He smiled. "In which case, you won't be able to sink a stob out there."

"You—you *tree huggers*!" Claire spat. "I'll sue!" Litigation, of course, being her ultimate threat; the Santimoke civil dockets were clogged with her connivings.

"Do you mean we may have saved White Marsh after all?" I asked, delighted.

Skipper sighed. "It would appear that way."

The door opened. It was Phillips. "Excuse me, sir," he said to H.P. "That state policeman, Lieutenant Friendly, is here."

FOURTEEN

•

Seduction and Betrayal

We all fell silent as Lieutenant Ormand Friendly walked through the door. He looked more than ever like Harrison Ford ridden hard and put away wet. I'd never seen a jacket that wrinkled in my life, and I had to wonder where he got a tie that featured Wyle E. Coyote.

Friendly's eyes ranged the room, then rested on me. "Well, Ms. Ball, you certainly do turn up in some interesting places." He smiled wearily.

"Arrest her!" Claire just had to say. "Arrest her now! She's trespassing here and so's he!" She pointed at Dartwood, who looked around himself, as if to see just who she was talking about; it couldn't possibly be him, could it?

"Howdya'do, Ms. Dupont." Friendly glanced at her warily. Apparently, he'd had dealings with her before. "Your security people called and told us that Ms. Ball was out here and that there was a disturbance," he said to H.P.

"Actually, we're not trespassing," Dartwood said. "We're here as contracted employees. We're the caterers." He withdrew a card from his wallet and handed it to Friendly, who glanced at it, then stuffed it in his pocket. "So you're Frank Dartwood," Friendly said. "The Greenhead Army?"

Frank nodded. "No outstanding warrants, I trust?" he asked.

Friendly rolled his eyes. "Anybody want to tell me what's going on?" he invited.

Bad move.

"Arrest these people at once! I insist on it, Lieutenant!"

"These people are in the house under false pretenses and—"

"This is a private family matter! I could make a few phone calls and have you busted down to highway patrol, young man!"

"Now, Lieutenant, be reasonable and—"

"Look, Friendly, is that really your name? These people have been developing wetlands without the proper—"

"Sam was a suicide, but I think one of these people killed Jason, if you'd just—"

Everyone had something to say, and we said it all at once. H.P. was demanding to know why the taxpayer's money wasn't keeping people from being murdered, Claire wanted Dartwood and me beheaded on the spot, Skipper was embarrassed about having the police in the house, Dartwood wanted an immediate restraining order put on Wescott Corporation, and I wanted the world to know I didn't kill Jason Hemlock.

"Okay, okay! *Okay!*" Friendly finally yelled, and we all fell silent. He glared around the room. "Anyone have any more comments to make?"

"Yes," I said. "I didn't kill Jason Hemlock. But someone in this room did—"

"Give me a nice quiet drive-by," he muttered. "No one said you killed anyone—"

"But—"

"Yet."

"I know she did it!" Claire muttered under her breath.

"And I bet you did it!" I retorted.

"Be quiet, both of you!" H.P. snapped. "Lieutenant Friendly, there has been a great deal of embarrassing speculation in the media about Hemlock's death and the family's involvement in this tragedy. Media people have had this house under siege for the past twenty-four hours, so you can imagine that our nerves are all on edge. I've had to hire a private security force to keep them off my property. No one could be more anxious to settle this than I am. This is a house of mourning, Lieutenant. I have lost a son in a tragic accident." Give the Old Man credit, he didn't skip a beat on that one. On the other hand, no one corrected him either. "If you need to arrest Hollis, then please do it quietly. I don't want to have to call the governor to complain about this intrusion, but—" The threat lay there, flat and heavy-handed.

Friendly didn't even pick it up. He just nodded, seating himself to the side of H.P.'s big desk. "First of all, since you called me, and I have you all here in one room, let's see if we can get a few stories pulled together." He flipped his notebook out of his pocket. "The murder of Jason Hemlock," he announced portentously. "Hemlock was killed with a single gunshot to the head, at close range, within a few hours of the time when Ms. Ball found him in the backseat of her car, about nine-thirty P.M. The ME can't pin it down any further than that. There was rigor, and the flies had only had time to lay eggs; the maggots hadn't hatched yet. For some reason, forensics really likes those maggots to determine time of death—"

"Please, my wife has a weak stomach," Skipper put in, but he was the one who looked green around the gills.

Dartwood, still looking at the Audubons, observed, "Our sources tell the Greenheads that Wescott Development paid Hemlock a lot of cash for his help in getting the permits for White Marsh Estates going." His smile was angelic.

"Claire?" H.P. said. "Is that true?"

She looked at her well-manicured hands. "So what?" she mumbled defensively. "So what if I did give him money? It was all in cash, there's no way anyone can prove it."

"Cash?" Skipper demanded. "Cash? Where did that cash come from?"

"I sold our Microsoft stock."

"You *what*?"

"You sold stock to buy off a politician? What do you think PACs are for?" H.P. demanded. "You never pay cash for a politician! They're tax deductible!"

"And I got into a rather unseemly melee with Hemlock because I thought you were having an affair with him!"

Skipper exclaimed. "If I'd known you'd sold the Microsoft stock, I would have killed him! My dear Claire, how could you? Sleep with whomever you wish, but *never* touch capital!"

For a moment there, it looked like Friendly was going to have another homicide on his hands.

But at least one thing was explained for me. Now I knew why Skipper and Jason were tangling in the job trailer. Still, the thing didn't fit Skipper; beige people rarely murder; they just steal from you with a computer.

"Ahem." Friendly cleared his throat. "Let's get back to the subject at hand, please."

Resentfully, they fell silent, glaring knives at each other.

"There's only one road in and out of White Marsh Neck," Friendly took up again. "No one who was at the job site says they saw Hemlock's Lexus anywhere on the causeway as they left. We found it in Jenkin's Creek, where it seemed to have been driven off the road and half sunk in the water. If there hadn't been an oil slick, we never would have looked for it, and it would have sunk into the mud. Okay. So let's trace everyone's steps that afternoon. At the site we had Mr. and Mrs. Dupont, Mr. Hemlock, Ms. Ball. There were four Ball Excavation people, all of whom can alibi each other, and none of whom seem to have had any interest in Mr. Hemlock. Mrs. Dupont left the site about three, three-thirty, and Ms. Ball saw her leave as she was arriving. Mr. Hemlock was last seen alive about three-thirty, four o'clock, on White Marsh Island, when the excavation crew saw him get into his car and drive away. Ms. Ball spoke to the excavation crew, then to Mr. Dupont and says she left between four-fifteen and four-thirty, to which Mr. Dupont agrees. He left about the same time as the crew, about four-forty-five, five o'clock. They followed one another into town, so they provide alibis for each other until approximately six, six-thirty. Both the construction crew and Mr. Dupont saw Ms. Ball's empty car on the side of the causeway at Jenkin's Creek bridge about five. Ms. Ball was nowhere to be seen. And frankly, the story she told about where she had been, with no corroboration, was fishy, to say the least." He looked at me. I was still puzzling this all out in my numb brain. I looked at Dartwood, and he looked at me.

"Ball, bless her heart, was trying to protect us," he told Friendly. "She was, er, visiting us at that point. We picked her up by canoe on the causeway and took her out to Greenhead Island, where she was with us until about nine-thirty, when we returned her to her car by the same route. We have an island in the marsh where we've set up camp. Until now, we preferred to keep our location a secret. But it would seem that doesn't matter if, indeed, the red-headed hawk has reemerged and established a breeding ground on the neck. A vast and important wetland has been saved from people like the Wescotts and will be preserved from environmental rapine—"

"Uh, okay," Friendly said quickly. "We can go into all of that later. In point of fact, the Department of Natural Resources clued us in about Greenhead Island."

"You don't say!" Dartwood sounded rather disappointed.

"Oh, yeah." Friendly nodded, looking at his notebook. "So you can vouch for Ms. Ball from about four-thirty to about nine-thirty?"

"Sure can." Dartwood beamed at me. "And so can the Greenheads."

"I did lie, but I wasn't sure what the Greenheads had done, and I didn't want to give them up if they were innocent," I confessed weakly. What a tangled web we weave. . . .

"Those times would still have given you opportunity to kill Hemlock. He was shot with a .38 and you had a .38 in your possession." Friendly frowned at me. "And that causeway's a long, lonely road. Hemlock could have stopped you on the causeway, you could have had a fight, shot him, dumped his Lexus into the marsh, then been stopped by the Greenheads who didn't see his body in the backseat."

"But—" I looked at Dartwood. I wasn't particularly

anxious to finger Jennifer, but my innocent behind was in the sling.

At that moment, the French doors to the patio opened and Jennifer herself burst in, accompanied by the rest of the Greenheads, who clustered around her in a protective phalanx. A couple of uniforms and a security guard or two were sort of hugging the edges, so, all of a sudden, the room was quite crowded. "It was my gun Hollis had," Jennifer said, looking very blonde and fragile as she stood dramatically in the doorway. "But she couldn't have shot Jason with it!"

Obviously, they'd all been listening at the window, which made me wonder who was serving the Daughters of Santimoke. Before I could mention this, everyone—and I do mean everyone—started talking at once, and when you have a roomful of people all pointing out why they couldn't have done what they were suspected of doing, and in very loud voices, the din gets pretty frantic.

"Enemies of the planet!"

"Hippie Communists!"

"Mr. Wescott, I try to keep 'em out, and they just keep comin' in!"

"Lieutenant, there's two TV trucks down at the gate. They're on the public road, but they're tryin' to film up the driveway—"

"If everyone would just calm down and listen to me—"

"I hope you at least got a receipt from Hemlock!"

"Our Microsoft stock! You spent capital! How could you?"

"I hate to disturb you, Claire, I really do, but poor Miz Godfrey's chokin' on a piece of fish bone, and none of us know CPR—" called Mrs. Baldwin.

I looked at the French doors and decided that I definitely needed a cigarette. I was going into serious nicotine withdrawal, and besides, it looked like it would be a while before Friendly was going to be able to restore order, if ever.

No one even seemed to notice when I slipped outside.

The night was dense with humidity and August heat. Just

breathing seemed like an act of faith, but I stood on the patio, looking out across the lawns and the river, straightened out a crumpled cigarette and lit it with trembling hands. The cacophony behind me was matched by the cacophony coming from the half-opened French windows of the drawing room, where the Daughters were listening to a talk by one of their number on how she had traced her descent from Thomas Jefferson's bookbinder's mother-in-law, and a state trooper was giving Miz Godfrey the Heimlich maneuver at the same time. Since half of the Daughters were deaf and the other half were not making any long-term plans, it probably didn't matter that much one way or the other.

In the glow of the fading moon, the world looked gray and silver. Somewhere off down the woods, I heard the lonely carol of bobwhites calling back and forth across the thickets. Saddest sound in the world, or it would have been if those damn people in the house would just shut up and let the night be.

In the heat, the boxwoods' dusty, sour smell curled through the atmosphere. It would probably never rain again. We would all just dry up and blow away.

I sucked on my cigarette, feeling the nicotine coursing its poison through my body. Yummy. One of these days, when my life is less stressful, I will stop smoking. Honest.

"Psst!"

At first I barely heard the rustling in the boxwoods, and when I finally turned to look in that direction, they were in the shadow of the house.

"Psst! Hollis!"

I peered into the dark, squinting around.

"Over here!"

I saw a dim moonlit shape about the size of a football in the midst of the boxwood hedges. "Hello?" I asked. "Oh, it's you."

Severn Capwell, state's attorney for Santimoke County, peered out of the boxwoods at me. "What's going on?"

"Sev?"

"Keep your voice down! This place is crawling with police and security guards."

"Well, as Santimoke County's top cop, you ought to be used to that," I said. "Why are you crawling around in the shrubbery?"

It seemed like a reasonable enough question to me, but Sev stayed where he was, looking over his shoulder. "Come closer, but make sure no one sees you," he whispered.

I walked to the edge of the patio and looked down at him. He was definitely hiding in the boxwoods. "What's going on in there?" he whispered. "What are you doing here?"

"Well, in our last exciting chapter of One Woman's Family, as you will recall, I was running from possible arrest for the murder of Jason Hemlock, which, as God is my witness, I did not commit. . . ."

Sev winced. "Hollis, I found the gun that killed Hemlock. You've got to get out of here with me now, or Friendly will arrest you." He beckoned to me. "This place is crawling with private security and state troopers, and down by the road, there are trucks from channels 16 and 13 just waiting for something to—"

"You found the gun? But the police have the gun." Having latched on to that piece of information, I wasn't going to let go of it.

"They have a .38, but not the .38 that shot Hemlock," Sev said grimly. "There were two guns. Come on, Hollis, you've got to get out of here."

I allowed him to help me jump from the patio into the box. "Sev, what's going on?"

"A lot, and we need to get out of here without being seen," Sev whispered. "Do you have a car?"

"There's the Greens 'n' Things van, over on the other side of the house by the kitchen. I think the keys are in it. But we can't just take it—"

But of course, we did.

We were rolling down the driveway in the dark with me

at the wheel and trays of unserved blueberry tarts rolling around in the back before I could bitch about the fact that I could now add Grand Theft Auto to my résumé. In the time it had taken us to walk around the house, ducking and weaving into the concealing shadows, I was soaked in humid sweat. Sev looked as if he had just stepped out of the shower, not so much as a hair out of place. I quickly filled him in on my adventures of the past twenty-four hours. I edited out Sam, but otherwise, it was mostly true.

"Do you want to find out who killed Hemlock?" Sev asked. "Do you want to go to jail for a crime you didn't commit?"

"No. Well, yes and then no."

"Okay, then, drive."

So I did, waving gaily at the troopers, security guards, and the handful of TV news trucks camped out by the brick pillars at the gate, all of whom assumed that I was just a happy caterer who couldn't drive a standard shift all that well. I couldn't believe how easy it was to roll out of the driveway and onto the county blacktop, a free woman.

Ha.

"Stop here for a moment," Sev commanded when we got about five hundred yards down the road and out of sight of the gates. He opened the door and jumped out. When the van light went on and I got a good look at him, I saw his spandex shorts and bright yellow nylon biking shirt. It was a wonder he didn't glow in the dark. He jumped over the ditch and wrestled his bike out of the underbrush in the woods.

"You came all the way out by bike?" I asked. "Is that what took you so long?"

"Hey," he grunted, lifting the sleek, thousand-dollar machine carefully into the back of the van, "I set a personal best! Also," he grunted again, steadying it carefully, "I was able to stash the bike and walk up to the house through the woods, thus avoiding any embarrassing interceptions." Sev patted the gleaming machine. "Damn mosquitoes," he said, slapping his well-muscled legs. They were fishbelly white in the moonlight, like his face. It gave him a ghoulish cast, an Aryan Count Dracula.

Sev slid the rear doors closed and climbed back into the passenger seat, digging in his belly bag as he fastened his seat belt.

"Okay," he said. "Let's get going."

I put the van into gear, and we lurched back onto the narrow road.

"So, where's this other .38, the one that killed Jason?" I asked.

"Right here," Sev said. "It's been in my belly bag all along." The silver barrel gleamed in the moonlight as he pointed it right at me.

FIFTEEN

•

Smoke on the Water,
Fire in the Sky

"If this is your idea of a joke, I don't think it's very funny, Sev," I squeaked. I sounded really weird, even to myself.

"No joke, Hollis, no joke at all. As a state's attorney, I've found it's a good thing to have a gun." Sev's voice was as cold as a Republican's heart. "Keep your eyes on the road, please!"

"Where are we going? Why are you doing this?" I squeaked.

"You ask too many questions, Hollis. You always have. Turn left up here. It's a good thing my biking has taken me all over these county roads. I know them so well I could travel them blindfolded." He sighed. "You know, I really do dislike the Eastern Shore. It's a very dreary, provincial place."

"That's like saying you hate Paw and Maw and apple pie, Joe Ben Billy Bob," I observed.

"Someday, your little cracks are going to get you into trouble, Hollis. Give me credit for eliminating one of the Shore's nastier denizens."

"Call me slow-witted and nail me to a fence post, but are you trying to tell me that you killed Jason?" I asked in what I hoped was a nice, conversational tone of voice.

"I thought you had already figured that out," Sev said, not unkindly.

"Uh-uh. I'm good, but I'm not that good." There was

still a part of me that thought this was all a joke and that Sev would soon give it up and we'd be working together as we fingered Claire or Jennifer or Skipper or Frank or H.P. or anyone other than me for Jason's murder.

"Sev, why are you pointing a gun at me?" I asked, not unreasonably.

"Because this way you will be able to say, in absolute honesty, that I forced you to do this, against your will. And, I want you to do what I tell you," he added in an equally reasonable voice, "so this is the best way to do it."

"Are you by any chance planning to kill me?"

"I *could* kill you. It's one of a number of options at this point. A morally repellent option, but an option nonetheless. However, the answer is no, I am not planning to kill you. In fact, I'm trying to rescue you."

I thought that one over for a while. I still could not absorb the idea that this was happening to me. "So how do you plan to rescue me?"

"Turn left up here at the crossroads."

I did as I was told, and we headed down a narrow road that wound between open corn and soybean fields. Far away, I saw the tiny, square lights of farmhouses we passed, distant havens. On the road, it was just us, racing with the moon as she hid and reappeared behind the trees.

Maybe it was moon madness, but my brain caught up with my mouth. "The bicycle! You came in and out of White Marsh on a bike!"

"I knew that you would figure that out sooner or later," Sev murmured. "Very good."

I was thinking very hard now. "People notice cars, but a bike is easy to conceal. You could get down off the bicycle and hide yourself and the bike in the marsh or the woods. No one would think twice about looking for someone on a bicycle." I swallowed hard. "You could have ridden all the way over from Watertown, met Jason in his car out on the road, shot him, driven him and the bike down the road in his car, looking for a place to hide them, and seen *my* car, just sitting there by the side of the causeway." I inhaled.

"Inspiration strikes. You don't see me anywhere around, so you dump him in my poor old Honda, drive his car back up to the island, dump it off the causeway, get back on your bike, and ride to Watertown, all without turning a hair. You're a long distance biker, you wouldn't even be breathing hard. You could be back in town before anyone even knew you were gone. Wow, Sev, that is so diabolical!"

Admit it, you had to admire his means, if not his ends.

He laughed softly. "Very good thinking, Hollis. Pretty much the way it went down, too. You know, no one looks twice at bikers. We all look alike in our helmets and goggles and spandex pants. You can barely tell a boy from a girl, did you ever notice? A casual witness would have had a hard time picking me out of a lineup."

"On a bike. Uh-huh. No one looks at caterers, either," I observed, based on recent experience. "Or anyone in uniform."

"Except I didn't know it was your car. I just knew it was a car. Believe me, I didn't intend to get you tangled up in this. Now I've got to try to get you out."

"How are you gonna do that?" I was pretty sure Sev wouldn't hurt me, but you never know. "And, more to the point, why did you kill Jason?"

"Because he killed Charles Coldstone. Just as surely as if he'd held the gun to his head and pulled the trigger," Sev replied thoughtfully. "And he would have gone on to hurt other people, destroy other lives, if he hadn't been stopped."

After a moment's thought, I had to agree with that. Jason was a destroyer, a man who could damage without conscience. Look what he'd done to me. God, what was it about me that I attracted awful men? I recognized that I was a bum magnet, and I mentally swore that if I ever got out of this mess alive, I would take a vow of celibacy.

"You know, I met Charles, biking," Sev reflected softly. "We both loved biking. It was a perfect cover for us to be together."

"Charles Coldstone?" Call me dumb, but I had quite a bit on my mind at that point.

Sev used the muzzle of the .38, a small deadly-looking .38, not a cumbersome old piece like Jennifer's, to scratch a mosquito bite on his arm. "Why, of course. You mean you haven't figured that part out yet?"

I had to look at him then. At least he wasn't pointing the gun at me anymore. "Sev, do you mean to tell me you and Charles Coldstone—you're *gay?*"

"What do you want me to do, drag up like Madonna? Hollis, not all homosexual men fit the effeminate stereotype of the screaming queen. Yes, to answer your question, I am gay."

I had to laugh, which was probably not the right thing to do, but when I remembered all the women who had pursued him since he'd landed in Watertown, the joke was pretty good. "I'm sorry, I really am, but many ambitious single—and some married—women in Santimoke County have been after you since the day you got here."

"And some of the men, too. You'd be amazed if I told you that some very high profile, so-called straight, macho males have come on to me in no uncertain terms," Sev laughed. But it wasn't a happy sound. I felt the cold muzzle of that .38 poking my arm, and it wasn't so funny anymore. He was using it to scratch a bite on his hand.

"For God's sake, Sev!" I cried. "Don't do that while I'm driving, or I might kill both of us."

"Sorry," he muttered, backing off. "I'm a little edgy tonight." I was just relieved that he wasn't pointing it at me any longer.

"I can't believe we're having this conversation, that's all. Do you really think I care if you're gay or not? It wouldn't have made any difference in our friendship, or the fact you are a damn fine state's attorney."

"Maybe not to you, but making my sexual preferences public knowledge would have caused severe damage to my career and my life. Look what happened to Charles when Hemlock outed him." His voice twisted.

"You mean, that story Jason was telling everyone about Charles Coldstone being gay was true?" Under the circumstances it was a miracle that my brain could catch up to my mouth at all. Give me some credit for something here. "You and Coldstone—"

Bugs spiraled into the beams of the headlights and splattered against the windshield. The air-conditioning had started to kick in, blowing cold air against my damp, sticky skin.

"I was an assistant SA in Baltimore County when I first met Charles. What I had with him was love, the real thing, the thing that comes along once in your life, if you're lucky. It wasn't easy for either one of us. He had buried himself so far back in the closet that he had married and even had children, trying to deny who he really was. If it's any consolation to you, the family never knew about us. It was a closed, private part of our lives. The world is not kind to homosexuals, particularly in politics. But I still wasn't comfortable with the role of homewrecker. I'm not totally without conscience. I even moved to the Eastern Shore to put physical distance between us. But that didn't work either. Charles was the great love of my life."

"Look, you don't have to tell me this, Sev. I'm not going to judge your love life."

"I need to talk. God, I've been quiet for so long." Sev's voice was moody in the darkness. Out of the corner of my eye, I could see the gleam of that .38. "We tried to stay apart. But after a while, well ... We were discreet, very discreet, almost to the point of paranoia. If we saw each other once a week, it had to be enough for both of us."

"I'm sorry," I said sincerely. "It must have been a very tough situation for both of you. Being gay in this culture is a hard thing. My cousin Barlow came out, and my family was pretty evenly divided on the question of what to do, when he announced he was marrying a guy named Dijskø Wöjånsku—"

"Hollis, please."

I shut right up. Having someone reveal they're a murderer can do that to you.

Clouds were drifting across the moon. Off to the west, I saw a flash of what I thought might be lightning. "I wonder if we're going to get a thunderstorm," I muttered distractedly. "Maybe we'll finally get some rain." I took a deep breath.

Some part of me was quite sure that Sev wouldn't hurt me; we were friends. We had eaten crabs together, after all. You don't kill someone who's sat up at a bar with you and three cops till two in the morning waiting for the jury to come in with a verdict, do you?

I was about to find out, I thought. I wasn't sure what his plan was. But there were other questions that needed answers.

"Aren't you going to ask me why I killed Hemlock?" he asked after a long silence, as if he read my mind.

"Jason exposed Charles Coldstone's homosexuality, and it drove Charles to kill himself rather than put his family though the scandal."

"Give the girl a prize. Do you have any idea what it's like to have someone you love commit suicide? Do you know what that loss, that guilt is like?"

It was a rhetorical question, but I had an answer. "Yes. I found out tonight that Sam Wescott, my ex-husband, killed himself."

But Sev was caught up in his own miseries.

"Hemlock was *gloating* when Charles killed himself. He sat at the bar in McGarvey's and boasted to anyone who would listen about how he'd removed a 'political enemy.' He never knew about Charles and me, thank God. But I knew I had to do something, anything to avenge what he had done to Charles. I just didn't—I couldn't—the idea of actually killing him was always there. But I found it morally repellent—at first. So, while I dithered like Hamlet, I worked to get close to Hemlock, to become his friend, to win his trust."

"And you did," I said.

"Oh, yeah, I did. It wasn't hard. Hemlock was very susceptible to flattery. He never knew how much I loathed him. I would have made a good actor."

My hands were shaking, and my stomach was clenching and unclenching, but I drove on. Sev no longer directed me; I think we both knew where we were going.

"In a way, it was White Marsh that convinced me that it was finally time to stop being indecisive and just do it. Just kill Hemlock. When you came into the picture, snooping around, he panicked. He knew that if anyone could dig up anything nasty to topple his house of cards, it would be you."

"Thank you, I guess, but I was being punished by Rig Riggle with that assignment. It was supposed to be a puff piece on the joys of living out at the end of a marsh in a four-million-dollar house. Nothing bad to be written."

"Yeah, but you're you, Hollis. If there was dirt to be dug there, and there definitely was, you would've rooted it out and seen that it was published. If the *Gazette* was too intimidated to print it, you would have found a way to get it out. You might have even come to me or Judge Carroll with whatever you'd found."

"True," I agreed.

"I knew about Hemlock's part in all of this; he kept me up to speed. He loved having someone to brag to, you see, and I was such a good listener. I even knew that he was a silent partner in White Marsh Estates. A definite conflict of interest, wouldn't you agree?"

"Yeah, that was made pretty clear tonight. But I'm not entirely comfortable with the idea that my appearance suddenly impelled you to kill Jason."

"You would have been the perfect scapegoat, Hollis."

"Sev, that is cold!" I exclaimed. "I would *never* have done that to you!"

"You should never say never. You don't know what you will do, given motive and opportunity. Believe me, though, the last thing I wanted to do was frame you."

"Thank you, I guess. Because I'm now eyeball deep in this mess."

"We're getting to that, in a minute. But let me tell you this: Your sudden involvement in White Marsh had Hemlock spooked. He had called me when he learned that H.P. intended to involve you, and told me that he was frightened about what you might uncover. 'That bitch is after my balls,' is how he so inelegantly put it."

"Sounds like him. Jason's vocabulary was limited."

" 'I need to Coldstone her,' is exactly the way he put it. 'I gotta figure out a way to Coldstone her so nobody will ever believe her again.' "

"Coldstone me," I repeated.

"Perhaps it was the way he used my lover's name as a verb for a particularly disagreeable activity that set me off," Sev murmured. "Perhaps it was the idea that he believed *everyone* as venal as him that impelled me to decide to kill him at last. And perhaps I wasn't willing to allow him to destroy you the way he'd destroyed Charles."

"I am not at all sure that I want to know how he planned to do me in," I said, well aware of my unfortunate choice of words.

"I saw very clearly that the world needed to be rid of Jason Hemlock. And I realized that I now knew too much and that I would inevitably be 'Coldstoned' in my turn."

"I need a cigarette."

"Those things will kill you," Sev replied briskly.

"Well, later rather than sooner," I choked.

"Maybe this will take your mind off nicotine. Listen, Hollis, I decided that Hemlock would die in the same way Charles died, with a bullet in his brain. I called him and told him I had the information he needed to 'Coldstone' you. I told him to meet me out on the causeway. I had no idea half of Santimoke County would be in and out of there that day. Claire passed me coming into town as I biked out, but she never even looked at a bicyclist." He sighed. "I am truly sorry, Hollis, that I made you think that the police were about to arrest you."

"How could you do that to me? I thought we were friends!"

"I'm sorry, Hollis. I had to. The lawyer's first commandment is 'Thou shalt cover thine own ass.' As long as you were on the run and the ballistics tests weren't completed and Ormand Friendly was seeing you as a prime suspect, I had time. Time to cover mine own ass, so to speak. And then look for a way to cover yours. I needed time."

"You lied to me, Sev."

"No, I didn't lie to you, I just didn't tell you I was the murderer."

I was really mad now. "You betrayed our friendship."

"No, I trusted you could handle the heat. And you did. You were within a hairbreadth of figuring it all out, you know."

"Not hardly, as we say down to the island."

"But now I'm going to get you out."

I was aware of another flash. Would it be a real thunderstorm, carrying rain, or just more heat lightning?

"The terrible irony is that I have spent my life upholding the law. And now I have committed the ultimate crime." Sev gave a low, unhappy laugh. "I'm a homicidal homosexual."

"I'm glad you said that and I didn't."

I rolled the window down a crack; I was feeling claustrophobic.

We drove on in silence, threading our way along the winding dark roads. The fields gave way to pine forest, then to greenbrier swamp, and then the open savannas of White Marsh Neck, streaked in tarnished moonlight.

Over the marsh world, the thunderheads were gathering, heavy, dark clouds that glowed behind the moon. Lightning, so close I could see the jagged edges, crackled over a cripple, throwing the world into brief, illusory daylight. A thunderbolt broke overhead. No mistaking it now; there would finally be rain. The heart of the storm was across the Devanau River, over Oysterback, moving this way fast.

Stray raindrops and hungry bugs splattered against the windshield.

"We're almost out of gas," I said, glancing down at the dashboard.

"That's okay. We're almost there." Sev's voice was distant, as if he were speaking from a dream.

I could have sworn that I saw headlights in the rearview, but it could have been a trick of the light. Who knew we were here? They were all back at Mandrake, fighting with one another, and I was alone in the marsh with Sev Capwell, boy murderer.

"Pull in here," he said after a few miles more, and I saw, through the drizzle and the bugs, the guardrails along Jenkin's Creek. This was where Sev had killed Jason.

"Stop," he said. "The killer has returned to the scene of the crime."

I did, and when I took my hands from the steering wheel, I noticed that they were slippery with sweat. The wind had picked up. Thunder rolled and exploded. A mosquito whined around the inside of the cab. Sev waited until it landed on his bare leg, then slapped it. I jumped at the sudden sound. "This is the end," he whispered.

I shivered. His voice was so detached. A bolt of lightning briefly illuminated his profile. He looked old and tired. "This is the end of the road."

"It doesn't have to be."

"Jason was waiting for me in his Lexus, right here." He gestured toward the steel guardrail. "I made him get out of the car and told him why he had to die. He begged for his life. Fell on his knees and whined for his pathetic, sadistic life. He was a coward to the end." Contempt curled the edges of Sev's voice. "I am not completely inhuman. When I shot him, it was a clean shot, to the head. He died instantly, begging words still forming on his lips. It was a more merciful death than he deserved. It was not the act of a sane or civilized man. But it was necessary."

"Sev, how could you say that when—"

"But worse than that, I *enjoyed* killing him." Self-loathing tinged his voice. "Severn Capwell, that most civilized of men, had murdered in cold blood. I loaded his body and my bike into the back of his car and drove down the road toward Watertown. I meant to dump him in a woods somewhere. Then I saw your car. A car. And, the rest you know."

Suddenly Sev leaned across me and opened the door. A cool wind, beaded with raindrops, blew across my face. "Get out," he commanded, prodding me with the gun to show that he meant business. Thunder cracked overhead.

"Come on, Hollis, move!" Sev commanded, and I clambered down out of the van, with him right behind me. A thunderclap burst directly overhead, like cannon fire. I started, but Sev was made of sterner stuff. "They're coming," he said grimly.

As I crawled out of the seat, I glanced in the rearview mirror. In the next flash of lightning, I thought I saw Sam standing by the road. But it must have been an illusion of the light.

I made up my mind right then. "Let's get your bike," I said.

My hands were shaking as I opened the back doors of the van and pulled the bike out. I set it down on the causeway. "You said yourself that no one sees bikers. You can hide, you can get away from here, Sev!"

"No, I can't let you do that. That's aiding and abetting. Then you would be involved, Hollis." He had to raise his voice to speak above the whine of the rain, coming down harder now. We were both getting drenched.

"It doesn't matter, Sev," I cried. "You've got a chance to run, Sev, a chance for a new life! Take it!"

"But Hollis, you can't—"

"That's between God and me. I've got a lifetime to figure it out! Just go!" I was yelling now, tears running down my cheeks.

The distant wail of sirens made us both turn.

Lightning flashed so close that it crackled inside my eardrums and lifted the hair on the back of my neck. A shaft the breadth of a man's thigh slammed into a dead tree twenty yards away. The pine, full of resin, flared up like a torch, sending sparks flying across the grass. The world was fire.

"Sev!" I cried. "Watch it!"

He turned to look. The sparks ignited, spreading like an illuminated stain across the marsh as it burned off the dry tops and moved on, leaving the damp sedge to smolder down to the mudroot, throwing off rolling clouds of blackish gray smoke. Wind blew the smoke and fire toward us. Cinders flew everywhere. Sev looked like a diabolical god. There was no emotion in those pale eyes.

Rain began to fall harder now, heavy, stinging drops against my skin. I watched as Sev shook his head.

All around us, the sea of grass was catching fire, long tongues of it spreading toward the causeway. Burning down to the tidal mud, it quickly smoldered into billows of thick gray smoke. "Run!" I cried. "Run, dammit, Sev! You've still got a chance!"

He started to shake his head, and I winced, expecting him to make some noble gesture, but his eyes were suddenly focused on something behind me.

His expression was weird; he looked as if he were seeing a ghost.

I turned to look behind me, and he grabbed my arm, dragging me toward the guardrails. "Remember, tell them I had a gun on you, that I forced you to drive out here! Keep your head down, right above the water so you can breathe!" he shouted. "It will be over soon." He gave me a push, just a light one, but I lost my balance, falling backward over the steel barrier, plunging into the dark waters of Jenkin's Creek.

"Have a good life, Hollis!" I thought I heard him say as I plunged backward into the black water and sank a long way down, clawing at unseen, slimy creatures in the darkness.

It was only about six or seven feet deep but it seemed like a hundred before I finally touched the slimy mud bottom and struggled to the top. I clawed for what seemed like forever, before I emerged, choking on water and smoke. The fire was eating steadily at the marsh grass on either side of the gut, flaring up hungrily as it ate at the drought-dry bayberry and phragmites, burning right down into the dessicated roots. I gasped for air, keeping my nose and mouth close to the surface. My lungs burned, and I tread water, gasping for precious oxygen below the smoke.

After forever, the rain began to fall across me in sheets, at last drenching the parched earth. The thunder and lightning had rolled away as quickly as they had come, heading across the Santimoke Bay toward Watertown. But the rains, heavenly, wonderful, blessed rains, continued to fall.

Sev was nowhere to be seen. I was blinded by my own tears and the torrents of rain.

Far away, down the road, I heard the sirens and saw the red and blue flash of lights. Shakily, I pulled myself up on the steep bank, clutching at smoldering clumps of baybush, trying to heave myself up on the blackened land.

The flaming pine had burned itself into a smoldering torch.

In the smoky rain, I thought I saw a familiar, silvery shape. "Sam?" I called, reaching out. "Sam?" But whatever it was, it faded away in the net of rain and noisy darkness.

I lifted my head to the rain, the cleansing rain, waiting for them to come and get me out of this.

SIXTEEN

•

Loose Cannons and Loose Ends

Four o'clock on a Saturday afternoon outside, but inside Toby's Bar and Grill—well, at Toby's it's always four A.M. in some dark night of the soul. Somebody kept the jukebox playing "Lawyers, Guns and Money," the Hank Williams Jr., version, not the Warren Zevon, over and over and over again. It made a nice contrapuntal harmony with the clack of breaking balls on the pool table.

Toby set a diet soda in front of me and went back to a conversation with a couple of watermen at the other end of the bar. The subject was Baltimore's chances of getting an NFL team; the answer: as soon as hell froze over, if you asked me. But no one wanted my opinion. I was putting out keep-away vibes like crazy.

I wanted to brood alone, but I also wanted Toby to be somewhere in the background in case I needed an ear to bend. I contemplated my reflection in the bar mirror and stuck my tongue out at myself.

Ever since my big adventure, I'd felt let down and restless and depressed. Maybe it had something to do with the fact that it hadn't stopped raining in two weeks. Buckets, floods, sheets, cats and dogs of rain. Once it started, it seemed like it didn't want to stop. Now the farmers were complaining about too much of it.

Behind me, I heard the door open and close, but I didn't bother to turn around, not even when I felt someone slide into the bar stool beside me.

"I'll take a draft," a familiar voice said to Toby. "And set the lady up again with whatever she's having."

I looked in the mirror and beheld Ormand Friendly looking back at me with a crooked grin. Today, it was a tie that featured Sylvester, worn with a plaid shirt and a corduroy jacket that looked like it had been pulled from the bottom of my mother's rummage sale pile. For a moment I thought about introducing them—he'd probably become her best client—but quickly tucked the thought away as too Dickensian.

"You're not trying to arrest me again, are you?" I asked his reflection in the mirror.

Friendly shook his head. Toby brought a beer over and placed it on the counter in front of him, glowered meaningfully at both of us, and ambled off again. "Actually," he glanced at his watch, "I went off duty about three minutes ago, so I thought I'd come by and have a beer. The fact I saw your car in the parking lot was just icing on the cake."

"I can't believe it came back so clean," I said. "Those lab techs really went over it with a fine-tooth comb. They even vacuumed it out. Why you'd hardly know there'd been a dead pol in the backseat. I guess I can get another few thousand miles off of it."

He nodded, sipped at his beer, and made a face. "They do do their job," he allowed. "You went and fetched back your daddy's duckboat today?"

I cast him a sideways look. He looked too innocent.

Suspiciously, I glanced at Toby, who was washing glasses, hanging them up in an overhead rack. He was doing his best to appear not to look like he was eavesdropping.

"Yeah. I brought it back. It's my day off." I turned to look at him. "The Greenheads were gone. They'd all cleared out. The place was empty. Not so much as a computer disk left. They never even said good-bye," I added sadly.

Friendly nodded. "Yeah, people will do that to you." He

tapped my cigarettes with his finger. "Mind if I borrow one?" he asked.

I shook my head. He lit it, exhaling. "I'm trying to stop smoking," he confided. "Used to smoke three packs a day. Stopped for thirteen years. When I got divorced, I started up again. Then I stopped again when I was transferred over here."

"Is that right," I said. I stubbed mine out in the ashtray. "The Greenheads may have been gone, but there were about a dozen ornithologists out there. They said they found not one, but *three* nesting pairs of red-headed hawks. It looks like the EPA and the DNR may be able to block any kind of construction out there for a long, long time, while the endangered hawk population is studied."

Friendly sucked on his cigarette and nodded. "I heard that someone had stopped up a waste pipe at a chemical plant up near Wilmington." He grinned at me and I grinned back. "The word I had this morning," he continued, "was that a retired secretary from Sam Wescott's lawyer's firm had located their copy of his will in some old file cabinets in storage. It looks like Mrs. Estelle Brooks has legal title to White Marsh Island."

"Yes!" I crowed. "Sometimes the good guys do win!"

Friendly nodded. "The Audubon Society and a couple of land conservancy organizations are anxious to buy it from her. Since she can't develop it, and apparently doesn't even want to, she's anxious to sell. She and her husband are looking at a comfortable retirement."

"Great!" I'd have to congratulate them in person soon.

Friendly rubbed his chin. He had a late-day stubble, I noted. It was not unattractive. "I'm not really sure about all the details yet, but it would seem that Wescott Development is in a lot of trouble. Apparently, they may have violated about eleventy-seven different laws, state, local, and federal. It looks like the federal prosecutors are going to say they'll have to pay big fines and also pay to have White Marsh Island restored to its original condition. Of course, it will take years to restore."

I whistled. "Federal court? That's the big time, the show."

"Apparently, they paid Hemlock a lot of money to fix things he never bothered to completely fix. It'll be a while before it all goes to hearings and gets straightened out, but it looks like we can expect to get subpoenaed."

"That means we'll be spending a lot of time sitting around the witness room waiting to be called to the stand."

"You can ride over to court with me. I'll have a state car."

"Thanks."

"Can you play courthouse pinochle?"

"Well enough to pass the time waiting to testify." Thinking of courthouse pinochle reminded me of Sev Capwell, and I felt sad. "I don't suppose you've heard anything about our former state's attorney, have you?" I asked.

Friendly shook his head, turning his beer mug around by the stem. It left wet marks on the bar. "No. It's like he just vanished off the face of the earth. Capwell and his bicycle. Some of the boys were thinking that we might try putting him up on one of those unsolved and wanted TV shows. At least, with your deposition, we were able to put the Hemlock case in the file."

"And there's no reason why anyone should ever have to bother the Coldstones. I think they've been through enough. At least Jennifer called her mother at last."

"I noticed they weren't in your reporting."

I put my chin in my hands and leaned on the bar. "My editor wanted to fire me for offending the advertisers with the story. Then I got a commendation prize for investigative journalism from the Regional Press Association, so he couldn't very well. Asshole. I ended up getting a quarter an hour raise from the Owner, though."

Friendly chuckled. "I hear Mrs. Dupont lost her real estate license."

"She was, however, elected president queen of the

Daughters of Santimoke," I pointed out. "That counts for something. I hear tell she's turned her attention to the decorative arts now. She wants to become an antiques dealer, they tell me." My diet soda made a gargling noise as I sucked up the last of it from the bottom of the ice.

"Don't worry about the Old Man and Skipper. Whatever happens, they'll land on their feet. A million-dollar fine is a blink of the eye to them."

Toby placed my second glass in front of me. I twirled the straw around in the ice. "How did you know that Sev had lured me away in the Greenhead van?" I asked.

"Mrs. Brooks—Estelle?—saw you leaving with him. She let me know at once. I was glad to get out of Mr. Wescott's study. It was turning into a brawl in there between the Wescotts and the Greenheads. So we followed you at a safe distance in an unmarked."

"It's all a nine-day wonder, you know. By the time everything goes to trial, it will be old news. And as a witness, I won't be able to cover it."

"Ah," he said. We settled into a comfortable silence.

Send lawyers, guns, and money.

Running into Friendly like that certainly gave me something to think about that night as I sat on the screen porch in the twilight, sorting through the mail. Another dateless Saturday night.

Rain dripped from the eaves, and down on the creek, the heron stood on one leg, looking in the shallow water for dinner. Off on the western horizon, a thin pinkish stain of sunset tinged the sky. Tomorrow might be a sunny day.

Venus, the cat from hell, squeezed through a hole in the screen, shaking off a light coating of rainwater. She jumped up on the glider and proceeded to groom herself right on top of a pile of bills. For a change, this month, I wasn't sweating payment. You had better believe that I cashed that nice large check H.P. had written. I'd earned the money, I thought, with enough left over to make a nice donation to

Friends of the Chesapeake. In Claire's name, of course; if you think I could resist jerking her chain, you don't know me.

Bills, bills, bills. I flipped through them. Then a postcard caught my eye. It showed some ancient Mediterranean ruins and a couple of good-looking, scantily clad young men lounging around in the bright sun. I turned it over. It was from some island in the Aegean Sea. The handwriting was neat and precise.

Having a wonderful time since you're not here.
(Just kidding, ha ha.)

It wasn't signed.

"Bet I know who that's from," a familiar voice said.

I should have known better, but I still almost jumped out of my skin as Sam settled down on the glider beside Venus.

"Where the hell have *you* been?" I demanded angrily.

"I'm so happy that you're glad to see me," he grinned.

"I thought you were gone, well, wherever you go when your mission's accomplished," I said. "Why did you scare me like that?"

"I didn't mean to. Sorry about that," Sam grinned. I could see the rain through him. He stretched out and began to pet Venus, who purred and rubbed against him, a look of feline ecstasy on her face. "This is a nice house. It's peaceful out here. I could get used to this."

"Wait a minute here, Sam. You and I have some unfinished business." I could not believe that I was shaking my finger at him, but I was. "It's about this suicide thing."

He had the grace to look uneasy. "Oh, that," he said, as if it didn't matter at all. "So, I forgot. Big deal."

"Big deal? Why did you send me on a wild goose chase when you knew who killed you—namely, you?"

Sam shrugged. He had the grace to look sheepish, if not downright guilty. "Oh, it's not that big a deal. Come on. I killed myself because I knew I was going to be dead anyway. I knew I was going to be in a lot of pain, and pain, my peach, is one thing I like to avoid—and I wanted to stay around you, and the rules say you have to want me to haunt you—" His gaze dropped to the cat. For once in his life, Sam had run out of things to say.

I had plenty of things I wanted to say, but I didn't even know where to start. Rage, frustration, fear, amusement, relief.

Comprehension.

"Have you no sense of adventure? What happened to you?" Sam demanded. "You used to be more fun than this." He is deft at changing the subject.

"Well, it sure beat sitting in front of a computer in the newsroom," I conceded, leaning back against the glider. "Or, having to cook up five thousand words of drooling prose about White Marsh Estates, the wave of the future in wealth care!"

"Damn right!" Sam agreed, floating toward me. He draped an arm around—or into—my shoulders. "This was like the old days, right? There we were, ripping across the waves, on our way to an adventure! This is what we *should* have been all about, Holl!"

"Yeah, with my ass in the sling, as usual," I groused, lighting a cigarette.

"Scratch a cynic and find a failed romantic," Sam grinned.

The fragrance of rain and salt water, a summer smell of ozone, filled my nose. It brought back memories. "Who made me that way?" I nonetheless snapped testily.

"Whoa," Sam said. His ghostly arm weighed as much as a down vest, maybe even less. Slowly, he leaned over and kissed me on the cheek. "I still love you, Holl," he said softly. "I'll always love you."

I stole a glance at him. "This is really perverted or something," I said. "You're dead and I'm alive."

"So it's a mixed marriage," he replied. His breath was as light as the breeze from a bird's wing.

"Hey, it's a *former* mixed marriage! You're ecto-plasmically challenged, remember? Living-impaired. And me, I'm still alive!"

"You need a life to be alive. Anyway, maybe marriage is a bad choice of words. But you weren't worried about that at Toby's the other night. Anyway, what do you think keeps me here with you?"

"I haven't the faintest idea," I said. "Stop that!" I swatted at him ineffectually. My hand went right through him. I had begun to notice that he could shift from solid to vapor at will. Seemed to me he was gaining control of his ghostly talents.

"I'm stuck to you because you want me to be," Sam sighed. "You've been hanging on to your thoughts about me for years, nourishing my connection to you like a grudge."

I opened and closed my mouth. It's true that one thing Beddoe's Island people are good at is nurturing a grudge. They can hold on to a slight through five generations. The Balls haven't spoken to the Gibbons in years. There was some truth to what Sam was saying; I had been clutching my rage against him for nearly a decade of my life. That's a long time. Too long.

"It's been poisoning you," he said conversationally. "Just like I've got to pay some dues, so do you, Holl. You have to learn how to forgive me for being a major idiot. You have to want me out of your life. . . ."

"And then you'll get out, right?"

Sam nodded. "Then I'll get out of your life."

I took a deep breath. "Okay. I forgive you."

Sam shook his head. "No good. You have to mean it."

"That will take a little time. Forgiving you, I mean. You were *such* a shit, Sam."

"I know that. And I'm sorry. I really am. That's why I'm here, Holl, to try and make it up to you."

"And look at all the trouble you got me into," I sulked.

"Admit it, Holl." Sam leaned forward. "You haven't had so much adventure in your life in years. We did a good deed. We saved White Marsh Island. Wasn't that about the most interesting thing that's happened to you since I left?"

"Yeah," I finally said, trying not to smile. "It was good."

"And?" I looked at the traces of his profile against the sun and realized we were losing the light. "Come on, Holl. Help me out here. The rules say because I killed myself, I'm stuck on this plane. At least until I learn my lesson. Then I can go on, if I'm a good boy."

"The rules! The rules! I think you make them up as you go along, Sam."

"The rules," he replied grandly, "are the rules. Anyway, who do you think kept Sev Capwell from shooting you out on White Marsh?"

"I *thought* about you," I admitted grudgingly. "I thought you might have manifested or whatever out there that night."

"I'm your guardian angel."

"More like my guardian devil," I said stubbornly. "Sev wouldn't have killed me anyway."

Sam smiled. He relaxed into the glider. Venus rubbed up against his thigh, demanding attention. He stroked beneath her chin. "Who knows what will happen next?" he asked. "You may be glad that I'm around."

"Do you mean you intend to keep haunting me?"

"Haunting is such a strong word. Let's just say that I'll be around whenever you need me or—"

"Now wait a minute, here," I said. "If you're going to be hanging around, we need to set up some rules of our own here. . . ."

"Now *you* wait a minute. First of all, there's this Lieutenant Friendly guy. What does he have in mind? Your track record with men is pretty poor, Hollis. You need me to be sure that you don't—"

"If you think for one New York nanosecond that—"

As the sun sank beneath the pine trees on the creek and darkness came on, we were at it again, going around and around in the usual circles. No end in sight; neither of us ever gives an inch. Maybe having Sam as a guardian angel wasn't such a bad idea.

I could live with it.

Los Angeles lawyer Nan Robinson
sees things as they are—not as the
killer *wants* them to seem.

The Nan Robinson mysteries
by Taffy Cannon

A POCKETFUL OF KARMA

Hollywood playgirl Debra LaRoche has
disappeared, confounding her former
boss, Nan Robinson: Debra is simply too
responsible to do that. Facing police
apathy, Nan must track Debra down. But
between Debra's many boyfriends and
her spaced-out friends at the Past Lives
Institute, Nan doesn't find out much.
She'd better act fast, though, because
there may be another disappearance
soon—Nan's, that is.

TANGLED ROOTS
by Taffy Cannon

In the second installment of the Nan Robinson mystery series, Nan must help her sister, Julie, out of a messy situation: Julie's husband, Adam, is accused of shooting Shane Pettigrew—the heir to a Southern California flower-growing dynasty—in his greenhouse. Since Julie had an affair with Shane, Adam's good reputation could clearly be ... soiled.

CLASS REUNIONS ARE MURDER
by Taffy Cannon

When Nan goes to her twenty-year high school reunion, all the stars are out: the Class Clown, the Cutest Couple, the Brain ... but the last person she expects to see is Class Tramp Brenda Blaine. But when someone murders bad girl Brenda, Nan sees her classmates in a new light. For among old rivalries and secret passions, one of them may have graduated to become a cold-blooded killer.

To meet Taffy Cannon's bright, clear-headed lawyer Nan Robinson, read on....

Nan was stunned.

She felt as if she were whirling on a carnival midway ride, plastered to the wall by centrifugal force while the ground suddenly disappeared beneath her feet. Until this very moment, the idea of any infidelity in the Chandler marriage had seemed utterly impossible to her.

Nan's own marriage had ended with more of a whimper than a bang, and her track record in subsequent relationships was somewhat less than inspirational. She was now at a point where she had begun to accept that not everyone was meant to be paired, that there was a certain dignity to maintaining total control over one's life.

She still believed in happy endings and the possibility of lasting, meaningful relationships. She even believed in white picket fences, and lived behind one. But she'd bought the house herself and lived there alone.

Adam and her sister, Julie, however, represented another type of life together, one that Nan had always subconsciously believed she would live herself.

There were virtually no specific details of their life that Nan coveted. She didn't want to live out in the country and raise flowers. She didn't want to anguish from month to month whether she could pay the light bill. She didn't want a small herd of pets, a freezer full of homegrown veggies, original needlepoint pillows, or slipcovers crafted for secondhand chairs. She most certainly didn't want to drive a twelve-year-old pickup truck.

But—at least until now—she had always been profoundly envious of the fact that Adam and Julie coexisted so gracefully.

**Nan Robinson tracks down the killer
and keeps her sense of humor.**

Read the Nan Robinson mysteries
by Taffy Cannon